IMMORTAL SORCERESS

BOOK 3

SHADOW OF THE SORCERESS

KRISTA WALSH

RAVEN'S QUILL PRESS

OTTAWA, ON

Raven's Quill Press

www.kristawalshauthor.com

Publisher's Note: This is a work of fiction. Names, characters, places, and incidents are a product of the author's imagination. Locales and public names are sometimes used for atmospheric purposes. Any resemblance to actual people, living or dead, or to businesses, companies, events, institutions, or locales is completely coincidental.

Cover Design: Deranged Doctor Design/2023

Shadow of the Sorceress / WALSH -- 1st ed.
Paperback ISBN: 978-1-7380240-7-0

For those who look to the past to see how far
you've come

1

Katerina

I STALKED THROUGH the woods along the back of my house in Spring Bay, Ontario, hunching low to stay out of sight. At the edge of the beach, a troupe of pixies bathed among the rocks, their high-pitched voices reaching me through the leaves.

I wanted them gone.

They'd taken up residence a week ago, mostly keeping to themselves. Then they'd dragged off my neighbour's yappy dog and picked the bones clean. Mrs. McCreary had accused me of the crime. That the woman disliked me had been common knowledge for years—the truth brought home when she'd joined the mob against me three weeks ago with particular enthusiasm—but her belief in my involvement in her dog's disappearance had solidified her bad opinion.

With as much diplomacy as I could muster—very much regretting that my housekeeper, Maera, wasn't home to people for me—I'd sworn I hadn't touched her dog, had failed to convince her, and was now stuck dealing with the true culprits before they caused enough trouble to trigger another mob.

I crept forward through the trees, conscious of every step to ensure I didn't give myself away until I was in place to take the pixies by surprise.

Two days ago, I'd asked them to leave. I'd put on my kindest, most reasonable voice and encouraged them to take their winged selves to the other side of the island. They'd refused. Unfortunately for them, that left me only one option.

I cleared the trees and tiptoed to the water's edge, staying behind the rocks that lined the curve of the shore.

Under the mid-April sunrise, the lake was too cold to tempt most people to go for a swim, but the pixies seemed to be enjoying it. Their splashes and laughter over their bawdy songs covered any noise I made as I dipped my fingers in the water. I called on my magic to absorb the heat, and the gentle lap of Lake Huron stilled against my palm. Frost spread across the surface, creeping towards the rocks and thickening into a thin layer of ice.

I remained where I was, pumping more power into the water, until shrieks of panic rose on the other side of the rocks.

"Get out! Move!"

Their tiny voices grew more agitated, and I urged my magic to move faster. I couldn't let them get out of the water, or I would have a bigger battle on my hands than I was prepared for this early in the morning. Before coffee.

"I'm stuck! Help me!"

"Everyone, *pull!* Gah!"

I peered around the corner. Of the dozen little biters that had set up camp, over half of them had been caught in the ice, which left five free.

Once I was sure the ones in the water would stay put, I focused on the others. I lifted my hand out of the water, smashed through the thin ice, and splashed them. Their wings fluttered as they tried to avoid the spray. I drew on my magic to pull the heat from the droplets soaking their tiny bodies, and two of them crashed to the ice with tiny grunts. The other three were mobile enough to turn towards me with rage in their eyes.

"Shit."

They bared their teeth and charged. I reversed the flow of my magic and summoned fire into my palms, holding on to the flames as they flickered over my gloved hands and hoping the threat would stop the creatures from attacking.

The damn things clearly had a death wish because they didn't slow down. Pointy teeth sliced into the bare skin that stretched between my T-shirt and elbow-length leather gloves. One of them wound up tangled in my hair.

I twisted around to get them off, cursing with every step that I hadn't been faster. My attack would have been so much smoother if I'd had a partner, but Maera and Rhys were in Muskoka, staying with Adrian until our greater problems were solved. Which left me alone to deal with these pests as best I could.

"I don't want to roast you!" I shouted. "Get *off*."

I summoned more fire, and a scream of pain cut through the shrieks of fear from the others trapped in the ice.

I snatched the burning pixie out of the air and held it tight in my fist, wincing as it cut its teeth into the fleshy part between my thumb and index finger.

"Will you cut it out?" I snapped. "Everyone freeze, or I'll squeeze the life out of this one."

"Ignore her," the captured pixie ordered. "I'll devour every bone in your hand before you kill my kin."

I huffed out my frustration. "Look, I don't want to kill anyone. But you ate my neighbour's dog, and now I have to clean up your mess. The longer you stay here, the more messes I'll need to deal with. I don't want you here. Leave."

The one in my hair chomped on my earlobe, and I screamed as I twisted around, accidentally increasing my grip on the one I held.

"This is our new home, sorceress," Hair Pixie hissed. "Who are you to make us leave?"

Who was I, indeed? That they knew I was a sorceress meant the odds were good they knew exactly what role I played in this world, but if they wanted to play ignorant, I'd indulge them.

"I'm the woman who stops the drakes from eating you by the swarm. That kelpie in Lake Manitou? Yeah, I sent her on her merry way as well. So maybe before you come picking fights, you consider *not* pissing off the person making your lives liveable."

I flicked Hand Pixie onto the ice and grabbed the one in my hair. The third one, who'd gotten stuck in my sleeve, tumbled to the ground.

Hair Pixie scowled at me. "You think you're the centre of the universe, sorceress, but one day someone's going to show you how wrong you are."

"Yeah, yeah." How many times had I heard that before? "Tell that to the harpy. I think bits of her charred remains are still near the falls. Now get out of here before I stop playing nice."

I melted the ice around me and left the pixies sputtering and gasping for air as they dragged themselves to the beach. With luck, they'd be gone before I returned home.

Pain pinched the back of my arm, and I hissed as I rotated my shoulder to take in the damage. Hundreds of little teeth marks marred my skin, and blood dripped off my elbow.

Great. Now I'd have to shower and change before I headed

to Muskoka. Because that was exactly the delay I needed. Emrick had left me this morning to escort some souls out of the living world, so I had to travel the old-fashioned way—a four-hour drive instead of the ten-second step through the afterlife.

Muttering under my breath, I stomped into the house and slammed the door behind me.

A morning of pixies to pave the way into an afternoon of banging my head against a wall as I tried to track down a witch who refused to be found. That was my life. It was great. I loved it.

But as I started the shower and stripped down, I couldn't shake the pixie's scathing words. I didn't think I was the centre of the universe—never had—but I was one of the few people in the world who stood between the magical and mundane and fought for the protection of both.

Somewhere out there, that missing witch was testing me. Twice now, Abigail had caused near-catastrophic magical events, and I feared what would happen if I failed to stop her.

A shiver ran down my spine as a sense of unease coiled within me. I stepped into the steamy shower, but not even the hot water could chase my dread away.

2

Katerina

I LOOKED AROUND the table at the team staring back at me. It was just past ten in the morning, and the coffee pot had already been refilled twice. The heavy curtains in the kitchen were pulled tightly closed to block out the sun, which did nothing to keep the night owls awake at this early hour.

Six of us sat here in person, with two witches joining us via video call on the laptop.

We'd gathered at Adrian's house in Muskoka to discuss our efforts in tracking down Abigail, but over the past hour we'd only made it so far as to agree she was a pain in the ass and we hated her.

Adrian, my two-thousand-year-old vampire bestie and unofficial therapist, sat to my left, inspecting his nails and pretending not to be invested in the war council taking place around his kitchen table. After all, he'd retired from his role of guarding the balance between magical and mundane and was now enjoying the peace and quiet of a well-deserving veteran. If he piped up to point out we'd veered off topic, he was only making conversation, or so he claimed.

"I don't know if wiping out every coven in the Toronto area would give you the results you're looking for, tesoro." He spoke with his barely-there smile that let me know he found my rage-induced suggestion amusing, but I wasn't laughing.

"Why not? Someone in this city knows where to find her, and if no one's talking, we need to make them talk."

I had no intention of doing any such thing, but frustration and my lingering crankiness over the pixie situation had pushed me to think beyond the boundaries of rational strategy.

James Barrett, Adrian's thrall, sat next to him. Made of muscle on muscle, Barrett looked like a walking shadow-weapon in his black T-shirt, black jeans, black combat boots. The lack of colour—or expression, or personality—made him a terrifying specimen of supposed humanity. And yet today he looked... softer somehow? No, not softer. That would imply the man had layers. But he looked alarmingly different nonetheless. Apparently our recent battles had dulled my view of his sharper edges, and I didn't know how I felt about that.

At my outburst, he grunted. "I can think of a few worse

options than storming the city. It might not solve our current problems, but it could prevent a few more from popping up."

I narrowed my eyes at him. There were those sharper edges of his. "Of course you'd hop on board with this plan. Maybe you should call up your witch hunter buddies and gather your pitchforks."

He held up his hands. "It was your idea."

Barrett hated all things magical—everything except for Adrian, anyway—so his enthusiasm for going after the witches didn't come as a shock, but it grated on me that the only idea he'd agreed to today was the one I hadn't been serious about.

"We'll try the tracking spells again, kitty Kat," Poppy spoke up from the laptop.

"Is there any point?" I asked. "You've tried dozens of times now."

She frowned. "She's blocking us somehow. If we could figure out how, not only would we find her, but we'd have some decent defence options on our side."

"The woman knows her way around a spell," Murisa agreed.

The necromancer and the tech witch had burrowed their way under my skin over the past few months and challenged my prejudices against witchcraft. As usual, appearance-wise, they were the light in the darkness. Poppy's tight curls bounced on her shoulders, but the tips had gone from being bright pink to a striking blue. The blue stood out against her orange top, and all that colour made her dark skin glow. Murisa was a picture in fuchsia from her long-sleeve T-shirt to the cloth headband in her thick brown-black hair.

I recognized the room behind them as Murisa's apartment in Oakville and wondered how much time Poppy spent there. Cuddles, Poppy's resurrected cat, sat on her lap, his yellow stare baleful, his long grey hair patchy but well groomed.

Poppy tapped a pink-tipped nail against her lips, then dropped her hand to clear Cuddles's hair out of the way as the cat stood to stick his butt in the camera. "You have to wonder where Abigail trained."

I had the same question, especially since I'd caught a whiff of sorcery within her witchcraft more than once. The woman was a force I hadn't seen in a very long time.

"Whatever her training, we can beat her. We just need to step up our game."

My housekeeper grumbled something about "doing it quickly" as she brought a tray of cookies to the table. By the number of different snacks already scattered across the surface, I suspected the woman hadn't stopped stress baking since she'd arrived in Muskoka. We'd agreed Maera and Rhys would stay here—away from me—until we found Abigail, but this crisis wouldn't be good for Adrian's electricity bill or the longevity of his oven.

Rhys sat to my left, and I couldn't help but notice he wasn't quite his exuberant self today. His recent possession by the fear demon, Shogaur, had shaken him more than he'd admitted, and the dark circles under his eyes gave away his difficulty sleeping.

I watched him now, waiting for him to offer his usual encouragement, but his attention had trailed off, so I let him be.

Across from him was Gavin, whose habitual glower burned with a bit less intensity than the last time I'd seen him. My hopes weren't high that he was coming around on accepting his identity as The Only Mortal Sorcerer On The Planet. More likely, he was tired. A bit of sleep and he would be back to glaring at me with all the loathing of his being. The man was a miracle. An impossibility. Aside from immortal me, the last sorcerer had passed out of this world in the sixteenth century. All that remained of our once-powerful bloodlines were the witches that tapped into the natural energies through external mediums like enchantments, potions, and rituals.

He resented me for putting a name to what he was. Sure, I'd saved him from a demon, but I'd also broken it to him that the fire that had recently started spilling from his hands was a permanent addition to his life and he'd better learn how to control it or risk roasting everyone he loved. This was not the news he'd wanted to hear.

Otherwise, though, he looked much better than he had when we'd found him strapped to a chair in an empty Hamilton storefront three weeks ago. The bruises and cuts he'd sustained under

Abigail's and Shogaur's cruel touch, still visible from under the hems of his sleeves and his collar, were healing, and at some point he'd cut his glossy black hair. Under Maera's watch, he'd gained a bit of weight, and it seemed to me his shoulders had filled out with muscle as well. That was probably Barrett's doing. The two magic haters no doubt spent all their time together complaining about my world while lifting weights.

My team was solid. We all knew what was at stake if we failed to track Abigail down, and there was nothing more I could say to make them work harder. In truth, I had no reason to be here. I'd made the trip so we could update each other in person, but mostly it had been an excuse to get out of the house—and out of my head. Everyone was already doing everything in their power.

I huffed out a breath and rubbed my eyes. "While she toys with us, the only advantage we have is making use of our time. No one knows who this woman is. She has to have been around for a few decades, she's powerful, she's wealthy, and yet not even the witch hunters have a file on her. I want to know how that's possible."

Poppy shrugged and scratched Cuddles's head, avoiding the notch in his right ear. "She's a witch, kitty Kat. Most of us who are out for power want to be in the public eye, but if she's working a long con, she could have found ways to cover her tracks. New identities, potions to hide her magic."

"Always hiding behind someone else," Barrett added.

Which we knew she'd done. She'd hidden behind the blood witch Mikhail for at least twenty years, feeding him information, teaching him rituals that should have stayed buried. After I'd killed Mikhail, she'd summoned Shogaur, once again staying out of the spotlight.

I wasn't about to let her hide behind anyone else. I was taking the fight to her this time—and I was going to end it.

If we could find her.

I slapped my hands on the table, making everyone except Adrian jump.

"All right, here's what we're going to do. Barrett, I want you on the phone with the witch hunters. If we can't track Abigail directly, maybe there's a different angle we can take. What about any of the other witches who survived Mikhail's ritual? Someone who followed him might know something about this woman. Murisa, Poppy, keep trying the tracking spell, but I want you focused on defence. Once we find her, she'll fight back. I want to be ready for anything."

"Already on it, kitty Kat," Poppy said.

Murisa nodded. "Give us until the end of the day, and we'll have a prototype for you." Her eyes gleamed. "I can't wait to show this off."

If it was anything like the magic Murisa had come up with to help against Shogaur, I couldn't wait to see it.

"Gavin"—I looked to him, and he narrowed his eyes at me—"you keep being you." He grunted, and I turned to Rhys and Maera. "You two will have to stay here for a while longer."

Rhys's shoulders slumped. "I can't wait until this is over. I love this place, but I want to go home."

My heart ached for him. Since I'd stabbed him in the gut to free him of Shogaur's hold, the poor guy hadn't had a chance to get back to normal. He'd gone straight from the Toronto hospital to Adrian's Toronto house until they'd finally come here two weeks ago while he recovered. The strain was showing.

I rested my hand on his where it lay on the table. "I know, Rhys. I promise I'm working as quickly as I can."

He gave a resigned nod and sagged back in his chair, then winced and sat back up as his healing wound pulled.

"What about me?"

Certain I'd misheard, I turned to Adrian and found him staring at me with his sharp brown eyes lined with amusement and something else I couldn't name. "You want to help?"

He drew his lips back to show off a hint of fang. "Is it such a surprise to you, mia Katerina? Abigail isn't some creature hiding in the mountains luring victims into her cave—she's actively making moves against one of the most important people in my life. I won't sit still and let that happen."

As he straightened his shoulders and lifted his chin, I saw the man who'd hunted beside me for so many centuries. He'd been lost for years beneath the veneer of a vampire happy with his books and blood, but this was the warrior I remembered.

Barrett's eye twitched at Adrian's announcement, but a thrill ran through me, and hope swelled in my chest. He was right that I was more than a little surprised. This was a man who'd sworn off the hunt for the past fifty years except for two exceptions—one of which had earned him his grumpy thrall. But I was more grateful than anything. He and I had been a team for hundreds of years. If he stood at my side, there was no way we could lose.

A hush fell across the table, and I turned to find Rhys sitting still, his green eyes white.

My breath caught in my chest. He hadn't had a full vision in three weeks, not since the one that had warned me of trouble on the way. Of an end. Of *the* end. My hands tensed on the table as I waited for him to drop another bomb on me.

But no empty, haunted tones spilled from between his lips. Instead, he turned to face me, and the smile that graced his handsome features was cold.

"There you are," he said, but his voice wasn't his own. It was higher pitched, laced with a tremor of age. "I wondered when you'd show up. Have you finished stealing pets from me? I think next time I'll take some of yours. See you soon, kitty Kat."

3

Katerina

MAERA RUSHED TO catch Rhys before her son fell out of his chair, but everyone else at the table remained still. All eyes were on me, and I didn't know what to say.

Abigail was coming for us, and she'd just shown us how ineffective we'd been at protecting ourselves.

There you are.

Had she been searching for me? Waiting for me to join the others so she could deliver her message directly? Or was she twisting things around to make us think she'd been spying on us through Rhys? It worried me how easily she'd been able to climb into his head. Doing so would require an incredible amount of scrying power.

My hands trembled on the table, and I tucked them between

my legs to hide the shake. I wasn't afraid—I was furious.

"That's the second time she's used Rhys to get to us," I said through clenched teeth. Last time, she'd pushed visions into his head, filling him with so much fear he'd run outside the ward and been ensnared by Shogaur. It had been luck he'd survived. "We can't let that happen again. Poppy, Murisa, what are our options on that?"

The witches exchanged a look, and Poppy cleared her throat. "I don't know if protecting his mind would work. She's not so much taking him over as using him like a radio. I think to keep her out, we'd have to block his visions."

"Find a way to do it."

Maera's eyes narrowed, but I ignored her. She was concerned for her son, but she had to know I wasn't about to let my friend take the brunt of Abigail's games.

"What about the rest of it, Katerina?" Adrian asked, his brown eyes sombre.

I chewed on the side of my thumb as I considered the situation. "I took out Mikhail and Shogaur, so now she plans to come at us directly. We got what we wanted on that score, at least."

It was small comfort, especially as I looked around the table at all the people I wasn't willing to lose.

"She's made it clear she won't come for me first. She wants to play, so she'll come for the people I care about. We need to make sure everyone in this room is safe."

Fortunately, there was nowhere safer that I could think of. Between Adrian's experience in fortifying his castles and Barrett's know-how in mundane traps, it would take more than a single witch to invade his territory.

I hoped.

Poppy and Murisa were the real concern. We had reason to believe Abigail knew how to get to Poppy—Poppy's occult shop had been well known before she'd handed the lease to a beribboned tea shop owner—but did she know where Murisa lived? If so, that meant she'd been paying attention to our movements far longer than we'd realized. Taking her by surprise would be next to impossible unless we levelled up quickly.

"We'll be all right, kitty Kat." Poppy grimaced around her nickname for me. None of us had missed Abigail's choice of words. She'd used the name to prove she'd been watching us, and her mindgames had worked. I found myself scanning the room, wondering just how close she'd wriggled into our lives. "We'll keep our heads down and let you know if we notice anything weird."

I started to argue, but Adrian rested his hand on my arm. "It might be for the best for now, cuore mio. If we start making immediate moves, we'll create openings she can manipulate."

I ground my teeth. "You're right. Fine. Stay where you are for now, but triple-check your wards and call me if anything happens."

"We will," Murisa promised. "We'll be in touch soon."

They ended the call, and I looked around the table. Gavin stood up and helped Maera carry the still-sleeping Rhys to the living room, leaving me with Adrian and Barrett.

"She wants us to panic," I said.

"She does," Adrian agreed.

"I won't do it."

"Nor should you."

The side of my thumb found its way between my teeth again. "I don't like this."

Barrett scowled. "Neither do I. I hate being played, and the woman's done nothing but own the board since Mikhail."

I met his eye. "Do you think Tony will help? Especially since Abigail's made it clear she's not going to up and disappear now that two of her plans have failed?"

The witch hunters were known for their heavy-handedness in dealing with witches, but right now maybe that was what we needed.

"I can ask. I'll make the call now." He shot Adrian a glance as he rose from the table, and my friend patted his thrall on the arm.

I frowned at Barrett's retreating back. "What was that about?"

"Nothing, my dear. James is simply fussing like a mother hen, as is his wont."

He stood up and gestured for me to follow him towards the stairs.

As we went up to his library, I struggled with the image of Barrett strutting about with a disapproving *cluck-cluck*, but I knew the man well enough to believe Adrian was right. The vampire had been around for over two millennia, but for the past ten years, Barrett had made it clear Adrian's wellbeing was his top priority. Some of that was the vampire-thrall bond that had formed between them, but I suspected even without the blood exchange, the ex-soldier would have been the same. Feelings existed alongside the magic, and they ran deep.

That being said, it wasn't often I saw Barrett worried for no reason.

"He certainly didn't seem happy about your offer to stand with me on this one," I pushed.

We entered the library, and I breathed in the familiar, warm scent of old books, extinguished fires, and the lake water that drifted in through the open window.

The fireplace was dark today, the hundreds of books on their organized shelves recently dusted. This room was a haven, as every library of Adrian's had been since I'd first met him eight hundred years ago. The nature of the tomes had changed, his tastes shifting with the times, but the warmth of the space—the heart of it—remained the same.

Adrian smiled as he settled into his armchair, the leather

creaking under his weight. "Barrett worries for me. Despite all I've seen over two thousand years, because he's taller than I am, he believes I'm delicate."

As I dropped into the chair beside his, I couldn't help but laugh. "Right. Such a delicate vampire. What does he think could happen to you?"

"What indeed?" Adrian asked, but again I caught the glimmer of something in his eyes, and I reached for his hand.

"Adrian, what is it?"

"Hmm? Oh, nothing, tesoro. Nothing at all." He raised our entwined hands and kissed the back of mine. "Just musing on life and the nature of the world. The danger this Abigail woman poses, the effect she's had on our lives. I thought I had rid myself of the weight of the darkness, but it turns out I've only been hiding in the light thinking it was gone."

I watched him closely, looking for his tells, but his features were as inscrutable as they ever were. "You'd tell me if it were something more, wouldn't you?"

Confusion flickered across his face before melting into understanding. "It's not me you're concerned about, is it?"

I forced myself not to drop my gaze. "Am I that obvious? I mean, of course I'm concerned about you. If there's something going on, I want you to tell me so I can help you fix it. We're in this together, Adrian. Just as we've always been. But…" I shrugged. "I'll admit, I'm also worried about the other third of our trio."

Adrian quirked an eyebrow in silent question, and I sagged deeper into my chair. "I don't suppose Emrick's confided in you lately?"

"Not since your death. You've both been too preoccupied to have time for your oldest friends." He winked at me, earning him a laugh, but my mirth quickly fizzled.

"He's changing. Faster than I've ever seen it happen. He knows it, but when I try to talk to him about it, he finds any excuse to change the subject."

After saving me from Shogaur's possession, Emrick's colouring had faded a few more degrees, leaving his once-pale skin deathly white, his hair less a straw-blond with its beautiful golden highlights and more an artificial bleach. His eyes remained the same, intense with their moonlight glow, but I wondered how long it would be before their brightness fled.

Rhys's warning, a gift from his second sight, echoed in my head that the end was coming, and I knew down to my marrow that if my end loomed, Emrick wouldn't let it happen without sacrificing everything he had left to protect me.

Our lives seemed predestined to come down to him or me, and I didn't know what to do. My heart was split between the selfish desire of leaning on Emrick to help me face whatever this threat might be and the wise decision of sending him away again to safeguard what remained of him.

"Now with the danger of Abigail hanging over us," I added, "I've got so much weighing me down I don't know how to start digging myself out."

Adrian stroked his thumb along my palm. "Emrick knows what's at stake. He won't push himself past the point of safety. If he's aware of it, he'll be careful—you have to trust him."

I did. With so many things. My heart, my body, my safety. But I didn't trust him to put himself first if my life was on the line.

Emrick was my everything. The source of my existence on a basic level, my heart and soul on the highest. I loved him beyond words, and even as Abigail had forced me to confront all the pains of my past, he represented all the fears for my future.

"Can you talk to him?" I asked. "I don't think I have the strength to send him away again—I don't know if that was ever the right solution—but I can't go after Abigail knowing he might put himself between us if things get bad. Not when we don't know who exactly we're dealing with."

"I'll do what I can, Katerina," Adrian said, my name dancing over his tongue in a way that was unique to him. "But you have to accept that, whatever comes, he's his own person. He'll make his own choices."

"But it's not just him, Adrian. You know that as well as I do. We're one and the same. If anything happens to him, I'll have nothing left of myself."

4

Emrick

K AT WASN'T HOME yet when I returned from my trip to the afterlife, and while I would have loved to lose myself in her arms, I was grateful for the opportunity to decompress and put my day behind me.

In my fifteen hundred years escorting magical souls to the afterlife, I rarely had to deal with more than one or two souls at a time. More when Kat was involved, as she rarely liked to do anything by halves, but that had slowed down during her decades of avoiding the hunt.

Today had been an exception. A shifter complex had caught fire out in Algonquin Park and swept up almost the entire pack before they'd had time to escape. I'd spent most of the night ushering their spirits across, answering questions, reassuring them that this end was far from *the* end.

And yet, I couldn't deny I'd been relieved by the excuse to stay busy. These days, when I had any time to think, I found myself worrying about problems with no easy solution.

I leaned on the balcony railing and stared at my hands. Not at the rough skin that marked my work as a farming sorcerer back in my mortal life, or the tendons or muscle or bone that reminded me I was still mostly human despite so many centuries playing spiritual shepherd, but at the near transparency of what should have been flesh and blood.

In the light of the mid-morning sun, I made out every tiny vein beneath the surface. My skin had grown so pale and thin it was almost chalky.

I thought I'd been careful in the fight against Shogaur, but somewhere between throwing myself into the forbidden river of the afterlife and dropping the protective talisman over Kat's head to shut the demon out of her mind, I'd lost more of myself than I'd realized.

As far as I could tell, my memories remained intact, but would I know if I lost them? Would I realize they were gone if I stumbled across the blank patches in my mind?

The lines Death had created around me had become blurred, and I was no longer sure when I crossed them. Given the number of times I brought Kat with me through the afterlife to some new destination, I suspected I was in the clear as far as that went—and if making love to her crossed that boundary, I would have lost my soul centuries ago. But stopping Shogaur from climbing into her mind and using Death's power to drive away the mundane mob closing in on Kat's house had cost me.

Now we faced some new threat—something that had the potential to bring Kat's end if Rhys's second sight was to be trusted—and I was stuck on the sidelines, forced to watch her handle it without my help.

I'd sworn to stand beside her against Abigail, and I meant it, but we both understood that was as far as I could take it. Kat was terrified I would drift too far away from her, and by the state of me, her fears weren't unfounded. More than ever, I understood just how fine a line I walked.

So I would stand by her, and I would support her, but I would remain hands off.

No matter what happened.

Even if Abigail pulled another demon out of her ass and threatened to drag my sorceress to the infernal realms, I could not step in to save her.

Gods help me, I was doomed either way.

5

Katerina

THE DRIVE HOME from Muskoka was long and too quiet. Way too quiet. Not even the music blaring from my speakers as I whipped along the highway was enough to subdue my raging thoughts.

Abigail was getting ready to make another move.

We'd known it was coming for the past three weeks, but there was a difference between planning for an abstract danger and an actual threat.

Poppy had described it well when she'd said Abigail was in for the long con. All her plans to date had involved a lot of thought and consideration, which meant whatever she planned next would be big, nasty, and unpredictable. We could do our best to get ahead of it, but it was like planning for a storm when you had no idea if it was going to be a hurricane or a volcanic eruption. Did we hunker down or run like hell and pray we could outrace it?

If we did outrace it, how many innocent victims would die along the way because we didn't stand and fight when we had the chance?

If we did stand and fight, what would we face? More demons? More witches? Something worse?

I didn't want to think too closely about that last one—my imagination had no limits as to what might fill the void.

It was a relief when my house came into view on its isolated country road. The mid-afternoon sun sprayed its shining light across the white walls, bouncing off the windows facing the driveway. It would have been a beautiful picture if not for the lingering evidence of the mob that had nearly destroyed it.

The front porch and picture window had been replaced, but my lawn remained a disaster of truck tire treads dug deep into the mud. Bit by bit, the ground was thawing, but we'd have to wait a while yet before the landscaping people could work a miracle.

I parked the car and dragged myself into the house. Maera had sent me home with leftovers, and I couldn't wait to toss them into the microwave, put on my favourite comfort film, and turn my brain off for a few hours while I subconsciously worked out the latest twist to our ongoing problem.

I made it as far as putting the bag of food in the fridge before I realized the house wasn't empty. The ward hadn't been triggered, which meant whoever was here was allowed to be, and my heart fluttered as I narrowed the list down to a single person.

Setting all thought of food and film aside, I hurried into my bedroom and found Emrick standing on the balcony. My skin warmed, my pulse raced, and I headed towards him with the full intention of throwing my arms around his waist and pulling him into bed—but I stopped when I came up beside him and caught the look on his face.

He hadn't heard me come in, his attention focused on the beach, with the glittering waters of Lake Huron beyond it. His posture was stiff, his knuckles as white as bleached bone where they clenched the railing.

I trailed my gaze up his bare arms, over his blue T-shirt where it stretched over his broad chest, up the lines of his neck to his tense jawline, to the anguish in his gaze.

I rested my hand on his arm, and he startled beneath my touch. If anyone else attempted to make contact, they would be nothing more than dust at his feet as their cells were jerked forward in time. I, however, stood outside time, immortal because of the bond to Emrick that should never have been possible but that I was grateful for every day of my eternal life.

When he turned towards me, the clouds across his silver

eyes cleared, and his smile was as warm as the midday sun. "You're home."

"Are you all right?" I asked.

His smile grew forced. "Perfect now that you're here." He bent to kiss me—a heated, desperate kiss. His tongue teased my lips open, tasting me, exploring me. Desire sparked within my tangled psyche and spread to consume everything except for the thought of him—

—and how he was obviously trying to distract me.

The need to hear the truth from his lips almost pushed me to press the issue, to force him to tell me what was on his mind, but I let it go. We both knew the burdens he carried, both in this world and the next. We both knew the price he paid to be here with me. To dwell on it would only make us miserable, so, like him, I chose to lose myself in his touch.

His hands skated down my back and drew my hips closer. I wrapped my arms around his neck, doing my best to remove every inch of space between us. Abigail's threat, Death's deal— they were problems that existed outside this room. Their reality would catch up to us soon enough, but they could damn well wait their turn.

His teeth skimmed down my neck, his tongue flicking out to taste my skin, and I gasped as heat spread through my body, molten and slow, seeping into my bones until my legs went weak and only my grip on Emrick kept me on my feet.

The temperature around us dropped, the mist of the afterlife cool on my arms, as Emrick stepped us through to the bed. In another heartbeat, I was on my back, and the weight of him pressed down on me, solid, protective. Nothing could harm us here.

His kisses continued downwards even as he slid his hands under my T-shirt and pushed it up over my breasts. His tongue circled one nipple as his fingers played with the other, and I arched my back against his mouth.

I twisted my fingers into his blond hair, holding him right where I needed him, and his free hand slipped under the waistband of my pants—then froze at the knock on my front door.

My breaths came in ragged pants, and I groaned in frustration as Emrick kissed the underside of my breast, then pulled away.

I was about to beg him to ignore the knock when it came again, and I bowed my head against his shoulder. He chuckled, the low sound vibrating right through me, leaving parts of me pulsing with pleasure, then rolled off and helped me to my feet.

"Whoever it is, I'm setting them on fire," I grumbled as I righted my shirt and stomped through the living room.

When I opened the door, I found Postal Worker Rita on my front porch. There was no shotgun in her hands this time, no expression of rage or terror on her face. In fact, she looked downright abashed. Her red curls were pulled back in a tidy bun, her jacket worn open to soak up the warmth of the late-April afternoon. She shifted her weight where she stood, digging the toe of her hiking boot between the brand-new floorboards.

Rita cleared her throat. "Hi, Ms. Palon."

I raised an eyebrow and crossed my arms.

"I wanted to come by and apologize for… you know. What happened. I don't understand what came over me. I've never had any issue with you, and Maera and Rhys are always lovely. It was like—I don't even know. I can't remember why I wanted to attack you like that." Her green eyes went wide, almost panicked, and I experienced a pang of sympathy.

She'd attacked me because Shogaur had stirred her latent fears that I was a danger. As a non-magical, she had no idea about my abilities or my immortality. All she knew was that I'd lived in this small community for ten years and had never connected with the people who lived here. Or aged.

Really, I was due for a move soon. But I'd gotten comfortable in this quiet corner of the world, and the idea of starting over somewhere else exhausted me.

"Don't worry about it," I said. "Consider the entire event forgotten."

She tried on a smile, but it looked a little snug. "Anyway, the other reason I stopped by was because a woman came to the post office this morning and asked for this to be hand-delivered. Not usually our job but, you know, it gave me an excuse to say sorry."

She held out a brown paper parcel tied with twine, and I accepted it without question. Only after I caught sight of the shaky *Katerina* written across the top did I stop to think maybe I didn't want to accept it. That the trouble I'd been braced for might have arrived in the form of a penitent postal worker.

I'd seen that chicken scratch writing before. It was the same hand that had drawn the runes on Shogaur's summoning circle. An aged hand. Abigail.

"Thanks, Rita," I said through numb lips. "I appreciate it."

She threw me a wave and rushed down the steps. "See you around!"

Her apology had been given, her task fulfilled, and now, I was sure, she never wanted to see me again. She climbed into her car and drove off, leaving me with what I couldn't help but see as a ticking time bomb.

Emrick stepped outside. "What is it?"

"I don't know." I frowned after the disappearing car, then dropped my gaze to the package. "But I don't think I want to open it in the house."

He followed me to the middle of the gravel driveway. Only then did I peel the paper away to reveal a small box of plain, untreated pine. There was nothing special about the box—it could have been picked up in the arts and crafts section of a dollar store—but it may as well have been a scorpion for the way I handled it.

Aiming the box away so it wasn't aimed at my face, I carefully flipped open the lid. Nothing happened.

Fighting my curiosity, braced for the whole thing to explode at any moment, I turned the box and peered inside.

All I found was a pale grey stone.

"What the hell?"

I picked up the stone and tossed the box a few feet away, still not trusting it. Not that I trusted the stone any more than I did the box, but I couldn't see anything special about it, either.

Emrick frowned. "More mind games?"

"It has to be. Or maybe a warning of some kind? She's going to tie a bigger version of this to my leg and hurl me into the lake?"

I ran my thumb over the surface of the stone and spun it between my fingers to check for any markings, but whatever message she was trying to send, it evaded me.

A low noise and sudden movement drew my attention to the trees on the other side of my driveway. Before I could make out what it was, the stone grew hot. I looked down and watched the shimmery specks across the surface take on a bright red glow.

I didn't think, didn't hesitate. I chucked the stone as hard as I could. It bounced off the base of a towering spruce tree, split open to release a vibrant spell circle, and engulfed the tree in a raging circle of fire.

6

Katerina

As soon as the shock wore off that my spruce tree was gone, I tugged my phone out of my thigh pocket and stormed into the house. I scrolled through my contacts to where I'd recently updated Barrett from **Satan's BFF** to **Annoyance Demon** and dialled his number.

By the time he answered, I had my keys and wallet in hand and was headed to my car. Emrick climbed into the passenger seat and eyed the tree as I drove wide around it.

"Looking for updates already?" Barrett asked without a hint of humour in his rumbling voice.

"Yes. Immediately. Give me a status update. The house and everyone inside it, and get the witches on the phone."

Without hesitation, Barrett barked, "Rhys, call Poppy."

"On it," I heard Rhys say.

"What happened?" Barrett asked me.

"Abigail sent me a gift. Some kind of… bomb in a stone?" I still couldn't make sense of what the hell that rock had been. Once the ground around my ex-tree cooled, I'd see if there was anything left of the stone. "If any strange packages come your way, don't bring them near anything flammable."

Barrett cursed, and I heard a door close. "Our security cameras show no movement around the perimeter, the ward hasn't been touched, and the traps are still set."

I released a breath of relief and pulled onto the highway. "Let me know if that changes. I'm off to the post office to talk to the woman who delivered the package. I'll call you if I learn anything."

I hung up, dropped the phone in the cupholder, and squeezed my hands around the steering wheel. "That bitch tried to roast me."

Emrick rested his hand on my thigh, and when I glanced his way, I found his silver eyes blazing. "And once again, she got too damn close."

I'd been trying not to think about what would have happened if I hadn't thrown that stone in time. If I'd still been holding it when those flames—I would never have survived. The spell had burned so hot and so fast, as though it had been pent up inside that rock, causing a flashover when it opened.

"How did she do it?" I wondered. "It looked like a regular stone. It wasn't even hot—until it was."

I'd never seen anything like it. There had been no runes etched into the surface, and I hadn't sensed any magic primed to go off.

Emrick squeezed my leg, and I dropped one hand off the steering wheel to loop my fingers through his. The car veered towards the edge of the road as we hit a sharp curve, and I reluctantly let him go to ensure we made it to the post office.

"She dropped the package off in person, which means she's here on the island." I had to stay focused on that and not on her near success. "Hopefully she thinks she cooked me on my front step and drops her guard so we can end this today."

I glanced at Emrick, and at the skepticism emanating from his quirked eyebrow and in the twist of his mouth, I sighed. "I know. But it's nice to believe that for once we're jumping ahead of her instead of trailing behind."

I parked outside the post office and hurried inside, wanting to beat the end-of-day rush.

Rita was alone behind the counter, but I couldn't count on the quiet moment to last long. It was a rule of post offices. Either you were at the back of the line or at the front of it, but a line there must be.

Emrick and I approached, and I watched Rita's customer service smile tighten, the lines around her eyes hardening.

Clearly her apology hadn't been an invitation for us to go for pints at the local pub.

"Ms. Palon, I didn't expect to see you again so soon! How can I help you?"

I flashed her my brightest smile, pointedly ignoring her silent plea for me to leave. "I have a quick question about the parcel you dropped off. I don't suppose the person who brought it to you left a name?"

"No, sorry." She sounded genuine, as though she wished getting rid of me would be that easy.

I leaned my elbows on the counter. "Could you describe them?"

She frowned and propped her hand on her hip as she searched her memory. "Older woman. Grey curly hair, lots of wrinkles. Her hand shook a lot when she set the package down."

If I'd had any doubts Abigail was my secret pen pal, they were gone.

"Did she mention where she was staying, or if she planned to stick around?"

Irritation flickered in Rita's eyes, and her attention shifted over my shoulder. I looked behind me, and sure enough there were at least five people lined up. I hadn't even heard the door open. Emrick edged closer towards me, keeping his distance from the others as best he could in the cramped space.

"No, she didn't say anything," Rita said. "Just dropped off

the package and asked me to deliver it. Is that all? Can I interest you in some stamps?"

As though me buying stamps would make me fit in around here.

I offered a perky shrug instead. "Nope, we're all set for stamps. Thanks, Rita. You know where to find me if you remember anything. House with the tire tracks in the front yard."

She flushed as she dropped her gaze to the counter, and I left her to her work.

Antagonizing the locals was probably not the best way to ensure something like Shogaur's influence was never directed my way again, but I was too frustrated by Abigail's cat-and-mouse game to worry about it. If I survived Rhys's premonition, it would be time for me to move, and if I didn't… well, it didn't much matter who I pissed off.

"What next?" Emrick asked.

"If we can't get ahead on facts, we'll have to settle for gossip." I swore Emrick paled, but when I looked again, his expression was blank. "We're going to visit the only woman who didn't rise to Shogaur's attempt to drive me out of town and, in my firm opinion, the only woman Death will never lay a hand on. Let me introduce you to Amelia the Indestructible."

7

Katerina

AMELIA CAPER, A contented widow of twenty-five years, poured the tea and set a blueberry-lemon muffin in front of Emrick. I'd already eaten two—mine and the first one she'd given him—and was eying the third on the plate in front of me. The tea was quite nice as well. This was a woman who'd perfected the art of steeping and preparing.

And of baking.

And of stained glass, knitting, crocheting, archery, wood-working, and video games.

For how busy she was, it amazed me she found time to gather all her neighbours' news, but without fail, whenever I ran into her, she was ready with the ins and outs of almost every person on the island. More than once, I wondered what information she had on me, but I was too terrified to ask. Especially since she'd earned my undying gratitude by not trying to kill me.

Rita might have no idea where to find Abigail, but if an unfamiliar older woman was wandering around the island, Mrs. Caper would know about it.

"I was so happy you didn't pack up and leave town after what Doc Emerson and the others did," she said as she peeled the paper wrapper off another muffin. I'd lost count of how many this was for her, though the crumb build-up across her cherry-dotted sky-blue blouse was impressive.

I broke a bite off the top of my own delicious snack. "I'm not the sort of person who lets a little mob scare her away."

"Which is why I'm glad you stayed. The island needs people like you to keep the blood moving. Otherwise, everything gets stagnant and we're left with a bunch of closed-minded fools who listen to rumour and ambush some poor woman in her home in the middle of the night."

I chuckled. "If my being here is supposed to prevent things like that, I'm not doing a good enough job. I'll have to get more unpredictable to keep everyone on their toes."

"Oh, please do. The stories around here are getting so stale. Like that muffin if you don't tuck in."

I complied and devoured half of it before asking, "Is anyone else injecting novelty into the regular goings on lately? Any unusual strangers keeping the bed-and-breakfasts busy?"

Mrs. Caper leaned forward with interest. "Unusual how? An extra finger? Green hair?"

"Too obvious," I said. "I came to you because you notice the people everyone else overlooks. And because you give me muffins."

She sat back, oozing an endearing smugness. "I do, don't I? All right, let's see. There's a couple in from Ottawa seeing the sights. They're lovely. She's pregnant, but neither of them knows it yet. Their dog does, though. Agnes Price's grandson is visiting from Nova Scotia. A biking tour is here from Sudbury—there's about fifty people in the group, and some of them are *quite* unusual." She gave me a knowing look, and Emrick hid a smile behind his hand. "But other than that, there aren't too many unfamiliar faces walking the streets. An older gentleman looking to get away. His wife passed a few months ago, so he's looking for a change. He's staying at an Airbnb close by. Pleasant chap." She tapped her finger against her teacup. "Oh! Someone's grandmother must be visiting. I've seen her around the Lodge a few times."

The delicious baked good turned dry on my tongue, and I forced myself to swallow it as I set down the other half. "She might be who I'm looking for. What does she look like?"

Mrs. Caper scrunched up her face and fluffed the top of her short white hair. "Grey hair. You can tell it used to be curly, but it looks thin and stringy now. Walks with a rolling gait, like her hip hurts. Bit of a stoop."

Visions flashed through my mind of a hunched figure, the hood of her black cloak pulled low, limping away from the top of a coven meeting before I could get to her.

Emrick rested his hand on my thigh, and his warmth chased away some of the chill that had set into my bones.

"And you say she's staying at the Lodge?" I asked.

She shrugged. "I saw her there once or twice over the past couple of days. Stopped to say hi to her when I was out for my morning walk, but she didn't give me much beyond a nod. Asked about the area, said she was here to visit family. She didn't say who." Her sharp brown eyes narrowed. "Are you her family? Kat Palon, if your grandmother is visiting and you haven't gone to say hello, then maybe I should have joined the mob against you."

I attempted a smile but suspected it came out more as a grimace. "Not my grandmother, no. Just someone I really need to talk to."

Mrs. Caper's jaw dropped, and her eyes shone with the potential of a good story. "Are you in trouble? Do you need a lawyer? Paul Oxford over in Gore Bay, he's the one to talk to if you need your assets covered. Here, I think I have his card."

She stood and bustled over to her kitchen drawer, rifling through the junk before she returned with a plain white business card with a plain white face staring at me from the corner.

I accepted the card with thanks. "I appreciate the recommendation. It's always good to have resources." I was dying to know what stories would spin from this conversation and hoped I didn't get a call from Oxford in an hour asking if I needed advice.

"If I see her again, I won't tell her we spoke," Mrs. Caper said, tapping the side of her nose. "You take whatever upper hand you can get to protect yourself. No one comes onto my island looking to cause drama for my friends. You can rely on my discretion."

"Thank you, Mrs. Caper. As always, you've been a highlight of my day."

She stood again and grabbed a tin from under the cabinet. "You may as well take some of these muffins home with you. I'm baking a lemon chiffon cake later for my quilting group, so I won't need all these extra carbs hanging around. You let Maera know the recipe is on the bottom of the tin in case she wants to try her hand at them. That woman can do wonders with blueberries, so I wouldn't mind getting the tin back if it comes full of her version."

"I'll let her know," I promised.

She returned with the muffins and eyed Emrick. "You're not much of a talker, are you?"

His silver eyes crinkled as he threw on his warmest smile. "Not so much, no. Especially not when I have someone so interesting to listen to."

She grinned and swatted her hand in his direction. "Oh, you're a charmer. You can come back any time. You don't like blueberries? That's no problem. I'll have some strawberry shortcake ready for you."

"That sounds lovely."

A shame for her he didn't eat.

"Now, I don't mean to be rude and rush you out the door," she said, "but I don't want to be late for my wall-climbing class. No better exercise for your core than scaling a colour-coded wall, am I right? Swing by again soon, Kat. A young woman like you shouldn't spend all her time cooped up in that house with no social connections. It's a good way to get people thinking you're strange, and then they show up at your front door with shotguns."

In a fluid motion of ushering us onto the porch and thrusting the muffin tin into my hands, she escorted us out, shut the door behind us, and disappeared into her usual whirlwind of activity.

"Wow," Emrick said to the closed door. "That was…"

"I'm telling you. If Death wants her, he'll have to catch her first." The muffins sat like a dead weight in my gut as I started towards the car. "Come on. We'll hit Muskoka first and get a quick game plan together, then we'll check out the Lodge before Abigail does another runner."

8

Katerina

SEVEN HOURS AFTER I left Adrian's Muskoka house, Emrick and I were back, this time stepping through the afterlife and avoiding the evening traffic. The late-afternoon sun cast its warm glow over the expanse of Adrian's beautiful garden, and I breathed in the sweetness of my surroundings to wash away the tension of the past few hours.

The earthly paradise stretched from the back of the house down to the lake, and although right now it didn't showcase much of the beauty that would arise in a few months, I could imagine what it would look like. Right now, in late April, so far north in Ontario, there was still some lingering snow, a lot of mud, and only the first shoots of greenery peeking through the brown.

And yet, the vampire's touch was all over the place. Last year's floral debris had been cleared out, and the ice sculptures were gone, replaced by stone sculptures that looked nearly identical to the frozen variations. On one side of the path stood a wolf howling at the moon; across from him, a dragon was wrapped around a lamppost. The designs of both were similar to the tattoo on Emrick's chest and the one on my thigh, and it never failed to warm my heart that Adrian liked to keep the two of us close, even when we weren't around.

At the end of the path, where in the winter a large half-igloo safeguarded a stone bench from wind and snow, stood a devil with its wings spread. Two tiny horns poked through its forehead, and its lips were parted in a smile that revealed its sharpened fangs. Its hands rested casually on the back of the bench, inviting any passersby to take a rest.

The piece never failed to make me smile, as Adrian had modelled for it himself. It portrayed the monster that many fiction authors believed him to be instead of the warm, welcoming man he was. Or at least, the man he was now that he'd overcome his bloodlust.

It had taken him hundreds of years to get his vampiric instincts under control, and the lives he'd taken in that time rivalled those he'd taken as a Roman tribune in his mortal life.

If the Adrian of yesteryear had been a tiger, today he was a house cat. Content in his retirement with his thrall and his books.

Though the cat wasn't without claws, as Abigail would find out in the days to come. I still couldn't believe Adrian had agreed to leave his library to help me, and again I felt that rush through my blood at the thought of once more fighting by his side.

Emrick and I started towards the back door of the beautiful two-storey log-exterior mini-mansion. The large windows that graced the back of the house, most of them covered at this time of day with heavy blackout curtains to keep Adrian safe, offered stunning views of the garden from almost every room. It was a magazine-quality paradise, and I hoped Adrian intended to keep it after he moved on, adding it to the collection of properties he owned across the world.

Emrick tugged on my hand to pull me to a stop, and I turned to look up at him, shocked once again by how the sun seemed to absorb him.

"Will you be okay if I head off for a bit?" he asked. "I have a few souls to bring over."

"Of course." I stood on tiptoe and brushed my lips over his, tasting the faintly chilled smokiness of his mouth.

He tightened his arms around me, slid his hand into my hair, and pressed his body against mine, drawing a gasp from me. I clung to his shoulders to keep my balance and lost myself in his hunger.

The moment ended all too soon, and when he pulled away, his silver eyes were hooded with lust. "I'll be back for you in an hour. Then I have plans."

He punctuated those plans with a slower kiss that filled my veins with molten heat, then disappeared.

After taking a moment to shake off the blaze of desire, I turned my feet towards the back door of the house.

When I stepped inside, I almost bumped into Rhys coming out of the living room. His eyes widened on seeing me. He shifted on his feet and dropped his gaze, then seemed to force himself to look at me.

Worry speared through my heart. "What's wrong?"

"Wrong? Nothing's wrong." He cleared his throat and shoved his hands in his pockets. "What are you doing back here?"

I'd called Barrett as soon as we'd left Amelia's house to let him know I was on my way, but Rhys obviously hadn't received the memo.

I narrowed my eyes at him, ready to push him for answers, but Maera popped her head out of the kitchen. "Kat? Oh good, you're here. We're waiting on you."

Rhys gestured for me to lead the way, his expression pinched, and I let my curiosity drop for now. He and I would have words before I left.

I found everyone exactly how I'd left them, with the exception of Adrian, who would have gone to bed after I left this morning. Barrett and Gavin sat on one side of the table, with Poppy, Murisa, and Cuddles's butthole on the laptop screen. Maera dropped into the chair at the head of the table with a cup of tea almost the size of her head and a plate of snickerdoodles in front of her.

Rhys grabbed a cookie before he sat beside her, not making eye contact with anyone around the table.

"What's this about a bomb, kitty Kat?" Poppy asked. She made a valiant effort to brush Cuddles's tail out of the way, but he'd decided now was the perfect time for a stretch and would not be swayed.

I settled in the chair across from Maera. "It was no bomb I've ever seen. It was a rock. Just a stone about an inch and a half wide." I raised my fingers to show them the approximate dimensions. "Something you'd find on the beach. And then it lit up like an ember, and if I hadn't hurled it at the tree, I'd have been charred Kat in a breath."

Another shudder ran through me. Almost nine hundred years old, and I still wasn't comfortable with the idea of my time being cut short that suddenly.

"I haven't had a chance to see if the rock survived the fire, but have you ever heard of anything like that?"

Murisa shook her head. "It sounds fascinating. Was it the rock itself that was enchanted? With a timing rune, perhaps?"

She chewed on her lip. "No, probably not. Not if you were the target. Abigail wouldn't have known when you would pick it up."

"Maybe it was attuned to Kat's touch?" Poppy suggested.

"It's possible. She would have needed to get Kat's fingerprints, but that probably would have been doable considering…" Murisa waved her hand in the air, gesturing to the numerous times Abigail and I had crossed paths without me knowing it. "We'll do some research, Kat. If that stone exists, someone had to have made it, which means their research exists somewhere. I'll find it."

I believed her. I just wished she could work a little faster. Abigail's message through Rhys and her attack on me were evidence enough that she was getting ready for a fight. As we stood now, we weren't ready—not if she had weapons like that stone up her sleeve.

"I think it would be best for you two to come here," I said. "If we're preparing for battle, I need my team together. We'd also have access to whatever prototypes you're working on."

Murisa's eyes lit up. "Already ahead of you on that one. As soon as we finished our call this morning, Poppy had our latest idea couriered to Muskoka."

Poppy grinned, a wicked slant to her smile. "You're going to love these, kitty Kat. Tell me you didn't toss them, Grumpy Boy."

I smirked at the nickname as Barrett rolled his eyes and rose from the table to step into the foyer. He returned with a purple cloth bag the size of his palm. When he tipped the bag, a dozen beetle-shaped metallic creatures rolled onto the maple tabletop.

Maera grimaced. "I really hate those things. Why did you have to make them look like bugs?"

"Because bugs are natural in the outdoors," Murisa said. "Also, I think they're adorable."

Cuddles meowed his agreement. Or his desire to eat them.

I reached for one. "What do they do?"

Barrett grumbled as he tugged a small remote control out of the bottom of the bag. It was a simple white plastic remote with three buttons on its smooth surface. He hit the first button, and the bugs lit up with barely visible lights along their backs. Their tiny mechanical legs stretched, lifting them up and carrying them in circles around the centre of the table.

He hit the second button, and the bugs stilled. Their backs split open as though they were spreading a set of fine metallic wings, revealing glass vials the size of my pinky nail within. The vials were filled with potions of various colours to do who knew what. I guessed it wasn't anything friendly.

"The third button sends the bugs flying to rain the potions down on the unprepared," Poppy explained.

I blinked. "That's epic."

Murisa clapped her hands. "I know, right?"

"The woman's a genius." Poppy pulled her in for a kiss—pushing Cuddles into an offended exit—and after a few seconds, I cleared my throat to remind them we were still here.

"All right," I said, "that's a good start. I want more. I want this house under so many safety protocols that if Abigail *thinks* about stepping foot on the property, she suffers serious bodily harm." I caught the arch of Maera's eyebrow and tacked on a quick, "Without, you know, maiming any neighbours or delivery people or anything. Barrett, where do we stand on that?"

"The property's ward has been refreshed and keyed to the people now here," he said. "Including Poppy and Murisa. No one else can get in without a DNA sample."

That was something, but I didn't trust Abigail not to get past our safety net. We'd already learned the hard way that wards only did so much.

"What about offense? Do we have physical traps beyond the ward? Cameras? Anything to give us early notice if she shows up?"

Barrett nodded. "Anyone who pulls up the drive without calling at the gate first will wind up with their tires shredded. It's linked to a remote, so I can deactivate the trap as needed. We've set up cameras, but—"

I pursed my lips. "We have to assume she'll navigate around them. I know." A groan of frustration escaped me. "All right. Our best chance is for me to catch her at the Lodge. That's where she was last seen, and she has no way of knowing we've learned that. As soon as Emrick's back, I'll try to pin her down."

Maera's eyes gleamed with worry. "Be careful, Kat. You don't know what she knows. We have no idea what's coming."

She shot a quick glance at Rhys, who was boring a hole into the tabletop with his stare.

I tensed. "Rhys…"

As he cleared his throat and shifted in his seat, an alarm sounded in my head.

"I may have tried to trigger a vision about what she's planning," he said.

Maera pressed her lips into a thin line, and my expression probably wasn't any warmer.

His cheeks flushed, and he ran his hand through his flop of red hair. "I know. It was really stupid. But no one else was making progress, so I wanted to help."

A string of expletives ran through my skull, but what was the point in getting angry after the fact? "I'm guessing by the word *tried* and the lack of a phone call, you didn't have any luck?"

His flush deepened. "Not exactly, but there was—just the once—I thought maybe I caught a glimpse of her. She was sitting in front of a scrying bowl. Or looking into it?"

The alarms in my head clanged louder. "Did she see you?"

He stretched out his fingers, then curled them in again.

"She might have. I might have woken up with a knife in my hand."

Maera huffed, and Barrett bowed his head into his hands. Poppy murmured a low, "My dude."

"I caught him before he did anything with it," Maera said, "but it was pure chance I did."

"Right." I rolled my shoulders and took a calming breath. "That's three times now she's gotten into your head. You were asleep when I said this last time, but you need to hear me now. We have to block your visions for a while. Poppy, Murisa, how is your brainstorming coming along on that?"

All trace of red faded from Rhys's skin as he paled whiter than Emrick. "Kat, no, you can't!"

"She can and she will," Maera said. "We know this woman is coming for us. The house is warded, but you're open hunting."

"At least until we have a way to protect you." I turned to the witches on the screen.

Murisa looked uncomfortable after Rhys's vehement refusal, but she said, "We have something that'll work. We'll bring it with us when we come."

I rested my hand on Rhys's. "It should only be for a few days. Then you'll have the upper hand on her. She won't see you coming."

He offered a weak half-smile and nodded. It hurt my heart to strip his ability from him, but I would rather have him flounder without purpose for a week than dead for a lifetime.

I looked around the table. "All right, everyone, let's get ready. When Abigail comes for us, she won't give us much warning. I want her caught in our trap before we're trapped in hers."

9

Emrick

I OPENED THE mists to the afterlife, and the soul of an older man followed me through. His form had faded into a pillar of shimmering light, his features brighter pinpoints where his face had been. Yet his voice remained, and he spoke of trouble.

"I don't suppose you could keep an eye on my granddaughter?" he asked. "Make sure she's all right?"

The love and concern in his tone made me wish I could say yes. "I'm sorry, but that's outside my role in this world. What is it you're afraid of?"

"Rumours. They've been going around my coven for a few years now, but lately they've gotten louder."

A rock formed in my gut. "What sort of rumours?"

"The immortal sorceress. Events are in motion now that

will push her to extremes. So many people are going to die."

He wasn't the first soul that had spoken to me of Kat carrying danger along with her. So many had feared for those they left behind. I'd hoped the rumours would fade now that Kat was back on her feet and regaining her magic, returning to her place as guardian between magical and mundane, but if anything they'd gotten worse.

"What events? What do you know?"

Now the soul crowded me, moving so close I could make out the shape of a face in the centre of the light. "You need to deal with her. Grab her and drag her to this place, remove her from the world. She brings nothing but chaos and destruction, and her power is growing. People who follow her have died and will continue to die, but it won't stop there."

It was the same warning I'd heard for the past few months. Talk of Kat bringing trouble, the magical community growing restless as the gossip spread of what might be coming. As yet, no one had been able to give me a clear idea of what this destruction was.

"What kind of trouble?" I asked, desperate for something more than vague worries. "What is it about her that's creating these fears?"

"It's her very nature. Everything I've heard, everything my coven has learned, proves that all she cares about is gathering magic. Something about undoing the past. How she's sworn to do whatever it takes to fix what happened."

I thought about reassuring him that somewhere along the line, the game of telephone had grown convoluted. From the time Katerina had accepted her immortal state, she'd sworn to continue the work Palonia had held sacred by protecting the mundane world from the dangers of the magical and the magical from the influence of the mundane. Every fight she entered into was with the goal of maintaining balance between both sides. But before I opened my mouth, I saw the futility of arguing with him. Whether people were confused or someone was intentionally maligning Kat's intentions, this man believed it enough to beg for his granddaughter's safety.

I guided him to the river where he would wait for the ferry to take him to whatever his next path would be, then drifted through the emptiness of the afterlife to recentre myself.

If Abigail was attacking Kat's reputation, I couldn't begin to guess why. To make it difficult for Kat to carry out her mission? To make it harder for Kat to reach Abigail? To turn people against her, increase the number of enemies gunning for her so she would be too distracted to stop Abigail from whatever the witch planned next?

Abigail had already taught Mikhail a devastating ritual that would have slaughtered hundreds of Toronto's witches, and she'd summoned Shogaur, who would have used his demonic influence to do the same.

Considering she was a witch herself, she seemed to have a deep hatred for her fellow practitioners. Unless it was all some power grab?

One thing was certain—Kat needed resources to track down Abigail and more to stop her, and for one reason or another, she risked losing both because of these rumours.

And there was nothing I could do about it but warn her and hope my warnings were enough.

I stared at the fields around me, the blades of dead grass and forked branches of barren trees leached of all colour, and cursed my fate that I should have so much power and be so limited in how I could use it. In my bones, I felt we were on the brink of war, and all I would be able to do was sit back and collect my friends' souls as they fell.

10

Katerina

WITH OUR NEXT steps lined up, I leaned over to turn off the video call. Before I could cut them off, Murisa threw up her hands. "Oh! Before you go, did Gavin tell you the good news?"

I looked to the sorcerer, who until now had remained silent, and watched his expression shutter.

"I'll take the silence as a no," Poppy said. "We've been working with him to drain more of Shogaur's energy from his aura, and the cleaner he gets, the more memories he's gotten back."

I looked at him with interest. Was that the reason he looked less ready to set me on fire today? "That's pretty huge. Do you remember anything about having magic?"

Gavin crossed his arms and glowered at me from under his thick eyebrows. "No."

I waited for him to say something else—anything—but he remained stubbornly silent. This man rivalled Barrett for aggravating behaviour. At least with Barrett, I knew why the man disliked me. I had magic, and he hated magic. I had a tendency to run into situations without thinking, and he considered my lack of strategy unprofessional and unimpressive. I got it.

Gavin's anger was less rational and more primal. I understood where the rage came from, but still. I wasn't the one who'd pulled him out of his happy life in Hamilton. I wasn't the one who'd tied him to a chair and abandoned him to the whims of a fear demon, going so far as to torture him when his mind proved too strong to give in to Shogaur's influence.

When the silence stretched on without any sign of breaking, Murisa jumped in. "Nothing about his magic, but about his family. I think it's fascinating."

I appreciated her efforts not to leave me out of the loop. While Gavin remained under Adrian's roof, he was part of my team, voluntarily or not. It was only right I knew the basics about him.

Or maybe I was just nosy.

"Family's always good." I looked at Gavin. "Any drama? An inappropriate uncle?"

Gavin's scowl grew deeper. "I know my name, my parents,

where I live. I got to call my mom and reassure her I wasn't dead." He scrubbed his hand over his face. "That was two hours of fun right there, let me tell you."

By the haunted look in his eyes, I assumed that by *fun*, he meant he would have rather scraped metal files under his nail beds.

"I don't suppose you had a chance to ask her about any magic in your family history?" I doubted it, but since he didn't seem ready to volunteer information, I figured it was better to ask.

He snorted, confirming my suspicion. "Not so easy to bring that up, no. 'Hey, mom, when dad moved here from Korea, did he talk about being able to shoot fireballs from his hands?' I don't see that conversation going well."

I shrugged. "How do you know it's from your dad's side of the family? What if it's your mom's?"

"She wouldn't know if it was," he grumbled.

"Why not? Family stories get passed down all the time. We don't always believe them or fully understand them, but there could be something buried in the bedtime tales your mum used to tell Baby Gavin."

He held up his hand, and his dark eyes burned as flickers of flame danced between his fingers. "I think she would have mentioned something like this if she'd known." He clenched his fist to extinguish the fire. "Even if you're right, Mom wouldn't have had stories to tell. My grandmother bolted when Mom was a kid, and Granddad never had much to say about her. They weren't exactly close."

"But oh my goddess, kitty Kat," Poppy squealed. "Speaking of Baby Gavin, look at this photo we found online!"

There was a sound of tapping on the computer, then the screen changed from the witches to a picture of a family in a park. At a picnic, maybe. A handsome Korean man sat with his arm around a slim white woman, who was trying to spoon-feed a much younger Gavin. The three were laughing, enjoying themselves on a summer's day, but I didn't have eyes for anyone except his mom. The way her brown hair fell over her shoulders, the curve of her eyes. The way her lips sat when she smiled.

In a flash, I was back on the street outside a burning new age shop, staring at an older, wrinkled version of that same smile through the smoke. The exact same smile. As though someone had copy-and-pasted it onto this younger woman.

A nagging thought in the back of my head told me I'd seen this smile somewhere else, but when I chased the memory, it evaded me, so I came back to the night of the fire. To Abigail— the witch with no history who created wards out of air just like the sorcerers of old, who'd created a spell circle so strong it had stopped my heart. Who'd somehow found a way to contain magic in a mundane stone.

A shiver ran down my spine, and I followed the trail where it led me.

"Do you know your grandmother's name?"

Gavin shook his head. "She's persona non grata at home. If Granddad mentions her at all, he calls her 'The Cow.'"

"Well, Gavin," I said, and my mouth was so dry the words felt like cotton around my tongue, "I think you might be part bovine. Because I'm looking at this picture of your mother, and I swear I'm looking at a younger Abigail. I know it might seem I'm grasping at air, but there's a good chance Abigail is your grandmother."

It made too much sense. Sorcerers were extinct, yet we had Gavin, summoning fire from nothing, and Abigail, creating wards the way my old teachers did. The odds were way too high for two bloodlines to have spontaneously revived.

Gavin blinked at me, his mouth opening and closing as he attempted to form his response. I didn't blame him for not finding one. The desire to deny it would be strong, but since he had no information about who his grandmother was, it wasn't like he could argue my theory.

No one else in the room offered anything to fill the weighted silence, all of them staring between me and Gavin. Barrett's jaw bulged as he clenched his teeth, and Maera reached for another cookie.

"We won't know for sure until we track her down," I offered by way of solace. "But based on your magic and the family resemblance, I would say I'm sixty per cent certain."

"But…" Rhys's brow scrunched in confusion. "If that's the case, she can't know, right? I mean, she tortured you. Would a grandparent do that to their own family?"

Poppy snorted. "Not all families are like yours, Rhys. You have a mom who loves you. My mother wanted to use me as a tool to gain power. Murisa's parents threatened to disinherit her if she kept using magic. A homicidal, power-hungry bitch like Abigail? She wouldn't care who she hurt to get what she wanted."

I hoped Rhys was right and Abigail didn't know. Either way would suck for Gavin, but how much worse would it be if she'd knowingly committed such cruelties to her own grandson? Sacrificing him to be host for a fear demon? Slicing into his skin to try to break his mind? He'd proved stronger than she'd expected, but the damage she'd inflicted was evident in so much more than the scars in his flesh.

But it also made sense as to how she knew what hid in his blood. She would have known exactly how to wake up his latent magic to use it for her own gain.

How furious she must be that he'd fallen into my hands.

I couldn't help but wonder how we might use this possible connection to our advantage.

As though Murisa had read my mind, she said, "If there's a DNA connection, we might be able to use your blood to help us learn more about her."

Gavin groaned. "Why is it always blood with you people?"

"Because there's power in blood." I shook off the shroud of shadow around my shoulders and refocused on the conversation. "But don't worry, they're not talking pools of it. A pinprick at most. Probably. Right?"

The witches smiled a little too brightly. "Sure," Murisa said, as Poppy spoke up, "Absolutely."

The temperature dropped and mist floated across the floor as Emrick stepped into the room. If possible, he looked more disturbed than he had when I'd walked in on him earlier today.

I rose from the table and backed towards him, sagging against his chest as his arm wrapped around my waist. "Wish me luck, everyone. If all goes well, Abigail won't be a problem beyond this afternoon. If it doesn't go well, you all know what you have to do."

"We'll be packed and ready to leave within the hour, kitty Kat," Poppy said.

Barrett jutted his chin towards Gavin. "We'll secure the house."

Good. Gavin would need something to take his mind off his homicidal possible-relation. At least with Barrett, he'd be in good hands to let off some steam.

"Make sure to update Adrian on all this when he wakes up. And you"—I pointed to Rhys—"no visions."

He dropped his head and nodded.

"I'll be in touch soon."

Emrick curled his fingers around mine and drew the mist around us. I took a deep breath and allowed him to guide us through, praying with everything I had that we'd be out of danger before the trouble really started.

11

Katerina

THE LODGE WAS a popular bed-and-breakfast during tourist season with its cozy aesthetic and proximity to the board-walk along Providence Bay.

In the winter, it was still one of the go-tos for people wanting to check out the winter sights and take advantage of the cross-country skiing trails.

In the spring, during the period when the woods woke up, the water thawed, and the first greenery peeked out over the melting snow, it was just shy of a dead zone. That someone was staying here should have been the subject of gossip for more people than Amelia Caper. There was no way Rita hadn't heard about it.

Which made me question what other stories Abigail had

spun about her reason for being here. Shogaur had sent these people after me. Was Abigail doing more to drag my name through the mud, or was her reason for sticking around more nefarious and more subtle? Did she expect me to discover her? Did she *want* me to discover her?

If so, it meant I could be walking into another trap.

Emrick brought us through the afterlife into the parking lot behind the ice cream shop along the boardwalk. The Lodge was visible from the beach, and I wanted to take a walk around first to get a feel for my surroundings and see if I could spot Abigail before she spotted me. It wouldn't do to go knocking on random doors trying to find her. And after my experience in the Toronto hotel, having been struck in the chest with so much power I'd literally met Death, I wasn't in a rush to follow the witch into more enclosed spaces.

"At least it's a nice day," I said as we sauntered towards the boardwalk. "And I have my weight in muffins to walk off."

As we strolled, I filled Emrick in on my theory about Abigail's magic and her connection to Gavin.

Emrick shook his head. "What a nightmare, knowing your grandmother might have thrown you to a demon like steak to a dog. How'd he take it?"

"About as well as you'd expect. But he held back from actually throwing a fireball at me, so I call that progress."

He frowned. "You don't think he's involved, do you? Lying

about his ignorance and working with Abigail in secret?"

I remembered the state Gavin had been in when we'd found him, stuck in that stinking room, covered in so many wounds his skin had been thick with blood. Bile crept up the back of my throat, and I swallowed it down. "If he is, he's more willing to throw himself into the mission than I've ever been, even at the height of my power. I think it's far more likely she saw him as an easily accessible tool. The guy's going to need more therapy than he'll ever be able to afford."

Anger simmered in my blood for all the crimes Abigail had committed. The people she'd hurt, the lines she'd crossed. I'd encountered enough evil in my long years, but she was among the closest to pure monster I'd ever met.

"I wish I knew who she was. She didn't wake up and decide one day to make me her enemy. We must have crossed paths at some point."

"You don't have any memory of this woman?"

I thought of the smile that had clued me in on the connection between her and Gavin, that teasing tickle at the back of my mind telling me I'd seen it somewhere before. Again, as soon as I reached for it, it flitted away.

"Enough to know we've met. Or I knew one of her ancestors. But nothing specific. Maybe I would have caught sight of her sooner if I hadn't buried my head under the pillows and tried to forget the world was turning around me, but there you have it. We've got to be looking at someone over sixty at the very least, right? If not older. So that's a forty- to sixty-year range in which I might have offended her. My memory's not good enough to whittle all those years down to one woman."

Emrick frowned. "She must have been aware of you, though, to have prepared all these attacks. Summoning Shogaur was more than a little personal, and now she's come straight to your door."

"Why now? If she's been around all these decades, what pushed her over the edge?"

"Retaliation for stopping Mikhail's ritual?" he suggested.

"Why would it matter to her? He might not have sacrificed her along with the others, but she fled as soon as things shifted against him, which suggests she wasn't aiming for immortality herself. Either this is a longer-standing grudge, or I'm missing something really freaking huge."

So many questions to lay at this woman's door.

The water lapped at the sand to my right, and I leaned on the railing to stare over the bay. The sky was overcast, obscuring the view in a hazy fog, and it was as though the world had closed in on itself. Emrick and I were alone, grabbing this stolen moment before the storm broke.

All too soon, the sensation of being lost in the mist dragged me into the memory of my near-final death at the hotel. How the fog had compressed around me with indecipherable shadows moving beyond.

I shook myself off, not needing the reminder that, difficult as I was to kill, Death was watching me. Maybe even waiting for the opportunity to pull me the rest of the way through.

Emrick slipped his arms around my waist. "Where did you go?"

His lips were close to my ear, his voice a deep rumble that vibrated down to my toes, and I leaned against him. "Just thinking about the nature of life and death. How unfair it is that after so many years of breathing, I don't know what to expect of whatever comes after."

"I straddle realms, and there are mysteries even I don't have the answer to."

I grimaced. "If that's supposed to make me feel better, it doesn't."

He laughed. "No, just commiserating."

I wished we could stand there forever, tasting the crispness of the air, hypnotized by the muted sunlight glittering across the surface of the water. But movement down the beach caught my eye, and I squinted to take in the dark figure lurching along the water's edge about a hundred metres off.

The breeze played with their hair, sending it whipping around their head, and their arms were wrapped around their middle to hold the edges of their grey sweater closed. Their rolling gait, the way their left leg dragged just slightly behind the right, made me stiffen.

"What is it?" Emrick asked, and I slid out of his grasp as I started towards the figure.

My footsteps echoed against the wooden slats of the boardwalk, and the sound carried over the otherwise silent beach. It must have been loud enough to catch the figure's ear because they looked at me over their shoulder... and I recognized the cruel curve of her mouth.

I pushed myself into a run and summoned my magic into my hands. Fire crept over my gloves, climbing to my elbows where the leather stopped. I pumped my legs to gain more speed and, with every step, closed the distance between me and Abigail. She was so close. The woman was moving at a snail's pace, so there was no way she would get away from me this time. If she'd wanted to taunt me, she'd misjudged.

Memories of the hotel in Toronto crashed down on me, and I opened myself to any sense of magic in the air. Abigail wouldn't catch me off guard this time. She couldn't hide a spell circle on a ceiling, and the sand would make an unstable surface if she'd tried to plan ahead. But I wouldn't put it past her to try.

I bounded down the stairs onto the beach and stumbled on the uneven footing. Before I could fall, I managed to find my pace across the rock-strewn sand and continued after her. Seventy metres. Sixty. When I was less than fifty metres away, the woman stopped and turned to watch me. Unease grabbed hold of my stomach. She didn't appear concerned by my rapid approach, but still I sensed no magic, no trap.

The breeze picked up and carried the scent of lavender on the air. It reminded me of screams. Of hundreds of witches crammed together in a warehouse filled with magic. Of Mikhail's mocking smile. And of rolling hills, bleating sheep, and the sense of home.

The sly angle of her smile grew wider, and the smugness in her expression made me try to slow down, but I had too much momentum to stop on a dime.

"Kat!" Emrick called out behind me.

I looked over my shoulder, but although he'd followed me, he'd kept his distance, running as far behind me as Abigail was ahead of me.

He picked up his pace, and I turned back to Abigail, again stumbling in the sand as my foot slipped in a divot. Rocks were scattered around me. They caught the light in ways that made my eyes glitch, and it took me more than a second to realize they weren't catching the sunlight through the clouds but were glowing from within.

Just like the one she'd mailed to me.

I cursed and tried to turn around, needing to run out of this minefield I'd found myself in, but there were too many rocks and the ground was too soft.

Abigail's mouth moved with silent words, and the glow in

the rocks grew brighter. I lurched away from the nearest stones as they split open. Magic released from within, and purple lightning exploded from the centre. I turned, but not fast enough, and a bolt caught me in the side.

I screamed as the power surged through me. Agony squeezed my heart, my head, my muscles, as I flew through the air into the freezing embrace of Providence Bay.

12

Emrick

THE STRENGTH OF the spell circle that burst from the stone threw me backwards. I braced for impact, prepared to hit sand, but found myself tumbling into the afterlife. I landed on the cracked earth of muted grey and, staggered by Abigail's magic and my unexpected trip through the barrier, struggled to regain my equilibrium.

Beyond my confusion, my anxiety rose. I had to get back to Kat. The last lightning bolt to hit her had stopped her heart, however temporarily, and I was afraid of what this one might do. So far, the tether that bound Kat and I remained intact, but I wouldn't relax until I saw her for myself.

I raised my hand to summon the mist, but for the first time since I accepted Death's deal, it resisted me.

I had to be careful. I'd made a deal to serve Death, not the sorceress, and I was running perilously close to breaking the terms of the arrangement.

The thoughts dropped into my head fully formed, as though some silent voice had spoken them. Impressions delivered straight from Death. I pressed my hands to my skull to block out the words and dull the deep throb that had taken up residence behind my left eye.

The only rule I had to follow was to not involve myself in the mortal world. I'd traded my wife's survival for that deal.

A vision of Gabrielle lying in our bed wavered behind my eyelids, her face pale, her sweat-slick hair sticking to her beautiful skin as she looked up at me with fever-glazed eyes. I hadn't wanted to lose her. I'd believed our love was worth forever.

She'd recovered and left me. Yet here I was, more in love than I ever imagined it was possible to be, desperate to return to the mortal world and fetch my beating heart out of the water. I had to make sure Kat was all right.

There would be consequences for my choices. They'd already begun to show. How far did I think I could push Death before Death caught up with me?

The thoughts bore down on me, the seriousness of Death's warning rumbling through my bones until I feared I would be torn apart right here, right now.

I knew how true the warning was. None of what passed

through my head was new to me, but I didn't care. I didn't need to change the world—I didn't need to involve myself in anything—but I had to find Kat.

More thoughts pressed in on me. Visions of me unleashing the full brunt of my power to protect Kat—expending my energy to turn anyone I wanted to dust with a wave of my hand instead of direct contact. I'd never done it, though I'd been tempted more than once. I was capable of so much more than opening a gateway to the afterlife. Death was a part of me, and with every fragment of myself I lost, the more like Death I became and the more power I developed. But the more I used it, the more I would forget who I was—what mattered most to me.

My desire for Kat kept me human and kept me from embracing the full potential of my nature. That wouldn't change.

More visions—me as nothing, as an empty-eyed wraith carrying out my duties without thought or emotion, no memories or ties to anchor me to this world. I would exist everywhere at once, no longer limited by my physical form, serving Death until the time it deemed my side of our agreement paid.

But I'd be without Kat. Her immortality would continue, the tether between us still existing, but she would be trapped in the mortal world without my company to help her pass her long, lonely years.

The image came with no associated emotion. There was no joy, no smugness, no satisfaction. A simple reveal of the future that awaited both Kat and me if I didn't smarten up.

After that final thought, I was thrown out of the afterlife and back onto the beach. I hit the sand with a grunt, and only when the grains stuck to my face did I realize I'd been crying.

I got the message all too clearly. The knife-edge I walked between who I was and what I was becoming had grown sharper. The next bad choice might be my last.

Knowing that, and having seen what my future looked like, I swallowed my rage as Abigail caught my eye from where she stood on the edge of the beach. I watched her turn and walk away, unable to go after her and put an end to the bitch like I wanted to.

From her, my attention jerked to the water, to where Kat drifted on the surface of the bay. Although drowning wouldn't kill her, she would be furious if she needed days to recover. I couldn't destroy Abigail, but I could damn well make sure Kat had the strength to fight her. Praying I made it to my beautiful immortal in time, I dove into the lake.

13

Katerina

C OME ON, KATE, *let's go!" My sister, Kyla, grabbed my arm and tugged me towards the door. "You can't hide inside during the harvest festival. Everyone else is already there."*

I laughed and shrugged her off, making faces at my nineteen-month-old son as I bounced him on my knee. "Go on without me, then. You don't need me to hold your hand."

She threw herself onto her knees in front of me, her brown eyes shining with sixteen-year-old ardour. "Katerina, this man is stunning. Have you no curiosity? By the time you get out there, someone else might have swept him away."

"I'm quite content with one husband, thank you very much."

"I'm sure Shep will be pleased to hear it," my mother said as she came in from outside. The scent of lavender water trailed after her.

She bent to press a kiss on the top of my head and scooped Rowan into her arms. "That being said, Kyla's right. Go out and enjoy yourself, love. There's food, and the rites have begun."

My smile turned brittle, and my hands grew cold as my heart raced.

She meant the demonstrations of power the sorcerers of Palonia performed to give thanks to the gods for our magic. The rites I hadn't been invited to participate in because I had no magic worth showcasing. They were a reminder of all the ways I'd disappointed my family and would keep disappointing my family.

The cottage faded around me, and I found myself outside, standing in front of a bonfire as high as my head.

"What do you think, Kate?" Shep asked. "What wishes should we cast into the fire this year?"

I turned my face into the sun as my husband wrapped his arm around my waist. "For my family to be together. For me to master my magic. For me to finally see what exists outside Palonia."

Shep drew his fingers down my arm and rested the chicken bones in my empty palm. "I second all these wishes. You deserve everything and more." He pressed a kiss into my neck. "Next year will be ours, Kate. You'll see."

His face was so full of hope and happiness it made me giddy. He was right. Of course he was right. What was stopping it?

Rowan babbled where he sat crooked in my arm, reaching for Shep's beard, and Shep grinned as he took him from me. "Mae says there's a big surprise planned for tonight at sunset. Wouldn't tell me what it was, but she seems excited about it."

"Why would she mention it to you so early?" I grabbed his arm. "Do you think it's about the journey to the continent? Did the elders choose you to be among the group?"

He laughed and kissed me. "Let's not get ahead of ourselves. Besides, even if they did, I don't know if I would accept."

"You have to. The travel, the knowledge. Think of all the languages you could teach me when you came home."

His laugh grew louder. "And let you butcher the German dialects as you did the French? I don't think the Saxons would thank me."

I gave him a teasing shove, which only made him smile more. With my heart lighter than it had been in weeks, Shep and I threw our offerings on the fire.

The fire faded, and I found myself among the trees, covered in blood, watching a cloaked figure move from body to body as he turned them to dust.

Consciousness came back to me wrapped in darkness and freezing wetness. I stretched out my arms and could barely see them through the water. Panic gripped me as I reached for something solid and found only more water. Nightmares and memories lurked in my periphery, turning with me whenever I wrenched myself to see them.

Where was Emrick?

As the memories faded, I forced myself to remember where I was and what had happened. The glowing rocks. The lightning strike. I was somewhere under the surface of the bay.

I clenched my jaw shut to avoid swallowing any more water, but already my lungs burned, and my legs felt miles away.

Which way was up?

The cold water tugged at my clothes, my hair, dragging me down. The bay wasn't deep here, but even so, I couldn't get my bearings. The burst of the spell had left me disoriented, clouding my thoughts and making it impossible for me to see straight. Light seemed to come through the darkness, wavering with the current, but every time I tried to track it, it shifted, leaving me confused as to what was real and what wasn't.

Water trickled through my parted lips, and in my desperate attempt to get rid of it, I inhaled more. My magic wasn't responding, my limbs weren't doing what I needed them to do.

My heart raced as I tried to kick my way to freedom and struck silt and rock along the bottom of the bay.

My arms grew heavy, my flailing becoming less focused, more desperate as consciousness slipped away. I struggled to hold on to it, knowing if I let go, I was done for. Drowning wouldn't kill me—I'd learned that the hard way when I'd first walked out of Palonia—but the oxygen deprivation would knock me out for a few days while I recovered, and I didn't have days.

Abigail had been right there. *Right. There.* I'd lost my chance because she'd taken me by surprise again with those rocks.

What the hell were those rocks?

The shimmer of magic within the stone, the murmured spell that had activated them and knocked me on my ass. They were the same as the one I'd held in my hand, but I was no closer to understanding them. What magic was the woman dealing in?

I needed to relax. Needed to let my body go limp so the water would carry me to the surface. But every time I tried, my body was wracked with shivers that made me curl up again. Exhaustion closed in on me, weighing me down, making it difficult to keep my eyes open.

Blackness closed in on me, and although I fought against it, the numbness overtook me, and my body gave in to the desperate need for air. With a last silent cry, I sank into oblivion.

14

Emrick

I CUT THROUGH the murky water with as much power as I could muster in the heavy darkness.

Kat had sunk out of view, and it took me longer than it should have to find her beneath the bay's surface. With a burst of speed, I wrapped my arms around her and tore us through the afterlife to the warmth of her house. The intact ward as we passed into her bedroom reassured me no one had breached it in our absence, but that was the extent of my relief as Kat's dead weight sagged in my hold.

Her eyes were closed, her clothes were soaked, her skin was freezing. The faint blue hue of her lips warned of more than the cold having affected her, and my pulse raced with worry. We didn't have time for her to recover. Not with Abigail so close—

not with me unable to do anything more than drag Kat back to consciousness.

"Come on," I murmured as I set her down on her bedroom floor and brushed her black hair out of her face. "Breathe for me."

I set my fingers beneath her chin, tilted her head back, and angled my mouth over hers. After five breaths with no response, I set my hands on her chest and began compressions. I'd never learned how to save a life, my role in this world being to bring magicals to the next one, but I'd watched emergency responders do it thousands of times and hoped it would be enough. A rib cracked under the heels of my palms, but I didn't stop. Her ribs would heal. She just had to breathe.

Her body spasmed beneath my hands, her mouth opened, and water sputtered up as she heaved out the contents of her lungs. I rolled her onto her side and held her hair back.

"It's all right, I'm here. You're safe now. I've got you. Breathe, Kat."

She sucked in air, then choked on a sob and expelled more water, this time from her stomach. I rubbed her back and spoke in soft tones, and as her retches turned to gasping breaths, I cradled her against my chest.

She trembled in my arms, her shivers growing so bad I struggled to keep my grip on her. Her teeth chattered too much for her to speak, but she curled herself into me. I held her tighter, rested my bare fingers on the back of her neck, and stepped us through the afterlife into her bathroom.

Without releasing her, I turned on the shower, making sure to keep the temperature warm enough to counter her chills but low enough not to send her body into shock.

For now, I didn't bother to undress her. She was already wet, and I didn't want to waste time fighting with the sodden rags. I carried her into the shower and sat on the floor with her. The spray washed over us, cool on my skin. After a few minutes, her shaking subsided, and she sagged against me. I inched up the temperature of the water little by little, never letting it get too hot, then turned my attention to the soaps and shampoos that lined the shower wall. How this woman kept them all straight, I'd never understand.

Choosing a shampoo that smelled of wisteria, I poured some into her hair and scrubbed my way through it, massaging it into her scalp to rid her of the smell of lake water and fear. She leaned her head into my hands. Her eyes were closed, her body relaxing, and I worked my fingers down her neck and between her shoulders.

As the shower rinsed away the last of the shampoo, I slid my hands under the hem of her T-shirt and tugged it over her head. She worked with me, raising her arms to help. She wasn't fully aware, which left me to do most of the work, but that was fine by me.

Once her shirt was off, I took in the healing burn on her side. By turning at the last second, she'd saved herself another lightning bolt to the chest, but the skin was blistered and ragged along her left ribs. It would take her at least a few hours before she made it through the uncomfortable stage of recovery.

Her leather pants were more of a challenge to remove, soaked as they were, but with some wrangling and a more revived Kat, we got them off. Her underwear I deemed a lost cause and tore away.

Her low chuckle caught my ear. "You've been waiting for an excuse to do that." Her voice was hoarse, and speaking must have been painful because she winced, but her faint smirk remained.

"You have no idea." I nuzzled the crook of her neck, trailing my lips over her warming skin. "I would have preferred us both to be dry, though."

"Next time."

"Next time," I promised.

I finished soaping her up, keeping her under the water until her skin had lost its deathly pallor, and left her in the shower while I gathered a pair of fleecy purple pyjamas with dragons on them and a thick, hooded blue housecoat.

The housecoat was Rhys's, but I doubted he'd mind lending it out. As for the pyjamas… I couldn't help but smile as I brought them into the bathroom. The Katerina I'd known centuries ago would never have worn anything so cute. I liked what this modern world had done for her.

Her cheeks flushed pink when she caught sight of them, and she kept her eyes averted as I helped her out of the shower and bundled her in a towel to dry her off. Her legs were steadier now, but she clung to me for support—emotional if not physical.

"Those aren't mine," she mumbled as she stepped into the pyjama pants.

"Oh no?" I asked, trying and failing to hide my smile. "Maera tucked these into your dresser by accident, did she?"

"They were a gift from Rhys. I've never worn them." A lie. "I usually sleep naked." A blatant attempt at distraction.

I lowered my voice as I spoke into her ear. "I remember." Goosebumps rippled over her skin, and my smile widened. "But it would be a shame to let such epic dragons go to waste."

She grumbled as I held open the shirt, and she slipped her arms into it. Her hands were still shaking, so I buttoned it for her.

Kat huffed. "In all my dreams of you coming back into my life, I never imagined you helping me *put on* my clothes."

I chuckled and bent to kiss her neck. "I dreamt of many things over the years without you, *ælfsciene*. Removing your clothes, putting them on… All versions left me aching for you."

A soft moan crept from her throat, but I wrapped the

housecoat around her and held the sleeves open so she could slide her arms in. I wanted her—of course I did; I always did—but more than anything right now, I wanted to make sure she was warm and safe.

She burrowed herself against me. "You're such a tease."

I hooked my arm under her knees and swung her up to carry her to bed, but she shook her head. "I don't want to sit here in the dark."

Understanding what she needed, I stepped through the mist and set her down instead on the soft couch in her basement rec room. While she flipped through channels on the large television, I went upstairs to make her a cup of hot cocoa.

When I returned, the TV was off and Kat was sitting where I'd left her, staring out the large glass patio doors, her gaze caught in the middle distance. She was so lost in thought she didn't notice I stood next to her until I pressed the mug into her hands.

With a blink, she looked up at me. "Thank you."

"Of course."

I settled on the couch beside her and pulled her feet into my lap, tucking the ends of the housecoat around her toes. She sat with her knees pulled to her chest, her mug clutched in both hands close to her so she could absorb the heat. I suspected her magic was still buried too far for her to access it. A good night's sleep would help, but more than anything, we needed to deal with Abigail.

Then we could talk about what the future looked like for us.

"What are you thinking about?" I asked as I rubbed my palms up and down her calves to work some warmth back into them.

"That there's something I'm missing here. No one levels up that quickly. If Abigail *is* a sorceress, why haven't I heard of her before? Even if she's a witch, those rocks—that's some serious power. She could have been dominating the magical community for decades, not hiding behind other witches or demons. If the power is new, how did she get it? Is there a whole coven behind her, and she's the figurehead?"

I continued my gentle stroking of her legs. "It could be the Death Raisers again."

She twitched. "I've wondered the same ever since I heard Mikhail had a patron, but in the chaos of everything that happened with him, then with Shogaur, I never poked into the theory. It's possible. No one's sent me more death threats in recent years than they have."

Kat had more experience with them than I did, but I knew the Death Raisers were a large coven out of Toronto that focused heavily on necromancy. They'd been around for over a century. Long before Kat had ordered me out of her life, she'd shut them down twice, and Adrian had kept me updated during my time away about how she'd dealt with them again in the eighties.

With the force she'd used, we'd believed they were out of the game for good.

"Poppy's mother was high in the ranks back then," she said. "I don't want to nudge that bear too hard in case it comes back on Poppy, but we might need to reach out. If Abigail is one of them—if they're supplying her with that kind of magic…"

"Rest first, then we can make plans. Maybe Poppy can get us an in with her mother."

Kat closed her eyes and leaned against the cushions, wincing against the pain in her side.

"Still hurt?" I asked.

"More itchy than anything. Always the worst part." She sipped her cocoa and relaxed into the couch. "I need to get back into my lightning practice. This bitch seems to have chosen it as her weapon of choice, but I'm feeling left out. I'll have to drag some of your training out of a very dusty mental trunk."

I stared at her, having no clue what she was talking about. What lightning training?

She opened her eyes and pinned me with a blue stare that grew increasingly more concerned. "Emrick?"

Her voice sounded far away, as though she were speaking to me from under the waters I'd rescued her from. Darkness swam on the edges of my vision, and I realized I'd lost myself to panic.

I dragged myself back from the fringes of madness and forced a smile, praying she hadn't noticed. "Good idea. We can't have this witch showing up the greatest sorceress ever to breathe."

She snorted and relaxed again, and I let out a quiet breath. Kat needed to heal, rest, and recover. She didn't need to worry about my sudden memory loss. Especially when it was a memory that involved her.

When had I lost it?

Two weeks ago when I'd pulled her back from going after a possessed Rhys? When I'd dropped the protection amulet over her head to prevent Shogaur from possessing her?

The uncertainty left me numb, and I slid my fingers under the hems of her pants to make contact with her skin. The foundations of my world were shaking, and she was the only person who could hold me steady.

Though at the moment, she didn't appear overly steady herself.

"Come back to me, Kat," I murmured. "Wherever you are right now, be here with me instead."

She jerked her gaze to mine. "When I was in the water, I was back in Palonia. Back to that night. There have been so many reminders lately, I guess it was bound to happen." Her throat bobbed, and tears welled in her eyes. "But it hurts so much."

I kissed the tops of her knees, giving her a moment to catch her breath before saying, "How can I help?"

"Be here and hold my hand? If things get as bad as I expect they will, I'll need your strength to keep me going."

I looped my fingers through hers and brought the back of her hand to my lips. "You have it."

"I love you." Her blue eyes shone, their depths overpowering me.

"Everything I am is you, Katerina. Whatever's coming, whatever she throws at you, you can face it."

A bitter laugh escaped her. "Can I? At every step, she's used my past as a weapon. It's the only enemy I've never been able to overcome."

I tightened my grip on her. "You can, Katerina. Our pasts may influence who we are, but they don't control us. Everything you've achieved since walking away from Palonia has prepared you for this."

She drew in a sharp breath and stared into her cocoa. I watched the battle in her head play out over her features, and after a minute, she sagged into her pillows. "If the clues to who she is, why she's after me, and how to get ahead of her lie in the past, then I have no choice but to follow her in that direction, do I?" Her voice sounded so small, desperate to have me argue with her.

"You might not."

I said it as gently as I could, but she flinched all the same. My heart twinged in response.

"Then I'll do it. As long as you're with me, I can do it."

I kissed her hand again. "I'm not going anywhere."

"I guess we should head back to Muskoka and talk to Gavin, see if we can drag any answers out of his blood." She frowned down at her dragon pyjamas. "But first I need to change."

15

Katerina

BEFORE EMRICK COULD take me to Muskoka, I had him detour us to the boardwalk. I needed to get my hands on one of those rocks for Murisa and Poppy. Despite my shaking hands and the chill that clung to my bones, I scoured the beach to see if any remained.

By luck, Abigail hadn't set off all of them, nor had she returned to reclaim them. I found six scattered in the sand and along the water. She'd been prepared for me to come after her, and no matter which way I'd run, I would have been caught.

Not that they were easy to find. The only reason they stood out was because of their consistency in colour. The same shade of grey, without any dings or dirt. Somehow she'd created them, and I intended to find out how.

I hesitated before picking one up, not wanting what had happened to my tree to happen to me… but then I thought of the moments before the spell circle had erupted. Abigail had said something to set off the stones.

A shudder ran through me. If the stones needed an incantation to go off, that meant she'd been on my property when Rita had delivered her package. She'd been watching when I'd picked up the stone—when my tree had burned down. She'd been so close, and I hadn't known it.

My revulsion swept into a determined rage, and I stuffed the stones into my pocket. "All right. Let's go so we can—"

The sound of sirens screaming down the road interrupted me, and the chill in my bones burrowed deeper.

I had no reason to think those sirens had anything to do with me, but the timing, the location, and the coil of dread that had set up camp in my stomach refused to let me ignore them.

Emrick took my hand and, without my having to ask, stepped me through the afterlife to the street where the emergency vehicles had stopped.

Right outside Amelia Caper's house.

We'd only been here three hours ago. So recently, the taste of her lemon-blueberry muffins was still on my tongue. Was she all right? Had she hurt herself during her wall-climbing and only realized it after she got home? Burned herself while making crême brulée? Anything seemed possible.

But not for the number of vehicles parked outside.

I held my breath as the front door opened and two people wheeled a stretcher out between them. The person lying on it was covered with a sheet, but her elbow remained visible.

A sky-blue shirt printed with tiny cherries.

I wobbled on my feet, and Emrick wrapped his arms around my waist to soothe my rising grief. I didn't need my spirit-herder to tell me she was gone.

Death had finally caught up with her, and Amelia the Indestructible was no more.

Tears spilled down my cheeks.

"Hours, Emrick. We were here *hours* ago, and she was fine." My head swam as a single conclusion dropped on the ground in front of me. "This is my fault, isn't it? We asked her about Abigail, and now she's dead."

"We don't know that," he murmured in my ear. "It could have been her time."

I shoved him away, anger rising within me although I knew he didn't deserve it. Given Amelia's eclectic hobbies, it was absolutely within the realm of possibility that she'd done something risky, and it had gone awry. But if it had been a sporting accident, she wouldn't have been at home. A kiln explosion, perhaps? But then she would have been wearing her smock. She'd forgotten to change out of it often enough when she went into town that I knew her habits as though I'd spent my life watching through her window.

"Can you go into the afterlife and find out?" I asked.

Emrick shoved his hands in his pockets. "Unfortunately, I don't have an in with the mundane collector. Also unfortunately, Mrs. Caper didn't have a single drop of magical blood in her veins, or else I would have been the one to escort her."

The thought gave my heart an unexpected pinch. "That's too bad. She was quite taken with you."

"That's because she was a wise woman with good taste." The glibness of his answer did nothing to remove the sadness that pulled down the corners of his mouth. "I'm sorry she's gone."

My anger returned in a wave. "I need to know what happened. If she keeled over from a heart attack while baking, fine, but I need to know. Can you get me into the house?" Uncertainty pulled at me, and I stared into his paling eyes. "That doesn't affect you at all, does it? Transporting me everywhere?"

It wasn't possible that every time he'd swept me away, he'd lost something, was it? How would he have anything left?

He kissed my forehead. "That, at least, I can do. But we'll have to wait until the house is empty."

I hated the need for delay. I didn't want to stand here calmly waiting. I wanted to rage at the Fates for taking a woman who should have outlived us all.

Well, maybe not Emrick or me, but she certainly should

have lived longer than the doctor with the smoker's cough and blue-tinged lips who had aimed a shotgun at my face two weeks ago.

We stayed by the side of the road until Amelia was packed into the back of the coroner's van. The empty ambulance left first, followed by the coroner. The officer lingered for a few minutes to have words with the crowd that had begun to congregate outside.

Amelia's neighbours were in shock. Their grief spoke volumes about the place the woman had held in her community. Tears were abundant, outright sobs came from a few. One purple-haired woman climbed the steps with the officer and used her key on the front door, a trusted neighbour ensuring no one accessed the house until next of kin arrived.

Fortunately, locks wouldn't keep me out.

Gradually, the crowd dispersed, heading to nearby houses to bury their sorrow in food, drink, and gossip. It was the way of the island, and I hoped it did them some good.

A few of them had noticed us standing back, but no one acknowledged us except for old Mrs. McCreary, whose glare was potent enough to pierce through flesh and sinew. As if she knew my being here wasn't a coincidence. Did she suspect me of having something to do with Amelia's death, as she suspected me of taking her dog? Would I need to worry about more shotguns and pitchforks storming my porch?

As soon as everyone was gone, Emrick tugged off his gloves. He stuffed them in his pocket and closed the distance between us as he cupped my face in his palms.

He said nothing, but the solidness of his warm body standing so close and the calmness in his silver eyes wove through my rising emotions. I realized how far my magic had climbed to the surface and tamped it down before fire licked over my fingers. That would certainly give these gossips something to talk about.

I closed my eyes, sucked in a breath, and leaned into his touch to ease the ache in my chest. Mrs. Caper and I hadn't been close, but we'd accepted each other's oddities. She was one of those rare people who made you feel like family even if you'd only spoken for five minutes. The woman had broken through the barriers I kept around myself simply by being her eccentric self, and now I was left to suffer the pain of yet another mortal life passing.

As I breathed, the world grew cold. When I opened my eyes again, we stood in the middle of the empty kitchen.

"We won't have much time," I said. "Depending on how she died, the police will be back to poke around. We should split—"

"Not a chance." Emrick's grip tightened on my shoulders. "Abigail has left multiple traps for you and already killed you once. You stand right here, and I'll take a quick look around. If I don't find any spell circles, then you can move."

I wanted to argue with him, but he was right. I didn't have time to be almost killed again. "Fine, but be quick."

He stepped through the mist, and I stood by myself in the kitchen, looking around to see if there was anything to find in the room where I'd so recently passed a lovely afternoon.

What had Mrs. Caper said? She was going wall-climbing and then baking a lemon chiffon cake. She'd been home, so she must have already come back from the community centre. Where was the cake?

As I turned in a slow circle to make out whatever details I could without breaking my promise to Emrick, I caught sight of the refrigerator door sitting at an odd angle—not open enough to turn on the light, but not sealed all the way, either.

Mrs. Caper would never have forgotten something so vital.

My ever-vocal gut screamed at me to check it out, if only to see what food I might take with me as a final farewell to one of the island's greatest bakers.

Paying close attention to my surroundings, opening myself to any hint of a magical trap on the fridge—or floor or ceiling—I hooked my pinky finger around the handle and eased it open.

The light turned on. No magical flares gave away any unpleasant booby traps, so I opened the door the rest of the way.

And had to lean on the fridge to hold myself up.

"Kat?"

Emrick was by my side in a breath, his large, warm hand on the small of my back grounding me as I reached into the fridge and slid an uniced cake on the top shelf to the side.

A card sat next to it with a dragon printed on the front—the same coiled design as the one tattooed on my thigh. A design no one except Emrick, Adrian, Maera, and Rhys could possibly know.

Not unless the design had been passed down over the years.

Was it possible? Could Abigail be a descendant of someone in Palonia?

My hands trembled, making it impossible for me to pick up the card.

Abigail had known I was coming. She'd known I would snoop around to find out what had happened to Mrs. Caper. How closely had she been watching me to time her visit so well?

Seeing I was unable to read the card myself, Emrick took it. He watched me as he flipped it open, his gaze only leaving mine when it dropped to the paper.

"I told you I'd come after your playthings," he read. "For all the trouble you've caused me, I'll give you triple."

It was true, then.

Amelia Caper, an innocent woman who'd had the bad luck to be kind and gracious to a lonely immortal sorceress, was dead because of me.

My mind, thoughts, body went numb, and when I roused

myself out of my shock, Emrick and I were in my bedroom at Adrian's Muskoka house. I clung to him, desperate to feel something real while the rest of my life slipped out of control.

If Abigail was willing to go so far as to kill a woman I hardly knew, what would she do to my family?

She wanted to play games, but I'd had enough of them. No one else could get hurt because of me. My soul weighed enough with the losses I carried. Any more, and I would never be able to lift my head.

"She has to pay for this, Emrick."

"She will," he agreed, pressing kisses into my hair. "You'll dance on her ashes before the end."

16

Katerina

Although I waited until my shaking had stopped, I was still frozen when I prepared to head downstairs to Adrian's kitchen.

More than anything, I wanted to be at home, bundled against Emrick in my ridiculous fleecy pyjamas, curled up safe in his arms. The events on the beach had rattled me more than I'd realized as I'd sat in the shower under Emrick's gentle touch, and Mrs. Caper's death had been another blow to my bearings.

As I breathed through the series of shocks the universe had dealt me today, the significance of Abigail's advantages over me sank in. She was armed with incredible power, she was prepared for every step I took, and she believed she would win.

The discovery of Mrs. Caper's death had made it clear the

woman was prepared to play dirty, believing it would throw me off my game.

So far, she was right about everything. The encounter on the beach had been my first real chance to take her down, and I'd never stood a chance. Even if I'd stopped running—even if I'd stepped carefully among those strange rocks—she would have activated them. If Abigail had made them herself, it meant she was capable of crafting similar enchantments. If she'd bought them from someone, it was a possible lead we could use to find her.

At the top of the stairs, Emrick stopped and kissed my forehead. "I'm going to go talk to Adrian. You'll be okay?"

"I'm not about to break down again," I reassured him. I was too angry to break down. Abigail was taunting me, laughing up her sleeve with every move she made. I was done being her squeaky toy.

Emrick squeezed my hand and headed down the hallway to the library. I walked downstairs and spotted the tin of muffins—our final gift from Mrs. Caper—on the kitchen table. I'd forgotten I'd brought them here on our last visit, and the sight of them nearly pushed me over the edge.

Maera was nowhere to be seen, but sugar and butter scented the air, so she couldn't have gone far.

Just outside the kitchen, the front door opened, and the tinkle of female voices drifted towards me from the foyer. Curious, I went to greet whoever had arrived and was hit in the face by the force of energy and colour spilling into the simple elegance of Adrian's home.

Poppy was excitable enough on her own, and Murisa was like bubble gum personified. Together, they were an entire boy band audience wrapped in two larger-than-life packages.

Poppy carried a duffel bag slung over her shoulder, glitter glue hearts drawn all over the canvas. By chance, the bright blue swirls matched her long, painted fingernails, and I had to wonder if it was coincidence or if she updated her bag every time she gave herself a manicure. Knowing her, I wouldn't be surprised if she did.

Murisa wheeled herself into the house with a smaller bag settled on her lap, and I might have believed she'd been more reasonable in her packing if Maera hadn't followed her in with a suitcase nearly as big as she was.

"I tried to pack light," Murisa said, her rich brown eyes glowing with eagerness, "but I didn't know what we'd need. The last thing I wanted to do was forget something important and have to go all the way back to Toronto to get it."

Poppy grinned. "She made me go back to the store three times as it is. I'm pretty sure my entire inventory is in that bag."

I raised an eyebrow. "Your store? Didn't you rent it out to the creepy tea shop lady?"

Murisa laughed as Poppy's smile faded into some serious

eye roll. "She took one look at Cuddles and bolted."

I was about to ask whether she'd brought her zombie cat with her when her duffel bag meowed. Barrett was going to be so happy.

I, on the other hand, was genuinely delighted. The undead cat had wormed its semi-decomposed way into my heart—and not only because it made Barrett's life miserable. Not caring about boundaries, I reached into Poppy's bag and pulled Cuddles free. His long grey hair had been recently brushed, with some attempt having been made to cover all the bald patches where clumps had fallen out. He was missing another bit of his tail, and his smell was still rough, but Poppy had taken good care of him.

He tilted his head towards me, and my hopes surged that he'd finally come around to me. But as I reached out to pet him, he pulled back his lips and hissed at me, swiping at my face with his claws.

"I missed you, too, Cuddles."

He twisted out of my grip and landed with otherworldly grace on the floor before padding into the living room. I hoped he found Barrett's favourite seat and made himself at home. All the cat hair would give the man apoplexy.

Murisa took Poppy's hand and looped their fingers together. "The situation with the store worked out for the best. Pop had her grand reopening last week and earned back everything we lost in the remodel."

"Murisa's a natural salesperson." Poppy smiled at her with a doe-eyed expression that was so sweet, I had a sudden craving for black coffee to kill the buzz.

"I don't suppose between mooning over each other and passing on your bags of oregano and thyme under the guise of fake curses you've managed to work your way through your to-do list?" I asked.

Murisa's expression grew brighter. "We did! We have something to help block Rhys's visions, and we think we know how to use Gavin's blood to dig up some dirt on our missing witch. We haven't figured out what those stones are, though."

"I guess it's good I brought you some samples to work with, then."

I pulled the stones out of the pocket along my thigh.

Poppy's eyebrows shot skywards as she recoiled. "Didn't you say those things explode? And you're just *handing* them to us?"

"Abigail spoke an incantation to set them off. They're stable on their own."

Poppy remained wary as she accepted one, and Murisa eagerly snatched the rest out of my hand. Maera huffed.

"Can we move this conversation into the kitchen? Or at least out of the foyer? I'll bring this bag to your room, then I have perogies to finish. Amelia gave me her recipe, and I need to tell her how they turned out. Which, between you and me, is a bit doughy."

In the rush of Poppy and Murisa's arrival, the recent sad scene at Mrs. Caper's house had fled from my thoughts. Before I could break the news to Maera, Poppy's cheerful tone cut in. "Perogies? You might be my favourite person in the whole wide world."

Maera flushed under the compliment as she dragged Murisa's bag towards the elevator at the end of the hall, and I opted to hold off on breaking her heart. She was worried about enough right now. I didn't need to ruin her day. Once everyone settled in, I would get her by herself and break it to her before she found out anywhere else.

Poppy took Murisa's wheelchair and pushed her into the kitchen so Murisa could concentrate on the stones. By the time we reached the kitchen table, she was almost vibrating with excitement.

"These are amazing."

They'd nearly killed me, but sure.

"At first glance, they look like spells in stasis," she explained. "Obviously, I'll need time to learn how it works and how it was made, but on a basic level, I'd say someone cast a spell circle and stored it in this enchanted casing. When the right words are spoken, the casing must disintegrate, unleashing the spell."

Poppy whistled. "That would take a huge amount of power to create."

"Not to mention control," Murisa agreed. "And to have more than one? It must have set her back a good chunk of change."

I frowned at the stone. "This is a fraction of how many she laid out for me as a trap. I'd guess she had at least fifteen lying around."

Murisa's face turned ashen, and Poppy blinked. "You're up against a real juggernaut, kitty Kat. I hope you know what you're doing."

At the moment, I didn't have the faintest idea.

"Can you create something to nullify them?" I asked.

Murisa frowned as she spun the stone between her fingers. "Not quickly and not easily. It would require breaking down the casing and cancelling the spell before it goes off. Without knowing the incantation that went into weaving the magic, unweaving it will be a challenge." She shrugged. "Not impossible, though."

Poppy nodded and tossed her stone into the air, catching it as it fell. "Leave it with us. We'll sort you out."

If I could remove Abigail's greatest weapon, I'd be closer to gaining the upper hand, and right now I needed all the higher ground I could get.

Poppy's frown deepened. "The magical signature on these is familiar. Don't you think, Ris?"

Murisa closed her eyes, and her dainty brow furrowed as

she concentrated. "You're right. It's faint because it's contained, but this is the same magic that's been outside your shop a few times."

My blood ran cold, and I curled my fingers around the back of the nearest chair. "Tell me."

"Twice last week we left the shop and traces of this magic were outside my apartment door," Poppy said. "Never inside, but close. Like someone had been standing out there for a while."

Poppy lived above her shop, the doors almost side by side at the front of the building. But even if the person who'd made these stones had been outside the shop instead of the apartment, it was more than a little suspicious.

"You don't know anyone who makes these kinds of enchantments, do you?" I asked. "Anyone who might sell them on the sly?"

The witches exchanged a glance. "Louay, maybe," Murisa said.

Poppy nodded. "For sure. He likes to dabble in all kinds of strange and unusual. But as far as I know, he's been out of business since the Mikhail fiasco. His coven was among those you cut down that night."

"Sad for him," I said, feeling zero sympathy that his dark magic coven had been terminated in its bid for power. Mikhail would have done worse if he'd succeeded. "Where can I find him?"

Poppy groaned. "You're going to get us exiled from the witch community, you know that? No one will want to talk to us."

"That's fine, you can talk to me." I flashed her my brightest, most sarcastic grin. "Address, please."

"We'll text it to you." Murisa rested her hand on Poppy's arm before the other witch could argue. "Along with the details of anyone else we can think of. Poppy can grumble, but these stones shouldn't be on the market. There's way too big a chance they'd end up somewhere they shouldn't be."

If anyone else had been on the boardwalk with me, that would already be the case.

"I appreciate your help on this." I prepared to go find Emrick when Poppy called me back.

"About Gavin."

I bit down on a grimace. "What about him?"

"Do you think he'd be willing to play guinea pig for us?"

I snorted. "I don't know if *willing* is the right word, but you might be able to bribe him into it. Cross your fingers he likes perogies." I looked between the two witches. "Why? Murisa said you have some idea—what do you think we could find out?"

The two exchanged a glance, and Poppy pursed her lips. "Maybe what Abigail's natural magic is. Where she's from."

My eyebrows climbed. "That's possible?"

Murisa slipped the stones into the bag hanging over the

back of her chair. "It's blood magic. Anything is possible with enough power and a clear intention. If we know where she's from, we could do some digging to find out more about her. Any other family she might have, or who she trained with."

Poppy cleared her throat and mumbled something that might have been, "Medical records."

I'd never seen blood magic as a dark style of witchcraft. Blood was as serviceable a medium as potions or spell circles. All of them could be destructive in the wrong hands. The biggest difference for me was the willingness of the donor, and I didn't think Gavin would rush to open a vein for these women.

"Only if he agrees. If he doesn't, we'll have to forgo that particular avenue." At the sly gleam in Poppy's eye, I held up my hand. "I'll talk to him. You two get settled, and when Maera gets back, ask her where you can set up shop that won't put the rest of the house at risk."

I left them to chat and went in search of Gavin. The living room was empty, and a quick look out back revealed no one in the garden, either. I was about to head upstairs when shouts and a thundering slam echoed from the direction of the gym.

Although Adrian had given up hunting with me, he ensured he had a training space in all his properties. As an ex-soldier, he wasn't one to let go of his disciplined regimen—even though, as a vampire, his perfect physique was a permanent fixture. He and Barrett practiced all sorts of self-defence training together, preparing Barrett for whatever supernatural battles he might have to fight either to protect Adrian during the day or out on a hunt with me. But as far as I knew, Adrian was still upstairs with Emrick.

More shouts reached me along with blasts of heat before the door came into view. Panic gripped me, thoughts filling my head of Gavin losing control of his power and setting the house on fire and of Barrett retaliating by cutting the sorcerer down.

I burst through the doors and released a cry as Gavin threw a fireball at Barrett's head.

17

Katerina

M Y HEART RACED, and I threw up my hands to send a blast of ice at the flames in a mad attempt to extinguish them before they struck Barrett.

I needn't have worried. With the perks of heightened reflexes thanks to his blood exchanges with Adrian, Barrett threw himself to the floor before the fireball made contact. He rolled on his shoulder, jumped to his feet, and rushed Gavin, wrapping him around the middle and tackling him into the wall. He managed to lodge his forearm against Gavin's throat and punch him in the gut before Gavin heated his skin to the point that steam seeped from the pores of his bare chest. Barrett fell back to avoid getting burned across his equally bare skin.

I readied myself to step in, but neither of them took

advantage of the vulnerabilities open to them. This wasn't a battle—it was a sparring match.

Barrett fell into a fighting stance, and Gavin stepped away from the wall, his hands raised, fire between his palms. I watched in awe. Both men hated magic. Even Gavin, who possessed it, carried a self-loathing that would have made me sad if he weren't such a pain in the ass about it. So to see them working with their strengths, learning how to offset each other's abilities, was more than a little impressive.

Also a relief. I would have hated to put either of them down to save the other.

The fact that they were practicing, however, told me how stressed they both were about the threat bearing down on us. Gavin would never have agreed to use his magic for a lark, and Barrett would never have agreed to spend so much time with a magical out of the goodness of his heart. They were preparing for war.

While they fought, I paid close attention to Gavin, searching his features for any trace of Abigail, and now that I was looking, the resemblance was uncanny. I'd only ever seen the woman from the nose down, but the shape of the mouth, the same as Gavin's mother's, was obviously a strong hereditary trait. It left no room for doubt that my conclusion was correct.

I waited until the fighters came to a natural pause, then stepped farther into the room.

Barrett wiped the sweat from his brow, the muscles on muscles on muscles in his arm flexing as he did, and turned to me with an emptiness of expression that would have wowed a blank sheet of paper.

"Here to give us more orders and disappear again?" he asked.

"Pretty much." I didn't have it in me to exchange banter with him. Mrs. Caper's death, after losing Abigail and getting hit by another one of her lightning bolts, were enough bruises for one morning. "No orders for you, though. You can carry on being your brooding self."

Okay, maybe I had it in me for a little fight.

With that out of my system, I turned to Gavin, who watched me warily over the edge of his towel as he scrubbed the sweat off his face.

"I'm impressed. You've been practicing."

He shrugged. "Like you said, I need to make sure I don't kill anyone by accident. If my training helps Barrett learn to destroy people like me, so much the better."

His self-hatred cut me like knife points flicking over my skin. Nothing I said would change his mind, but it pained me that his introduction to this world—with all its beauty and wonders—should have been so crushing.

But if I couldn't convince him otherwise, I could lean into it to get us what we both wanted. "Do you want to destroy people like us in another way?"

He narrowed his eyes. "How?"

"Donate a few drops of blood to Poppy and Murisa so we can trace your ancestry and use it to take down your demon-summoning, murdering grandmother."

Barrett crossed his arms, and I braced for more attitude about the evils of using magic to fight magic. "Digging up background information on your enemy? That's almost strategic of you."

I barked a sharp laugh. "Did I just hear the hint of a compliment? That's almost human of you."

Gavin tossed his towel into the hamper beside the door. "What good will it do to know where she came from?"

"If we can learn where she grew up, we can learn who trained her, which will give us a better idea of her skillset—and maybe explain how she knows things about me that should have been impossible to discover. That information would have been passed down through twenty generations without losing detail. Have you ever tried playing telephone with twenty people? It's nigh on impossible to get so much of the message correct."

Gavin grunted. "If you think it'll help, I'll give them the blood, but I'm not sitting through any more spells. They make my teeth hum."

He grabbed his shirt and headed upstairs, but before I could follow him, Barrett took my arm. I stiffened under his touch, my body reacting to him as it would to an enemy. When I met his gaze, though, the concern I found shining there pushed me to drop my defences.

"Have you spoken to Adrian lately? Alone, I mean."

I frowned. "Yes, why?"

His gaze darted around the room before landing back on mine. "Did he tell you what's bothering him? If he did, you have to tell me. Please."

Barrett saying *please* was as terrifying as it was novel.

I eased my arm out of his grip and leaned against the wall by the door. "He didn't mention anything." His furrowed brow suggested this was not the answer he'd hoped for. "Why? What has you so worried?"

He walked away to grab his shirt from the bench along the wall. "I've been with Adrian for ten years, and in all that time, he's never kept secrets from me. Not ones that affect our relationship, anyway. But lately I've caught him looking at me like he wants to say something. Or moments when he thinks he's by himself, and he just looks… I don't know. Sad. I ask him about it, and he shrugs it off, but whatever it is, it's got its hooks in deep."

I'd spent every one of those ten years wondering how Adrian could stand keeping Barrett around. The man was grumpy, argumentative, had the personality of a concrete wall, and hated everything magical with such intensity I was amazed Adrian hadn't turned to ash.

Yet in this moment, I got it. Barrett might hate magic, but he loved Adrian with a depth I hadn't known he possessed. He and I might be oil and water, but he and Adrian clicked. And now he felt the same way I did about Emrick slowly fading away—knowing something was wrong and unable to stop it.

"I noticed the same," I admitted. "He said everything was fine."

The furrow on Barrett's brow deepened. "I think Maera and Rhys know what's up. Lately, they haven't been able to look me in the eye."

"I'll talk to them. If he's in trouble, we won't let him face it by himself."

Barrett nodded, but the furrow didn't fade.

Maybe it was the stress hanging over me or the result of getting slapped in the face with my past, but in a moment of sentiment, I rested my hand on his arm. "I'm glad he has you. I've always worried when he was by himself that he would get tired of having nothing to do, but he's been happy with you. For whatever reason."

Barrett's mouth twitched in a smirk. I gave his muscles a final pat and left him to his concerns, needing to clear my head of that moment of camaraderie. It felt strange and unusual, and I didn't think I liked it.

The feeling was made worse because I also hadn't hated it. The world didn't sit right when James Barrett and I were on the same page.

It made me feel like the end times were near.

18

Emrick

I PACED THE length of Adrian's library, unable to stand still.

"You're making me dizzy, my friend. Come sit down and tell me what's bothering you this time. Between you and Katerina, you're keeping me busy. When I told Kat I would help her in the hunt for Abigail, I expected more fighting, not so much brooding."

I tore my hand through my hair. "I don't even know where to start. Between Kat's problems and mine, I don't have space to think."

Adrian rose from his chair and joined me in the centre of the room, leaning his shoulder against the mantel of the darkened hearth. "She says much the same, and now that I see you for myself, I agree Kat's fears are well-founded. When you stand in the light, you're barely there."

"It's getting worse. My memories—I *forgot* that I taught her how to access lightning. The way she talked about it… it wasn't a small event. What am I supposed to do, Adrian? I can't leave her. I *won't* leave her. My life is as good as over if I do. But if I stay?"

The options bounced around me, none of them tolerable. If I stayed, I'd have to keep my distance. Watch from afar as Kat put herself in danger time and time again and do nothing to help her. Every incident would test my fortitude, and I didn't think I had much left in me.

Adrian pursed his lips, crossed his arms, shifted his weight, and with every tiny delay, I was driven to shake him. I didn't want to see consideration from my oldest friend. Adrian was the one with solutions, and I was in desperate need of one.

When the silence stretched on too long, I broke it again. "My third choice is that I stick around and do nothing. A long-distance relationship for eternity. That's not fair to her or to me. She deserves someone who can support her, and if I can't be that, what good am I?"

"She needs *you*, Emrick." Adrian's shoulders relaxed, and his arms fell to his sides. I hoped that meant he saw some way forward, but the expression in his eyes was apologetic. "I'm sorry you want the world and you feel the world is denied you, but the truth is you have everything you want. You and Katerina are together. Whether it's every day for the rest of your existence or once in a while when her situation and yours allows it, it's something. You have forever ahead of you to be more than two passing ships."

I dropped into one of the armchairs and scrubbed my hands over my face. "For us to have anything else would require Kat to follow in your footsteps. To retire from the hunt and relax. But I don't know if she would be as content with it as you are."

A fleeting expression of regret passed over Adrian's face, but it was gone before I could pin it down. He smiled. "Not everyone can embrace the joys of a simple library, it's true. But you never know. This trouble with Abigail might be the push she needs. More than that, if she deals with Abigail and can finally put the past to rest—for good this time—maybe she won't feel the need to keep proving herself."

I sagged back in the chair. "Abigail got to her again. Another spell circle. Kat survived this one, but a few inches to the left and she might not have. It took everything in me not to run after the witch and turn her to dust."

"I'm impressed," Adrian said with his barely-there smile. "Every time I think you've grown as much as is possible for an immortal, you take another turn. The Emrick of old wouldn't have hesitated."

"The Emrick of old thought he could get away with it." I raised my hand to make my point. I could almost see the blood flowing through the blue veins. "I'm walking proof that's not the case."

Adrian frowned, his jaw flexing with unspoken worry. He settled in the chair beside me and stared into the middle distance at the clock on the mantel ticking the seconds away.

When he spoke, he left the subject of my condition behind us. "Abigail is on the island, then?"

Part of me was disappointed, not wanting to give up on discussing my doomed future, but the rest of me accepted the truth—there were no other options. Kat and I would have to sort this out for ourselves. Which meant we'd need to sit down and talk about it.

"She is. She killed one of Kat's neighbours as a message, spreading her evil all over Kat's territory. The woman's begging to be torn apart."

"What will Kat do next? Will she try again to confront her?"

"Not until I know I can get around her weapons," Kat said as she walked into the room.

Although I'd only left her a few minutes ago, my heart leapt at the sight of her. Love pulsed through me, and I suspected it was almost as visible as the blood beneath my skin. I stood and made my way to her side, unable to not touch her.

She leaned into my embrace, and I felt whole. No, I couldn't leave her. I would need to find a way to keep myself solid that didn't involve disappearing again.

"Poppy and Murisa are working on shutting down her portable spell circles and sending me in the direction of people Abigail might have bought them from or worked with to make them," she continued. "The next time I see her, you can be damn sure I'll start the conversation with a fireball aimed at her head or an ice spike at her throat, but I'll feel better if I'm not dodging camouflaged spell circles to do it."

Adrian nodded, and the smile he directed at her was full of pride. "A wise move. How far you've come from the young immortal who climbed a basilisk with her eyes squeezed shut."

She laughed, and the sound was as sweet as music, free of the bitterness and stress of our situation. "One of my finer moments. Give me credit, though. We did take it down."

"We did, indeed." His smile faded. "And you'll take down this witch as well. She believes she's dealing with the same sorceress you were a year ago, and that belief will be her downfall. I see the Katerina of centuries ago shining from you again, cuore mio, and it does my unbeating heart a world of good. You've grown into quite your own woman."

Kat stiffened in my arms. I looked from her to Adrian to find out what I'd missed, but it escaped me. My friend sat in his favourite chair exuding love and welcome, as he always did.

"Adrian, are you all right?" She stepped towards him, but her grip on my hand remained tight. "You have Barrett worried, and that man doesn't worry."

Adrian waved a hand in dismissal. "Nonsense. He worries over me more than you ever have. I'm fine. Never been happier, actually."

Now I was the one worried. "Why's that? What's changed?"

"Nothing." Adrian bestowed on us a smile both rueful and amused. "That's just it. I'm surrounded by the people I love with a life full of my greatest pleasures. What need have I to be bothered or upset by anything?" He approached Kat, clasping her free hand in both of his, linking the three of us together. "If anything is wrong, it's that I feel for you, mia Katerina. I know how hard it is to wake up each day not knowing how your past is going to inflict itself on you. Abigail is using it to torture you. You must not let her. We are not our pasts. Or our futures. We are only who we are in this moment—fighting for what we have right now. If that's not enough, nothing will ever be enough."

His dark eyes clouded for a moment, then his smile returned. "I'm happy because once again I'll get to fight by your side to show this woman she made a mistake in targeting you. Let the magical world see one more time why they should never cross us."

19

Katerina

I LEFT ADRIAN'S library feeling no more at ease than I had since leaving Barrett. I should have felt relieved by Adrian reaffirming his desire to hunt with me again, but instead, his declaration had delivered a lead weight to my stomach. A sense of inevitability.

A sense that Rhys's The End was coming faster than I was ready for.

"Barrett's right. Something's wrong," I said.

Emrick nodded and looked over his shoulder at the closed door. "I didn't notice it before, but it's true. He's not himself."

If Adrian were mortal, I'd worry he'd been given a terminal diagnosis and didn't want anyone to know. But he was a vampire. As long as he kept anything sharp away from his chest and maintained a healthy distance from fire, he would be around as long as I was.

Emrick pulled me to him and kissed my forehead. "Don't stress, Kat. He might have a lot on his mind, but we've seen him like this before. He's lived here for ten years. He might be itching to move on, start fresh somewhere else. I bet the reason he says he's so happy is that he found the perfect new home to add to his collection."

I latched on to the answer like a life raft. It made sense, especially given my own recent urge to leave Manitoulin behind.

Before I could relax, however, Emrick's brow furrowed, and he glanced again at the closed door.

"What is it?"

"Probably nothing. A conversation Adrian and I had a few weeks back. He said he felt change in the air. Maybe it's connected? He didn't seem worried about it, though."

"He said something similar to me during the Shogaur mess."

"I don't suppose our old friend has developed psychic visions?"

Barrett's concerns about Rhys and Maera came to me, and I frowned. "No, but we know someone who does. Maybe it's time to take my prying questions elsewhere." I tilted my head, considering. "But if Adrian isn't worried... maybe it is time for a change? It could be something we all want to consider. After we deal with Abigail."

"After Abigail," Emrick agreed.

Feeling better but knowing the conversation was far from over, I met Emrick's eye. "You two seemed to be having an intense conversation before I walked in. Are *you* all right? Adrian isn't the only one keeping his thoughts to himself right now."

Emrick pulled off his glove to make contact with my bare hand and led me down the hallway to the room I claimed as mine whenever I stayed in Muskoka. I loved it—the large windows overlooking the garden, the canopied bed with its thick burgundy comforter, the heavy antique wardrobe stuffed with cozy sweaters and leggings so I never needed to pack when I came to visit. This was my home away from home.

I hated that the tension pouring through the hallways had tainted everything about it.

As soon as Emrick shut the door behind us, his silver eyes went dark, and he pulled my body towards his. Burying his hands in my hair, he claimed my mouth, pouring everything he was into his kiss. Confused by the suddenness of his ardour, concerned by his desperation, but too overwhelmed by the spike of my own desire to stop him, I allowed him to back me towards the bed until his familiar weight pressed down on me. His hips rolled against mine, one large hand hooking under my thigh as his lips and tongue trailed from my mouth to the crook of my neck.

With miraculous effort, I stifled my lust. Going still, I

stroked his hair off his face. "Please talk to me."

He tucked his forehead where his lips had been, and his fingers relaxed their hold on my hair as he glided his other hand to my hip and let it rest there.

"I don't want to burden you with more than you're already carrying," he said against my skin, "but I also can't handle figuring this out on my own."

My throat grew thick as his meaning sank in. "You're fading."

He nodded into my neck, and I wrapped my arms around him, holding him tightly against me.

"I don't know why putting that talisman around your neck took so much from me, but it did. More than I realized at the time."

"The sacrifices are getting bigger?" I was amazed I could get the words out, each syllable as painful as a knife to the chest.

He pulled back to meet my eye, and a tear streaked down his cheek. "I don't remember training you, Kat. It's gone. Like it never happened."

My heart fractured. Visions of a future without this man stretched out like a wasteland. The pain I'd felt in my empty immortality would be nothing compared to the agony that awaited me if he were no longer here. When everyone else passed into the afterlife, it would be me and Adrian alone together, both of us mourning. Adrian might move on, find another Barrett, make another friend, but half of myself would always be missing—a wound that would never heal even as my body continued to function.

I rolled Emrick onto his side and pressed my forehead against his. "You can't step in anymore. My life might hang in the balance, but you can't. If I die, I die. I'll move on, and you can follow me when you can. We have to agree to that now, or I won't be able to face Abigail. I can't worry about losing you."

He squeezed his eyes shut tighter. "And the thought of losing you…"

"Temporarily, *mîn hiertan*." My heart. "Death might escort me to the next world himself, but no matter where I end up, you'll find me when you can." The idea made the possibility less terrifying. Less lonely. "But the only way that happens—the only way you'll remember to look for me—is if you stay yourself. So promise me, Emrick. And this time I'm begging you not to break it. If you do, it might just break me."

He leaned in to kiss me, and my heart, my blood, my bone cried out with love and longing as they were carried through time and gently returned. I kissed him back, dragging him to me, stoking my desire with every dance of his tongue. His hands slid under my T-shirt, and he swept it over my head as I undid his belt and drew out his hardened length. He moaned against my mouth and rolled onto his back, taking me with him.

The rest of our clothes followed my shirt, and just for now, I followed Adrian's advice and left the past and the future outside this room. Here, only this moment mattered. My connection with Emrick was everything. No matter what happened next, I'd stolen this glimmer of happiness and would wield it as armour as I faced the nightmares ahead.

20

Katerina

I SLEPT LATER the next morning than I'd intended to, but everything that had happened yesterday—the day of a million years—had knocked me on my ass. Once I felt ready to face the world's problems again—or at least mine—I got dressed, tugged on my gloves to prepare for battle, and went in search of Rhys and Maera.

Emrick left me to it, disappearing again into the afterlife and assuring me he'd be back within the hour to take me home. After we'd both caught our breath, we'd agreed it would be wisest to return to the Lodge and take another stab at finding Abigail. This time being on the watch for enchanted stones or any other tricks she might have thrown around.

I passed by the living room where Gavin sat with Poppy

and Murisa and continued into the kitchen. Shockingly, it was empty. The perogies were finished and nothing else had been started. As if I needed something else to worry about.

Leaving the kitchen and its eerie stillness behind, I extended my search through the rest of the main floor. When I passed by the garden, I spotted Maera strolling along the path. She wore a ratty denim jacket and jeans, oversized gardening gloves, and a hat that sagged over her eyes.

The sun shone overhead, and a sweet breeze brushed through the spruces that wrapped the property where it led to the lake beyond the garden. I closed my eyes to drink in the serenity of the space, then started down the path to catch up with my housekeeper near the stone wolf.

As soon as I came within earshot, I said, "Taking over Adrian's garden? I don't know how he'll feel about that."

She bent down to clear a few dead weeds from a vegetable patch. "I checked with him before I started. I need to keep busy, or I'm liable to lose my mind."

"Baking's not enough anymore?" I asked, half in jest. If she was keeping secrets from me, her break in habit seemed like a good place to start poking around.

She tossed the weeds into the path to pick up later and stretched her back as she straightened. "It's not my kitchen. It's nice enough, and the oven heats to a consistent temperature, but it's not home."

I understood that well enough. "You won't be here much longer. For the first time in two months, we're making progress on Abigail. Every day we get closer. This will be over before you know it, and you can bake enough food for the whole island to celebrate."

A shadow passed across Maera's green eyes before she smiled. "I have full faith in you, Kat."

I crossed my arms. "No, you don't. Or you do, but there's something else. What's going on, and what does it have to do with Adrian?"

Apparently I was too impatient today to beat around the bush.

She frowned. "Adrian? What makes you think anything I'm worried about has to do with Adrian? If anything, it's Rhys."

She turned away from me to attack the next bed along the path, and I followed. "What about Rhys?"

"I know Poppy and Murisa have a plan to block his visions, and as far as I'm concerned, they can't do it quickly enough." She held up a hand. "I know, we agreed he needs to learn how to use his second sight, but with Abigail climbing into his head, I don't want to think about what she might make him do. It's bad enough that over the past few weeks, his visions about what's coming have gotten worse."

My stomach dropped. "More visions? You didn't mention them."

Maera's cheeks flushed. "He didn't want me to tell you. There's been nothing concrete, nothing to give you any insight or new information, or else he would have. It's been more of the same. Bolts of lightning, fire, screaming, you falling. The same scenes, but more horrific every time. The poor boy's afraid to go to sleep these days."

That explained the dark circles under his eyes.

"Hopefully the temporary block will give him a reprieve," I said. "It won't be comfortable—it'll be a constant hum in his head he can't shake—but his thoughts will be his own."

Maera puffed out a breath and stopped by the next bed. "I appreciate all you're doing, and I know this can't be easy for you, but I'm proud of you. You're putting everything you have into stopping Abigail before she hurts anyone else, and we all see it. You've come a long way in the past couple of months. I'm glad I'm getting to know the woman my grandmother told me about."

I grimaced. "I'm sorry that woman vanished for so long. Maybe Abigail wouldn't have been able to get a foothold if I hadn't slipped so far."

Maera pulled me in for a hug, a gesture so rare between us these days that I stiffened before melting into the comfort of her embrace. "You may be immortal, but you're still human, Katerina. You're allowed to fall apart every now and then. The goal isn't to not fall—it's to pick yourself up after. You're doing well."

"I'm not. Not as well as I should be." I held my breath for a count of four to work up my courage, then said, "Amelia Caper is dead."

The blood rushed out of Maera's face, and I rested my hand on her arm, escorting her to a bench nearby. She dropped onto it as her legs gave out.

"What? How? Was it a wall-climbing accident? I told her she shouldn't keep doing it until she got her hip looked at."

"It was Abigail. I went to speak with Mrs. Caper to ask about any strangers she'd seen on the island, and somehow Abigail knew it. She did it to spite me, just because I liked the woman."

In a flash, my shocked housekeeper became a raging nemesis. She sat up tall, and her green eyes burned. "That bitch. She comes onto our island and thinks she can steal our treasures without consequences? Whatever fears I have for you, Kat, they don't include worrying you'll fail to kill her. All I ask is that you make it hurt."

I had no problem making that promise. After all the harm Abigail had caused, I didn't feel magnanimous enough to offer a quick death.

I left Maera to grieve with her gardening and returned inside to find Rhys.

He was easier to track down than his mother had been, being exactly where I'd expected him. Because of course the gamer had found the only television in the entire house, and of course he'd brought his gaming console with him. He wouldn't have suffered being away from it for three weeks. It would have been like asking Poppy to leave Cuddles at home—though at least Rhys's console didn't come with the stench of decay.

The cat in question was stretched out in a sunbeam on the floor, a low rumbling purr emanating from his scraggly frame. When I walked in, he raised his head and flicked his tail in warning, then relaxed when I held up my hands in a show of surrender. I wouldn't approach. I knew better.

Rhys started to pause his game as I came in, but I gestured for him to continue and sank onto the couch beside him.

For a while I said nothing, taking in the shadows under his eyes, the slump of his shoulders. He was struggling, all right, and I longed to put my arms around him and bundle him close, reassuring him that everything would work out.

But not for the first time, I reminded myself he wasn't my son to coddle—and he wasn't a child. Not that eighteen was so very grown up, but it was well into the age where he felt the need to sort his problems out for himself.

I understood that, but if there was any way I could help, I wouldn't shy away from it. And if he was holding something back to prevent me from worrying, I wouldn't shy away from that, either. Not if it meant he could finally close his eyes and rest.

"Have you talked to Poppy and Murisa yet?" I asked.

The corner of his eye twitched. "Not yet. They asked if I wanted them to start with me or Gavin, and I told them to go nuts with Gavin. Whatever they need him for is probably more important than blocking my visions."

"It's not." I pulled my knees to my chest. "Protecting you is more important than tracking down some guy's grandmother."

"Yeah, like that's all this is," he said, refusing my attempt to downplay the stakes involved.

"You're still more important. You should go find them."

He shrugged, his thumbs never slowing as his character leapt over rooftops. "I still don't know why I have to. The visions are useful. What if I See something that could help you against Abigail?"

"Have you Seen anything lately other than fire and torment?"

His character tumbled from the roof into the ocean, and the option came up for Rhys to reload the game. Instead, he set the controller down and turned to face me. "You've been talking to Mum."

"Maybe a little. She's worried about you. And Barrett says you've been acting weird. Like you can't be in the same room with him."

Rhys's pale skin flushed, and he shifted carefully on the couch. "I don't know about that. I haven't really been in the mood to talk to anyone lately. For the first few days after I left the hospital, everyone acted like I was about to break. Mum wouldn't stop fussing, and even Barrett treated me like a kid. Then all the visions." He paled further, going so white I worried he might faint. "It's bad, Kat. I can't make out half of what I'm Seeing, but if that's what hell looks like, I wouldn't be surprised. I can't tell the difference between dream and vision when I sleep. Demons and fire and my friends falling. Is it going to happen? Is some of it going to happen? Is it something we can stop? I don't know, and it's driving me crazy."

I frowned. "Demons?"

He shrugged. "I'm guessing. Grey, flaking skin, antler things, sharp teeth."

The description was close enough to Shogaur's demonic form that I couldn't argue his conclusion. Were we dealing with more demons on the horizon, or was he picking up on some lingering imprint of the fear demon?

Rhys curled his fingers into his hair, and I suspected it had become a regular gesture. Unable to keep away, I slid close to him and put my arm around his shoulders. "Give me a week, Rhys, okay? We'll block your visions for a week, and you'll drink some of Poppy's sleeping tonic. Get some rest, let your body heal, and we'll see where we are then. You went through more than physical trauma when Shogaur was here—is it any wonder your mind is still seeing demons? You were possessed."

He shuddered. "I know."

"When you're ready to talk about what happened, I'm here, but until then, you have to give yourself a break."

Rhys nodded and sagged against me. "I know you're right. I hate not being helpful, but—"

I pressed my fingers to his lips. "You being here is helpful. Seeing your handsome face is helpful. You don't need to torture yourself to be useful to me, okay? You just need to be well."

He wrapped his arms around me, and I squeezed him right back.

I didn't know if there was more to what he and Maera were saying, but what they told me sounded true enough. Everyone was stressed, and until I sorted Abigail out, tensions would continue to rise. The only way to ensure everyone stayed safe was to put an end to the witch.

Which meant I needed to get moving.

21

Katerina

As Rhys and I walked out of the living room, the temperature dropped and Emrick stepped out of the afterlife into the hallway. Dark circles lined his eyes, and I started. I hadn't thought it possible for a servant of Death to look exhausted, but he had all the hallmarks of someone who'd pulled an all-nighter and was dragging himself home to bed.

He mustered a smile for me and kissed my forehead. "That was a rough one."

I wrapped my arms around him in silent support. In all our years together, I'd learned not to prod him about his Deathly obligations. Most of what he did wasn't for me to know as a living, breathing person. Once in a while, he came back with stories, and if he learned anything that helped me on a hunt, he shared without me asking. If he offered nothing, I knew his mood was simply a side effect of the job. Not even a servant of Death could be immune to every loss.

Together, the three of us walked down the hallway to the living room at the front of the house where Poppy and Murisa sat with Gavin.

Maera had come in from the garden while Rhys and I chatted. She sat on the couch next to Poppy. Murisa had pulled her chair close to the large coffee table and was mixing something with her marble mortar and pestle. Gavin sat across from her looking grim.

"How are things coming along?" I dropped onto the couch on Murisa's other side. Rhys sat beside me, but Emrick, as usual, preferred to stand, taking his place at my back with his gloved hands on my shoulders.

"Slowly," Poppy said. "This isn't a spell we can rush."

Gavin scowled. "You said they'd only need a few drops."

I caught the bandage on the inside of his forearm and flinched. "My mistake."

Murisa's brow furrowed in concentration. "We needed more than usual because we're following more than one line of inquiry. We have to search backwards through Gavin's history and his mother's to get to his grandmother's. Traces of Abigail's DNA exist in him, but we need to parse it out if we want to get accurate information."

Spread out across the coffee table was a world map. If the witches weren't limiting themselves to one area, this spell would take a lot of energy from them. Worth it, I hoped. Within the hour, we could be armed with all the information we needed to tear Abigail to pieces.

It was a long shot—we all knew it—but I was ready to grasp at straws if straws were all we had left.

Murisa's foresight in packing more than she thought she'd need proved to be lucky as the spell she'd come up with was more complex than anyone in the house was prepared for. Three potions, six different powders, many drops of Gavin's blood, and an invocation later, we were only at the starting point of their spell.

"It gets simpler from here," Poppy assured everyone as Murisa mixed everything together.

Despite Gavin swearing he'd leave once the magic started, he stayed where he was. Rhys leaned in, riveted. His green eyes followed every movement, and I wondered if he was paying so much attention out of curiosity or a wish to learn. Barrett sauntered in during the third stage of the spell, but he remained in the doorway, wearing his usual disdainful expression whenever magic was involved.

Even Adrian came down to join us, standing behind Barrett in the shadows of the windowless hallway.

Maera's features had twisted from interest into a familiar

wariness that I tagged as her "how much of a mess is this going to make" face, and I didn't blame her. I'd seen these spells go wrong often enough to believe these powders might end up scattered across the room, covering every surface with a glitter-like stickiness that would linger long after the foundations of the house had crumbled to dust.

With every passing stage, my patience strained. Thoughts of all the other steps I could be taking to deal with Abigail gripped me. Going back to the Lodge, talking with the witches Poppy and Murisa had listed as possible sellers of those enchanted stones—returning to Palonia to see how Abigail had managed to dig up so much information about me—anything would be better than sitting here.

And yet I couldn't get up and leave. Not when there was a chance we might be about to unravel the mystery of the woman who'd hounded us for so many months.

Emrick rubbed his thumb in slow circles across the back of my neck, the gesture soothing my need to take action. Even so, I found it increasingly difficult to sit still. The seat of my chair pressed uncomfortably into the backs of my thighs, my neck was stiff, and my back was sore. I wanted to stand up and walk around, shake out my arms, stretch, but I worried any move-ment would throw off Murisa's concentration and delay things further. So I sat statue-still, afraid to breathe.

Finally, Murisa recited the last incantation. As Poppy tugged the curtains closed, sealing the room in darkness, Murisa picked up the bowl now containing a purple gloop that cast an otherworldly glow over her skin. We watched in awe as she tipped the bowl over the map, spilling the contents across the surface.

I crossed my fingers so hard my joints complained, praying we hadn't wasted an hour on a failed ritual.

After thirty seconds passed with no result, Rhys opened his mouth to speak. He hadn't gotten out more than a "What—" before the glowing gloop began to shift.

I'd watched Poppy cast a similar spell the last time we'd attempted to track Abigail, what felt like decades ago but was only a couple of weeks. This version was Poppy's basic magic packed with steroids. The light coming from the gloop grew brighter, in a shade of purple that was far outside the spectrum of human understanding. Bit by bit, the purple mass slid across the map. As it homed in on the epicentres of its purpose, the remnants evaporated, leaving only a small globule in central Ontario as more travelled across the ocean.

The light flared bright enough that I had to look away, and the stench of smoke and burning paper irritated my nose. A shout of alarm sounded from Maera, but Murisa was quick to put her at ease.

When I opened my eyes, the tiny fires had gone out, the gloop was gone, and all that remained were the burn marks that were supposed to give us the answers we sought.

The largest target was in Ontario, which made sense. It was where Gavin and his mother lived. "You were born here?" I asked him.

He nodded, his face blank. "In Hamilton. Mom is from London."

Which fit within the same target.

Gavin pulled the map closer to him, blocking my view. "There's nothing else in Ontario. So this burn mark over here must be where my grandmother's from?"

Poppy leaned in. "It must be. England. Cool."

A shiver ran down my spine, and Emrick's hands tightened on my shoulders.

Murisa pulled the map towards her and squinted at the dot. "I thought the spell would be more precise than that. It was supposed to pinpoint the exact place of birth, but there's no town marked here."

"Maybe it's really small? England's full of little villages, isn't it? Maybe it's not big enough for a world map." Rhys pulled out his phone, brought up the map and zoomed in close on the area.

"Is it possible the spell carried too far back?" I asked through numb lips. "To a more distant ancestor?"

Poppy shook her head. "If that were the case, we'd have way more burn marks on this map. Unless everyone else was born in the same place, which I guess is possible. Not likely, but possible."

She pulled the map towards her so she could see better, and my view was once more unobstructed. Right to the burn mark in the middle of the Lake District.

"Magic binds us to our birthplace," Poppy said. "Which makes sense if you think about it. All the energy that lingers in the air becomes a part of you when you take your first breaths. In a way, it helps form you. No matter where you move or where you live, your origins have a claim on you. You and your mother were born here, so that mark in England has to be where Abigail is from."

Her words floated around me as though I were still trapped under the waters of Providence Bay. I heard them but couldn't process them. My attention was fixed on that small mark tucked into the hills near Ambleside.

What were the odds that Abigail had been born so close to my old home? Had the long line of descendants remained in the area, biding their time? I couldn't see it. Twenty generations without a single person taking flight and starting a new life for themselves?

Nine hundred years passing down history, waiting for an opportunity to strike?

It didn't make sense.

Which left one possible explanation. One that I never would have believed possible but couldn't set aside with the evidence staring at me.

Nothing about this moment felt real. It was as if I'd stepped out of the living room and into a dream, as if I'd fallen asleep while waiting for the spell to work, and this was me walking through my worst nightmare.

The dragon symbol on the card I'd found in Amelia's fridge should have been the biggest clue. No one else could have known about that symbol. Not unless it had been pressed into their own skin as well.

Not only the card, but the magic. The strength of the spell circle in the Toronto hotel room. The strength of the air-manipulated ward Abigail had thrown around Mikhail to keep him safe. The strength of the spell circles crammed into those enchanted stones. I'd thought her power bewildering because it hadn't been witchcraft—it had been sorcery.

Not inherited, passed-down-through-centuries magic, but original, channelled-from-the-earth sorcery.

Everyone looked at me, and I felt as targeted as I had when I'd realized what Mikhail's intentions were in gathering his covens and draining their blood. The ritual that had destroyed Palonia—the ritual Emrick and I had never been able to find because it had been lost with the women who'd cast it.

Barrett stepped farther into the room and stood behind Rhys. "Let me guess, it's another connection to your past?"

I swallowed hard, needing to find the words that I was too

terrified to utter.

"Not *a* connection." I looked beyond him to where Adrian stood just past the doorway, his dark eyes sharp, knowing. "*The* connection."

"What do you mean?" Poppy looked from me to the map and back. Her jaw dropped. "You can't be serious."

I nodded, and Emrick rested his forehead on the top of my head. "That's Palonia. That was my home. And Abigail… I don't think she's a descendant. I think she's…"

Murisa's eyes widened, and I watched the pieces fall into place. "Another one of you?"

Another Palonian. Another immortal sorceress. I should have suspected it the moment I'd pieced together the connection between Gavin and Abigail. I'd started down the road but hadn't pressed far enough. Nothing else explained how Gavin possessed such strong magic when every other sorcerer bloodline had died out centuries ago. He wasn't twenty-two times removed from my old village—only two.

Silence fell on the room as we considered the significance of Murisa's conclusion.

If we were right, I wasn't the only person to have outlived the ritual that had taken everything from me. It meant someone else had survived—and she'd made it her mission to destroy me.

22

Katerina

I STOOD BETWEEN *Shep and my mother as the chosen performers of tonight's demonstration tossed balls of fire into the air. As they reached their peak, the fireballs transformed into great swaths of flame that raised sweat from my pores and brightened the darkening sky. Beyond them, the setting sun cast a secondary fire through the trees, throwing the audience into shadow.*

Everything about tonight was beautiful, and everything about it made me ache.

I buried my sigh into Rowan's hair where I clutched him against my chest, and Shep slid his arm around my shoulder. "You all right, love?"

I raised my head and forced a smile. "Fine."

No one in my family was fooled by my lie.

My father tilted his head, reached behind Mother to take my hand, and tugged me towards him. "Walk with me."

I kissed the top of Rowan's head as I passed him to Shep, then left them to enjoy the demonstration. Side by side, my father and I passed beyond the bonfires and walked up the incline to the top of one of the fells that contained our village. It was a beautiful view with all the fires scattered across the open dale. Herdwick sheep bleated around us, and the mere below reflected the sun with such fiery brilliance I couldn't look at it long without stars dancing in my eyes.

"Times like this, I feel like the luckiest person in the world," Father said, breathing in the sweet, crisp air.

I tried to rise above the weight pressing me down. "I know I should feel the same. I have everything I could want. A good match with Shep, a beautiful son. I just…"

Father moved so he stood in front of me, blocking the light from the mere, leaving me nothing to look at but the seriousness of his brown eyes. "Katerina, you are my daughter. From your first skinned knee and the first time you summoned fire into your hands, I knew you would be a force. I hope you know you've never let me down."

Tears welled in my eyes. "But my magic—"

"It's there. You'll find it." He wrapped his arm around my shoulders and turned me to face the village below. "Look at them. Three hundred sorcerers with various abilities and degrees of control, but all of them a facet of this village. Just as you are. Remove any one of us and the nature of Palonia shifts. We all have our roles to play.

You've spent your entire adult life believing you don't fit in because you can't master your magic, but you've never taken the time to figure out what you do contribute to our lives. You give Shep a reason to come home from every hunt. You're raising Rowan to be a fine young man." He brushed a loose hair off my cheek. "You have a purpose, Kate. If you don't come to see that, you'll waste away, and it would break your family's heart to watch it happen."

I stared out over the hundreds of people wandering between the bonfires. I spotted Alodie, Mae, and Blythe going into a cottage on the far side of the village. There was my family—Gran, Shep, Kyla, my mother, my brothers—standing near the food.

Father was right, of course, but in my soul I knew something was missing. That my potential was there, just out of reach, and to pretend otherwise would be to leave an important part of myself behind.

He kissed my head. "You have time, my girl. We Palonians are of long-lived stock. Never stop working to become the person you want to be, but never for a minute believe who you are now is any less. Your mother and I love you. We're proud of you, and we can't wait to see the woman you become."

I opened my eyes to find everyone watching me. Emrick was crouched at my side, his hands curled around mine. Murisa had made space for him, her expression full of concern.

Maera was in the process of leaving the room—no doubt to go make tea—and Gavin sat uncomfortably in his chair.

"What does this mean? My grandmother is immortal like you?" He blanched. "That doesn't mean I'm immortal, does it?"

I curled my fingers into my hair. "I don't think so. I don't know. I can't begin to figure this out. Give me a second. Everything is such a jumble." I looked at Emrick. "How could it be possible? We were both there. I watched them fall. All of them. We would have known if anyone survived."

He reclaimed my hands and clasped them between his. But he looked just as lost as I felt.

None of this made sense. If someone else had survived, why would they have it out for me? Wouldn't they want to reconnect, having something in common no one else could understand? I hadn't been important enough in Palonia to make enemies among my kin.

The only people I could think of who might wish me ill were the three women who'd cast the ritual—the ones who'd craved immortality so badly they'd sacrificed their entire community to achieve it. Only to fail. Because they had failed. Hadn't they?

"All right," I said, hating every shaky syllable. "Palonia. September 1147. The bonfires are burning, the three traitors are around the cooking pot." I spoke without picturing, pulling facts without returning to the past. The memories were so ingrained in my mind that it was possible for me to spit those details out without trouble. But the next part wouldn't come as easily. I knew what I *thought* I'd seen, but had I missed something? "They looked so… triumphant." The back of my throat burned with rising bile. "But at the last minute, they weren't. They were screaming with the rest of us. Then they fell. I swear I saw it. Their spell backfired, and they died. Isn't that what you saw?"

Emrick's forehead creased as he cast his memory back. "I was too focused elsewhere. There were so many, Kat." He spoke gently, walking carefully across the eggshells of my fractured emotions.

He wasn't exaggerating. Three hundred sorcerers dead over the course of a few minutes. He'd spent all night escorting everyone across and cleaning up the scene, laying hands on the bodies to turn them to dust so no passing mundane would walk by and discover the carnage.

He'd escorted my parents, siblings, grandmother, husband. I'd never asked him about it. Especially not about Rowan. It did soothe my pain, though, knowing he'd been the one to bring them to whatever came next. He wouldn't have led them astray.

The furrow on his brow deepened, his face going blank before life returned to it. He turned his gaze on me, the silver sheen filled with pain. "It's also foggy. I remember it happening, but the details are gone."

I swallowed the lump in my throat and focused again on the current issue. We didn't have time for me to panic about his fading memories or my rioting ones. "There were no other survivors. I'm sure of it. Their demon either double-crossed them or they messed up, but they fell."

But we had never confirmed it. Emrick had gone corpse to corpse to usher their souls into the beyond, but he didn't know who anyone was. And everyone was so covered in blood that even if I'd described the three women in detail, I doubted he would have picked them out.

If one of them—or all three—had survived, where had they been for the past eight hundred and fifty-odd years? Lying in wait for an excuse to come after me? It made no sense.

"What am I missing here?" I asked the room. "If Abigail is breathing, she's immortal, right? I don't care how many Wheaties or how much kale you eat, nine hundred years is an extreme life extension. So how has she aged?"

"Maybe something went wrong with the ritual," Emrick suggested.

He turned my hand over and hooked his fingers through mine. I hated his stupid gloves. I wanted the rush of contact, skin to skin, but no, I didn't want anyone else in the room to accidentally suffer the consequences. So I tolerated the rough leather and stared into his moonlight eyes, seeking the comfort of connection there instead.

"Something *else* you mean," I said.

I was the biggest, most unexpected side effect of Alodie, Mae, and Blythe's horrific plan. By all accounts, I should have died along with my family, my blood pulled from my veins to fuel the spell that was meant to summon the demon they would bind themselves to.

It was the same ritual the blood witch Mikhail had attempted to perform a few short months ago.

He, too, had failed, but only because I'd accidentally turned him into the Human Torch. As the youths of some generations would say, my bad.

"Yes, something else," Emrick agreed, pulling my attention back to today's problem instead of the one I'd already resolved. He slid onto the couch beside me. "Something makes sense now, though. For months, the souls I've escorted have talked about trouble following the immortal sorceress. They've been terrified for their families and everyone left behind. I thought they were talking about you, but it must be the other woman. Abigail."

"Or so she calls herself," I spat.

Gavin stood up. "I need to go hit something. Three weeks ago, I had no idea magic existed. Then I find out my grandmother is likely some murderer. Now I learn she's some *immortal* murderer? What the fuck, Kat? I don't have room in my life for this shit. Can I go?"

My head reeled, my entire world turning on its axis.

Maera returned with a tray in her hands filled with tea and cookies. She set it down across the map, blocking the hard truth from me. "I think everyone needs a snack. We're all—"

She fell silent on a gasp, and I looked up to find Rhys sitting rigid in his seat, his green eyes muted under a film of milky white.

"I felt that, Katerina," he said. Although the voice was his, the quality was different. Not his usual emptiness when touched with second sight, but higher pitched, shaky. "Playing with your tracking spells. Picking away at my hiding places. Teach your witches to hide themselves better. They give away all your secrets."

Poppy sucked in a breath through her teeth, and Murisa went pale.

"But I suppose it's only fair that I learn yours as you learn mine. Dragon's out of the bag—that ritual didn't fail as completely as you thought it did. After nine hundred years, I look forward to taking back what you stole from me."

23

Emrick

R HYS FELL INTO a doze after Abigail left his mind. Maera refused to leave his side, terrified the sorceress would come back and do something worse than use him as a mouthpiece.

"As soon as he wakes up, we'll block his visions," Murisa reassured her. "She won't get through to him again."

While they fussed over him, I watched Kat from where I'd settled against the wall.

She'd risen from her place on the couch to make room for Maera, but otherwise, she'd shut down. Her gaze was stuck on Rhys but unseeing. She'd wrapped her arms around her middle as though she were holding herself together and had pressed her mouth into such a thin line her lips were white.

Barrett and Gavin made their escape, but Adrian remained

in the doorway, a faint crease on his brow as he stared at Rhys.

Despite the ward, Abigail had found a way to infiltrate our safe space, and I understood why every person in this house felt violated.

As the first rush of chaos died down, Adrian made his way towards me. "Take her away," he said, softly enough that only I could hear. "She needs to process this. Despite the pain it will cause her, it's the information we need to beat this woman. Unfortunately, we don't have time for Katerina to dwell."

I hated that he was right. After so many revelations in such a short amount of time, Kat deserved the opportunity to sit with it all, but any delay might cost her so much more.

Pulling off my glove, I slipped one arm around her waist, rested my bare hand against the back of her neck, and stepped us through to her bedroom upstairs.

The change of scene shook her out of her stupor, and she sucked in a breath.

"What could I have possibly stolen from her?" she demanded, jumping right into the conversation as though we were already in the middle of it. "If anything, *she* stole from *me*."

I brushed her hair out of her face and maintained my grip on her as shivers took over her body.

"Every step of the way, it's another knife to my gut." She sounded desperate, her expression begging me to make every-thing right.

I wished I could. I wanted nothing more than to track Abigail down. A few days ago, I would have thought the traitor's immortality meant I could carry out whatever vengeance she deserved, but now I stayed my hand, uncertain what would classify as breaking Death's rule.

All I could do was serve Kat as she'd asked me to—holding her hand and lending her strength.

Kat gripped my arms. "I need to see her again. Now that I know she's one of the three, I need to look her in the eye and know who I'm dealing with. Right now, she's a faceless figure stalking me from the shadows, and I can't fight shadows. I need her out in the open. I need to know why she did what she did. Where she's been. Why now? Why Shogaur? I have so many questions, but I also don't want to know the answers. I don't want to give her another moment to breathe. But if she's immortal, how do I stop her? How do I kill her? How has she *aged?*"

Tears streamed down her face faster than I could wipe them away, so I gathered her against my chest and gave her space to vent the maelstrom storming inside her.

Her pain radiated through my bones as though it were coming through the tether that bound her to me. My frustration rose to meet it, lined with rage at how useless I was to help her. I was a servant of Death. I had the power to manipulate life itself, and in this I was impotent.

Being here for Kat didn't feel like enough—not nearly—

but if that was the limit of my purpose, I would do everything in my power to walk her through this.

I rubbed her back, trailing my fingers up and down her spine, trying to focus her thoughts on this moment instead of the thousands of others vying for her attention. "We both know immortality has its limits. She has a weakness. Once we figure out how she survived, we can think of ideas about how to stop her."

"How are we supposed to find out without tracking her down and asking?"

An idea played in the back of my mind, and I latched on to it. "She said the ritual didn't fail, but what if it went sideways? They needed a demon to finish the spell. We thought they didn't get as far as the binding, but what if they did?"

She drew in a shuddering breath and pulled back so she looked up at me. "But the demon didn't make them immortal the same way you did me?"

"Maybe not on this plane of existence."

Her red eyes widened, and the flow of tears stopped. "You think they were dragged to the infernal realms? Is that possible? How would any of them have lasted so long in that place?"

I kissed her brow and stroked the backs of my fingers along her cheek. "I don't believe it would be possible for any mortal. Certainly not while hanging on to any facet of humanity. Clearly only one of them survived."

The idea was horrific, but it answered too many questions.

Abigail would have been locked in a world without sunlight, without human contact, with her soul-bound demon for eight hundred years.

"It would explain Abigail's absence," I said. "She didn't come after you sooner because—"

"Because she wasn't in this world," Kat breathed.

"And if her immortality is tied to a demon… well. We know demons are difficult to kill, but not impossible."

"Once the demon is dead, we can get to Abigail."

Hope flared in Kat's expression where before there had been despair, and warmth hugged my chest that I'd offered *something*, even if it was only a theory.

She set her jaw and drew her shoulders back. "Okay. This is good. We can see if Murisa and Poppy—Muroppy?—can look into the demon angle, and they're already working on ways to nullify Abigail's spell circles. At least with that, we'll be able to get close enough to pin her down. In the meantime, I should play investigator. We need to cut this sorceress off from her resources."

Another furrow formed between her eyebrows as her concentration deepened. "So far, except for the ward Abigail cast around Mikhail, she's only worked with witchcraft. It's all been spell circles. Strong ones, sure, but still secondhand magic. Does that mean she lost her power at some point, or that it's weaker? Or did she just not want to give herself away? We'll have to work on the assumption it's the latter, which will make our defences more difficult. We don't know what she's capable of."

Fear fought against the fledgling hope, but this one I couldn't battle. She wasn't wrong to be afraid. It was likely we were up against one of Kat's teachers, and if that were true, she packed a lot of power inside that frail frame.

"What do you remember about the three women? She might have learned a few new tricks since then, but likely she'll focus on her strengths, the same way you do. It might be enough to let us prepare."

My chest tightened at the thought of Kat battling this woman, but there was no other way forward. No one else was strong enough.

She paused to gather her thoughts. "Most of the Palonian sorcerers focused on fire. Alodie and Mae were both good with lightning. Blythe was a deft hand with air. But there's more to it than their magic. There's the way they thought."

I rubbed my hands up and down her arms. "Talk it out."

She frowned. "If it's Alodie, we need to brace for a straightforward attack. She was always loud and abrasive, but she wasn't clever. More likely to use a hammer to open a locked box, regardless of the damage it caused. I've always suspected the idea for the ritual was hers. Why gain power the old-fashioned way through experience when you could simply summon a demon and force everyone to your will?"

Her gaze shifted into the middle distance as memories took hold of her again. "Blythe was the patient one. She'd try to pick the lock, even if it took hours or days. If I had to guess, she was the one who thought to put the potion for the spell in the shared drink that night. Those cups circulated throughout the community, all coming from the same pot, and tradition dictated that everyone take a sip to honour the gods. Mikhail used the same trick to spread his potion around, which makes sense if Abigail taught him everything he needed to know. If Blythe is Abigail, we need to be prepared for her to wear us down. Everything so far would be only a taste of what's to come. She'll keep the pressure up until we're too exhausted to keep looking over our shoulders, and that's when she'll strike."

"And Mae?"

"She'd overlook the locks and go straight for the hinges, getting into the box backwards. Clever, quick. She's probably the one who suggested the ritual be carried out the night of the festival, when it was a guarantee everyone would be home and their chances of success at their highest. If we're dealing with her, then the dragon, Mrs. Caper's death, talking through Rhys—they're all distractions while she plans something unrelated and a million times worse."

Three women with three different angles, and so far everything we'd seen could fall into any one of those categories. Everything came down to the motivation behind them.

I scrambled to come up with a way to stand by Kat, to ensure she had everything necessary to win. "We'll train. You and me. We'll make sure if it comes to a face-to-face battle, you're in a position to take her by surprise."

Kat pressed her hand against my cheek, and I leaned into her palm. Her love for me wrapped around my shoulders and drew me to her, and I met it with every ounce of my love for her.

She bowed her head against my chest with a groan. "I feel like I'm facing off with Cerberus, and I don't know which one of his heads wants to eat me. If I make the wrong guess, I leave myself open to attack from either side."

I tucked my fingers under her chin and made her look at me. "You won't be left vulnerable. I'll be there to watch your back no matter which way you look. I can't act, but I won't let her sneak up on you." I brushed a loose hair behind her ear, and her eyes closed at the vibration that hummed under our skin. "It's a small comfort, but at least we know who we're dealing with now."

Kat grunted. "Once—just once—I'd love it if my nightmares would stay dead."

24

Katerina

I FELT BETTER for having talked out every facet of my problem with Emrick—and for having a horrifying working theory about where Abigail had been hiding all these years—but the weight of what we faced dragged on my shoulders.

Another immortal sorceress.

Someone like me wandering the earth, bound to a demon instead of Death, searching for an opportunity to destroy me.

I paced the length of the hallway as I attempted to settle the maelstrom of thoughts rushing through my head. With every turn, I danced around Cuddles, who'd chosen the middle of the floor as the perfect spot to laze about.

Emrick had left again, and everyone else was downstairs. The hum of magic tingled over my skin, and I guessed Muroppy were working on saving Rhys from playing unwitting host to a homicidal immortal.

Good. It had been bad enough hearing Shogaur's voice come out of his mouth, but for Abigail to reach through him like that was a whole other level of disturbing. The poor guy was only just learning how to control his second sight. It wasn't fair that someone with more power could hijack him to mess with me.

I reached the end of the hallway, then turned and started in the other direction, avoiding the knife-laden paw that swiped at my ankle as I passed.

So many memories of the ritual in Palonia had resurfaced over the past couple days, each one hurtful, each one tugging me forward with possible clues of who I might be dealing with.

And what she might want to take from me. No matter how much I wracked my brain over that question, no answers appeared, only more questions.

A door opened behind me, and I turned to find Adrian standing in the doorway to his bedroom. Mozart's "Eine Kleine Nachtmusik" drifted from the stereo within. He tilted his head in appraisal and must have found me wanting because he opened his door wider in an invitation to join him.

Desiring nothing more than to get his views on this latest disaster that was my life, I accepted, entering the massive space he shared with Barrett.

The curtains were pulled tight against the afternoon sun, the room lit with soft table lamps that warmed the oak-and-green decor. A canopy bed similar to mine sat against the wall to my left, green curtains falling around the bedposts. In front of me was a sitting room, with a sofa and armchair set up in front of the large fireplace, the hearth currently dark.

Adrian settled on the sofa and extended his arm along the back. "How are you coping, tesoro?"

I dropped beside him and rested my head on his shoulder. "I'm able to put one thought in front of the other, which is better than I expected to be an hour ago. I don't suppose you have any words of wisdom?" At his silence, I sighed. "My mind is in such a tangle. I don't know where to start picking the knot apart. Emrick thinks she might have spent all these years in the infernal realms, bound to her demon. A nightmare of an idea, but there's logic to it. It explains why we've never heard of her in all our years hunting. But if it's true, how long has she been back? Or an even bigger question—how did she get back?"

Adrian laid his cheek on top of my head. "There's one simple answer."

My mouth went dry. "Someone summoned the demon she's bound to." I sat up to look at him. "Another coincidence?"

His eyes shone with amusement, but I sensed the vibration of anger hidden beneath it. "They seem to be piling up, don't they?" He clasped my hand in his. "What of your plan to track this woman's history? Why does that have to change now that you know who she might be? Whoever summoned her demon might still be out there. The more you learn about where she's been, how long she's been back, and who's hiding behind her, the better idea you'll have on how to stand in her way."

A shudder ran through me, and I returned my head to his shoulder. "Finding that out might mean returning to Palonia, and I can't go back there, Adrian. When I walked away from those hills, it was for good."

A noise escaped the back of his throat that might have been the start of an argument or merely disapproval, but he swallowed it before any other syllables followed. "I suspect, if you want to win this, you'll need to lean into your past instead of avoiding it, Katerina. Into every nightmare that's chased you, every bad memory you've run from. As long as you're afraid of looking back, she'll remain the lurking monster waiting to strike. She's using your fear against you. You need to grow bigger than she is, armed with your pain and your history."

Every word landed like rocks in my ears. It was everything I'd been working so hard to deny. Now that Adrian had said it—Adrian of the calm, rational thinking, who I loved, admired, and relied on—I couldn't ignore the truth.

"I wouldn't know where to begin." My voice sounded small in my ears. "Thinking about that night, opening myself up to those memories, feels like plunging my hand into a fire. The deeper I wade into them, the more they consume me, and I don't know if I can pull myself back a second time."

"You won't be alone," he reminded me. "Back then, you had Emrick, but who was Emrick to you beyond the man who wouldn't let you find a way to die? Now you have family. We'll be here for you every step of the way, tethering you to what matters. Which, despite everything, cuore mio, is not the past."

I shifted on the couch so I could wrap my arms around his waist, and he folded me into a hug. "I don't know what I would do without you. Aside from Emrick, you're the only person who understands what it's like to be chased by so many lives. So many different versions of yourself it's difficult to remember sometimes which person you're supposed to be right now. Every time Abigail draws my attention, I become Katerina of Palonia all over again—the poor, scared woman-child who saved herself as her family died. Thanks to you, I've lived so many lives since then. Amazing lives. I need to step into one of those the next time this bitch comes calling."

Adrian tightened his hold on me. "It's as you say, my beautiful one. Every decision we make, every loss, every addition changes us. The past may hurt, the memories may burn, but it's when we stop changing that the real problems begin. I wonder if that's the challenge Abigail currently faces. She gave up so much for her immortality, believing eternity would be her answer to everything. Perhaps she now realizes immortality is only worthwhile when you stay open to the wonders life offers. Perhaps what she hopes to steal is your ability to live all these lives you've had."

Something in what he said made me sit back to look him in the eye, but all I found staring back at me was the fondness that had been there almost from the day we'd met.

A strange hum ran over my skin, and it was only when it ended that I noticed the sudden lack of magic in the air.

"The witches just finished their spell. I guess that means they're ready for us." I reluctantly extricated myself from Adrian's embrace, and we both rose from the couch. "Thank you for listening. Again. I feel like all I do these days is drop by to lay my problems at your feet. When this is over, we'll dance like we used to. Think Emrick remembers how to play the pipes?"

My smile faltered when I realized how possible it was that he might not, that Death might have already stolen that from him.

Adrian offered a sad smile in reply. "We'll find out, tesoro. When we finally get that moment of peace, we'll take time to draw on the good memories. Goodness knows they outweigh the bad by no small amount, even if right now it doesn't feel that way. And goodness knows there will be many more to come, even in the middle of your darkest days."

He kissed my hands and slid his arm around my waist, directing me towards the door. "I'll check in with Barrett while you see to Rhys. We'll ensure you stay ahead of this."

Together, we turned our steps towards the stairs, and I hoped Muroppy could put my mind at ease on the dozens of problems nipping at my heels.

25

Katerina

WHEN I ARRIVED downstairs, I bumped into Rhys as he walked down the hallway towards me. He was leaning his weight on his mother's shoulder, his face pale, his shoulders hunched, as though his energy had been drained from him.

"Are you all right?" I asked.

He lifted his gaze, and his green eyes were empty, haunted. "No." It came out as barely more than a whisper. "It's worse than I thought it would be. Worse than you said. It's like part of me has been cut off. I can't think straight."

I took his hand and gave it a tight squeeze. "Only a week, okay? I promise. We won't leave you like this."

He sagged against his mother, who cast me a pained glance. There was nothing accusing in her look—she knew as well as

I did this was our best option to keep him safe—but I experienced a pang of guilt nonetheless. My decision had caused my friend this discomfort. It was on me to resolve the problem so I could undo it.

Drawing my shoulders back, I marched into the room.

Poppy and Murisa were tidying up the candles and ingredients they'd used to complete their tracking spell. An empty vial sat on the edge of the table, and a pale blue tinge stained the bottom. My chest tightened at the sight. I'd expected them to create an amulet to protect Rhys, like they'd done to protect us against Shogaur, or maybe a warding spell. I wasn't comfortable with the idea of Rhys ingesting some kind of anti-Sight potion.

"You can undo it, right?" I asked. "When this is over, you can give him a counterpotion?"

Murisa's gaze drifted to the vial, and her eyes widened in understanding. "Of course! That's if we need to. The potion hasn't actually blocked anything. We worried if we cut him off altogether, the effects might be too severe. So the potion sort of…" She pursed her lips and looked to Poppy.

"We've redirected his second sight, forcing it along the temporal line to See what's in the present instead of what's ahead. Abigail shouldn't be able to reach him because he's not able to look for her, but it will only last a couple of days."

Murisa nodded. "If you haven't found her by then, we can brew him another dose."

I glanced over my shoulder, staring in the direction Rhys and Maera had gone. "He looks really out of it."

Poppy stuffed a few more vials into her satchel. "Imagine walking around cross-eyed. That's basically what we've done. He'll have headaches, dizziness, but nothing worse than that."

I trusted them to know what they were doing, but the timeline stressed me out. A few days to bring Abigail to an end, or make Rhys suffer to buy me another opportunity.

I'd find a way to make it happen, and any plan I hoped to form started with these two.

"With everyone here as safe as they can be, how about we talk about next steps. I have a laundry list for you."

Murisa's eyes brightened, but Poppy crossed her arms and tapped the tips of her neon-yellow talons against the fabric of her teal T-shirt. "We haven't finished the last load you gave us. I thought you wanted us working on nullifying those enchanted stones."

I sat down and crossed my legs, aiming for a pose of relaxed authority. Anything to fight the apprehension tying my guts into intricate knots. "I do. Top priority."

"What else do you need?" Murisa asked, shooting Poppy a look that made the other witch press her lips together.

"More defences," I said. "If Abigail's been hiding her power to keep her identity hidden from me, then we need to be prepared for her to unleash it now that her secret's out. We have to assume that anything I can do, she can do a hundred times better. Fire, lightning. Based on the ward she put around Mikhail, she must have learned how to manipulate air as well. What can we do to protect everyone from that kind of magic?"

Poppy blanched and sagged onto the end of the couch. "You might be asking for the impossible, kitty Kat."

Murisa offered an apologetic nod. "Creating the talismans to keep a demon as strong as Shogaur out of your head was challenging enough, but to ward off that level of magic? I don't know how we'd do it."

The two women looked at each other, and Poppy canted her head as an excited gleam entered her eyes. "We'd need a lot of supplies. More than we have on hand here."

"And it wouldn't be quick," Murisa warned.

"And we'd need a lab."

I raised an eyebrow at Poppy. "Isn't that a bit extreme?"

She shrugged. "It'll involve a lot of experimentation. There will probably be some explosions. Bad smells. Maybe a small fire or two. I have space behind the shop, but—"

"No, you need to stay here. Abigail's already killed one woman, and I barely knew her. And she's made her presence known at your shop. If you make yourselves an easy target, she'll come for you." I ran my palms over my hair, thinking things out. "I'll talk to Barrett, and we'll get you set up somewhere. Whatever you can come up with, I want you to try it.

Amulets, potions, whatever. If she hits Maera with a fireball, I want Maera to brush herself off and walk away."

"We'll see what we can do," Murisa said, but her tone was lined with caution.

I appreciated how slim our odds were, but I was ready to gamble everything I had to protect my family. A chill ran through me at the thought of what might happen if I couldn't. Goosebumps pebbled my skin, and I rubbed my arms to warm myself.

"What about supplies?" Poppy asked. "We'll need to drive into town to get what we need."

Murisa grimaced. "Probably farther. No offense to the area, but the city would be our best bet to find everything—especially in the quantity we'll need."

Poppy scowled. "Again, *my store* is fully stocked."

My patience grew frayed. "Make me a list. I'll have Emrick take me to your store to pick it up. This can't wait. For Rhys's sake—for mine—for everyone in this house, we need to be ready to face her again. I'll go tonight."

"Tomorrow."

Only when Emrick spoke did I realize my goosebumps had been a reaction to the sudden drop in temperature and not my rising anxiety.

I turned to face him. "Excuse me?"

"You need to sleep."

With the adrenaline running through me, I doubted I'd be

able to close my eyes for a second.

"I can't, Emrick. We don't know when she's going to disappear again, and we don't have time to track her down from scratch. Who will she come after next? On top of that, we only have so many days before Rhys's potion wears off, and I won't put him through any more pain."

Emrick took my hand and pulled me towards him. His silver eyes were filled with so much love my heart bled, but love wasn't enough to quash my stubbornness.

"I watched you get zapped with a powerful spell yesterday, Kat. You almost drowned. You found a friend dead. You need to sleep, or you won't be able to cope with whatever else Abigail throws at you."

Tears pricked the corners of my eyes as fear wrapped its fingers around my throat. "But what if she—"

"I love you, Kat, but you are an infuriating woman." He kissed the backs of my hands. "Yes, you're immortal, but you're still human. You need to sleep."

As his words sank in, his concern washing over me like a warming touch, I sagged against him and bowed my head against his chest. "I know. You're right." With a sigh, I turned back to the witches. "For tonight, work on nullifying the spell circles, make the list of supplies, and also the list of people who might be selling those enchantments. First thing tomorrow, Emrick and I will go to Toronto."

"Absolutely," Murisa said. "Whatever you need."

Poppy blew me a kiss. "You can count on us, kitty Kat."

Emrick pulled off his glove and tugged me forward, bringing me through the afterlife to my bedroom upstairs. Evening had found us between the time I'd spoken with Adrian and now, and although the curtains were open, little light spilled in from outside.

The thought of climbing into bed made my muscles tense with the need to keep moving, but Emrick gave me no space to turn around and leave. He tugged off my shirt and threw it in the corner, then pushed me onto the bed and pulled off my boots and pants. Once I was naked, he drew back the covers and tucked me in, laying gentle kisses across my face until my eyelids sagged.

"You're not joining me?" I asked, though it came out more as a murmur than the seductive invitation I'd intended.

His low laugh hummed through my blood. "Not this time, *ælfsciene*. You sleep. I won't be far."

My thoughts began to drift. "I forgot to mention your demon theory to Muroppy."

He kissed my temple. "It can keep."

I didn't think I'd be able to sleep on my own, afraid more memories would pop up as soon as I closed my eyes, but Emrick traced his fingertips over my brow, down my nose, across my cheeks. Under his gentle touch, all awareness drifted away.

26

Emrick

AFTER KAT FELL asleep, I stayed beside her while I debated my next move.

The smartest step would be for me to return to the afterlife and stay out of everyone's way, but Kat's fears had leached into me, making me all too sensitive to the destruction bearing down on us. Kat needed to sleep, but we couldn't afford to lose time going after Abigail's demon.

I stroked my fingers through Kat's hair—my paper-white skin against a deep black canvas.

My heart thudded in my chest as I considered my precarious position. There wasn't enough of me left to risk a single piece, but I couldn't lie here and let a critical piece of information sit idle.

Praying I could play this smart, I carefully pulled myself away from Kat and headed downstairs to the witches. When I walked into the living room, they broke apart, surprise written on Murisa's face, curiosity on Poppy's.

"Not often we see you without your better half," she said.

I found my place against the wall and tucked my hands behind my back. "You have another job to do."

Now curiosity lit on both their faces. Poppy shifted on the couch to face me, and Murisa pulled a notebook out of the bag she kept slung over the back of her wheelchair. Poppy raised an eyebrow, and Murisa blushed. "I have a limit of three tasks before I need to start writing things down."

Poppy winked at her, then crossed one leg over the other and looked at me. "What do you need, reaper?"

I cringed at the title. She wasn't wrong, but the image of the grim reaper was too close to the wraith I was all too quickly becoming. "I can't tell you. I can't help you with this at all."

The two exchanged a glance. "Oh… kay…" Poppy said. "I can see this being an issue."

I shoved my hands through my hair. Every word out of my mouth was another potential fragment of soul lost. I felt like I was moving through the steps of one of Adrian's dances. Put my foot in the wrong place, and the entire performance was ruined.

Searching for a way forward, I cast my gaze around the room and found Cuddles sitting like a meatloaf on the couch, his yellow eyes fixed on me. He flicked his kinked tail to the side, and I got the impression he was debating launching himself at me. I hoped he didn't. He might be undead, but I'd still turn his resurrected corpse to dust.

I couldn't believe Kat had let Poppy keep him. But then, the witch was obviously good at working with loopholes.

At the thought, a loose plan arranged itself in my mind. Muroppy had proved they were good at assembling whole pictures from tiny details—maybe I could work with that. After all, giving them information they already knew couldn't be seen as interfering.

"Abigail is immortal."

Poppy leaned forward, waiting for me to say more. When I didn't, impatience flickered across her face as she tapped her nails on the table. "Right?"

I met her eye. "She performed a ritual to bind herself to a demon to gain her immortality."

"Yes, we know that." Poppy huffed and looked to Murisa, but Murisa was watching me. Her eyes were narrowed, her posture leaning slightly towards me as she clasped her pencil between her fingers.

"She survived," I added.

Poppy blinked. "Wow. Thank you for the summary. Now, if you don't mind, we have—"

Murisa's eyes flew wide, and she grabbed Poppy's hand. "She

bound herself to a demon. That part of the ritual didn't fail. She did it."

My heart raced as I watched them, doing my best to keep my expression neutral. Nothing I said or did could influence their conclusions. But that didn't mean I couldn't stick around to see if they got where I'd led them.

Poppy frowned, trying to catch up. "We're not just dealing with the sorceress, we're dealing with the demon, too." Her eyebrows rose. "Get rid of the demon, the sorceress is vulnerable."

"It's brilliant," Murisa said.

Poppy remained skeptical. "If there's a demon wandering around this plane, wouldn't we have heard about it? They're not exactly subtle, what with the craving death and destruction and all that."

"They're not, but I don't think we're dealing with another Shogaur." Murisa flicked the end of her pencil against the notepad. "If we were, Abigail wouldn't be bothering with enchanted stones, right? Besides, if I were going to bind myself to a demon to become immortal"—she held up a hand towards me—"I wouldn't, that's gross—I would want it to be something I believed I could control. I'd guess it's low- to mid-level. Strong enough the traitors believed it would endure, not so strong that it would constantly be challenged by other demons or likely to be summoned or destroyed by someone else."

"But someone obviously *did* summon it," Poppy said. "Otherwise, how is it here?" She shot me a look. "I know you have a theory in that gorgeous head of yours about where it's been all this time, but I'll wait for Kat to tell me." She wiped her hands on her thighs. "Okay, so someone summoned a low- to mid-level demon who *happened* to be bound to a woman out to get our sorceress. Everything about this screams conspiracy. Am I wrong?"

Murisa shook her head. "You're not. Maybe this is the piece we were missing to get to the heart of this mess." She scribbled in her book. "Banishing this demon should be the same process we used to get rid of Shogaur, but we'll need more information. Its name, for starters. I can go through the books I brought with me, and I'll add a few more titles for you and Kat to pick up from the shop when you go for the rest of our supplies. Maybe we'll stumble on a few possibilities."

My shoulders sagged in relief, and I leaned my head back against the wall. At no point during their conversation had I experienced that disturbing *suction* of some new piece of me fading away. I hoped that was true—that I'd managed to navigate my way through without breaking the rules—but all that mattered was I was still here. Still me. One more strike.

Poppy grinned at me as though she'd read my every thought. "You're a clever one, reaper. We'll take it from here." She resumed her tapping against the table. "We could probably do some digging in the astral plane, but not without Abigail noticing. She made that clear enough with Rhys poking around."

I rubbed the back of my neck. "I can't tell you what to do. Or what not to do. Hypothetically, though, it might not matter anymore how much she catches on to what we're doing. She came after Kat on the beach, and she killed Kat's neighbour. She's not trying to hide. At this point, I'd guess she's waiting for another opportunity to come after you. If it doesn't come soon, she'll create one."

"She won't find us unprepared." The line of Poppy's jaw grew hard. "We'll make her regret everything she's done."

I wished we had more to rely on than pep talks and plans. I wanted guarantees that Kat would be safe. That the people she cared about would be safe. That Abigail would burn for what she'd put my sorceress through.

But until we knew more, nothing was certain. I'd pushed my hand as far as I dared go; now I had to hope everyone else had what it took to take us the rest of the way.

27

Katerina

I FELL ASLEEP with Emrick beside me and woke up alone. He'd told me that would be the case, but his absence felt like a hole in my chest. Not least because my dreams had been haunted by visions of life without him.

I'd been in Palonia again. Not the community of my past but a version my subconscious had drummed up, filled with endless hills, dozens of bonfires, and a shadow of Emrick trailing behind me, making no contact, always out of reach.

All my worst fears crammed into one nightmare because my brain was a bitch.

I pressed the heels of my palms into my closed eyes, then blinked my eyes open to stare at the ceiling, trying to embrace the solitude now that I felt somewhat rested. While my to-do list for the day was eye-wateringly long, another few minutes wouldn't make a difference. What *would* help was putting together some of these puzzle pieces.

First, a devastating part of my past had stepped into my present. Not the first time that had happened in the last two months, but a living, breathing sorceress was not the same as a ritual or a demon. Someone I'd known in my mortal life meant a personal connection, which meant associated emotions I was not ready to deal with. Especially since I intended to kill her.

Second, this woman had waited almost eight hundred and fifty hundred years to make an appearance. That was a long time to sit around and plan. Emrick's theory about her being trapped in the infernal realms was twisted beyond belief, but it would also explain her unhinged behaviour.

Third, she was old. I hadn't aged a day since being bound to Emrick, so either a bond with a servant of Death was better bang for your buck than binding yourself to a demon, or Emrick was right that something else had gone wrong during their ritual.

The next question would be harder to answer—where did I stand in all this?

Muroppy would be busy for the next few days working out how to keep everyone in this house safe from Abigail's power. Rhys's second sight had been blocked, which would protect him from Abigail's manipulations but also prevent us from knowing what was coming.

I had to talk to the people Murisa and Poppy suspected might be supplying Abigail, but the longer I sat with the idea, the more my gut told me there was no point. Considering how long it had taken us to dig up the tiniest details about this woman, she didn't seem like the sort to make deep connections within the local witch community. She'd stayed close to Mikhail for her own purposes, but after his death, she'd switched to demon summoning instead of raising another coven against me.

Still, if it meant preventing anyone from working with her and maybe discovering information to use against her, it would be worthwhile to do the rounds and make my opinions of the woman known.

I also had to ask Muroppy to look into Abigail's demon. I would owe them so many of Maera's cookies when this was over.

With my game plan laid out, I threw back the covers, ready to start my day. But as I attempted to climb out of bed, panic curled its talons into my chest and froze me in place.

The intensity of the past few days swept over me in a rush. I'd fought many enemies over the years, some of whom had been cruel, some wily, some terrifying, but rarely had those qualities been combined in one person, and never in such a personal capacity.

Shogaur had been close, but even with him, I'd had some emotional distance. He was a moment in my past that had brought Emrick and me closer together and made us realize how tenuous my immortality was.

Abigail was a connection to the life that defined who *I* was. My reason for becoming a hunter, my reason for still being alive, breathing this air, walking this earth. She was a connection to my parents, my training, my magic.

And instead of seeking me out to rekindle those memories or rediscover the values that made Palonia so wonderful, she was murdering people because they'd spoken to me. She was terrorizing me and threatening my friends.

What kind of fiend did that to someone who shared a history like we did?

But what did I expect from a woman who believed the lives of three hundred men, women, and children were worth the cost of unending life?

I couldn't wait to track her down. She wanted to frighten me? She was the one who should be frightened. She thought she was some badass bitch because she was able to sneak around and leave messages with my postal worker or in a dead woman's fridge, but she didn't have my friends at her back.

It wouldn't be long before she realized she had miscalculated by coming after us.

Determination and rage overpowered my momentary anxiety, and I leapt out of bed and into my usual uniform of black leather pants, black T-shirt, fingerless leather gloves. I was in full hunting mode, and I wouldn't sleep again until I had that bitch's head on a plaque.

"Did you get some rest?" Emrick asked as he came into the room behind me.

"Enough to charge my batteries. I'll sleep better when Abigail's corpse is dust." I finished tying my hair up in a ponytail and turned to face him. "I need the lists from Muroppy, and we're good to go."

Emrick flicked a piece of paper between his fingers. "All set."

I frowned at it. "How did you get that?"

"I went downstairs to see how they were getting along. Happened to overhear a fascinating conversation about Abigail's demon and the connection to her immortality. So they're also working on that angle."

Another wave of apprehension gripped me, and I latched on to his arm. "What did you do?"

He picked up my hand and pressed a kiss into my palm. "Absolutely nothing. I pointed out a few facts they already knew, and they worked it out for themselves. You have a great team here, Kat. They've got this."

I breathed until my heart rate settled. Emrick wouldn't take unnecessary risks. Not anymore. I had to believe that, or I'd lose my mind. But if the witches were already running with the demon idea, that was worth my heart attack.

I plucked the paper from him and scanned the names written in a neat script. The top sheet listed the witches who might have worked with Abigail. There were only three to check out. A grand underestimation, I suspected, but if Poppy believed they were the only likely candidates, I was inclined to believe her. The rest of the page, written in cramped writing to fill every last white space, was their ingredient list. Some of the herbs and potions leaned into very murky territory but didn't quite cross into dark magic. Given what I was asking of them, I wasn't about to judge.

Emrick ran his fingers from the nape of my neck down to my tailbone. "You sure you're up for this?"

I arched an eyebrow at him. "If you try to stop me again, I'm leaving without you."

He extended his bare hand, and I placed my palm on top of it, sucking in a breath as the tips of my fingers stroked his skin, the contact making my cells play jump rope.

"We wouldn't want that," he murmured in my ear as he pulled me towards him.

The mist formed around us, and a moment later, we found ourselves in an alley on a downtown Toronto street. The sign of a new age shop flickered above a darkened storefront.

I pulled out my phone to check the time. It was a little past eight in the morning, but although the sign on the door said they opened at eight, I saw no movement within. Curious, I searched the store's website and let out a grunt as I took in the latest update on their home page. The store was permanently closed following the death of the store owner. They'd tried to keep it going without her, but after two months, it was time to say goodbye.

The image below the announcement was of a smiling woman, her brown hair cut short, her green eyes bright. I recognized her, and it took me a moment to remember her as one of the witches protecting Mikhail in the warehouse.

"I guess that was my fault," I said with a grimace. "On the bright side, we can cross this one off the list and try the next place."

Emrick did his best to hide his amusement, but his eyes sparkled. "Even when you're not trying, you're a scourge on the magical community."

I huffed as I looked up the website for the next name Poppy had offered. "If they want to keep breathing, they shouldn't get involved with people who want to make them stop. That's just logic. Okay, this online store looks like it's still open—oh, no. They shut down after their apartment was firebombed during the witch riots. That one's Shogaur's fault."

I didn't want to say I had my enemies to thank for helping me clear out the riffraff of Ontario's magical population, but I did make a note to raise a glass to them for making my life a little bit easier.

That left Louay, the witch with the highly reputable shop

who sold griffin testicles and wyvern scales out of his back room.

According to rumour.

Emrick stepped us through to another area of Toronto, and as we walked inside, I looked around the shop shining brightly on the overcast day. Louay had set up The Zen Toad to focus on spiritual care—yoga, tarot, meditation—and the floor plan was spacious and minimalist with sage green and soft maple notes.

The man himself stepped out from behind the counter dressed in loose linen trousers and a billowy purple shirt. His smile was wide, his eyes warm… until he saw us and made a break for the back room.

I tore after him as Emrick stepped through the mist, and in another second, Louay was backing away from him with his hands raised.

"I don't have what you're looking for, I swear."

I met Emrick's confused gaze as I crossed my arms and planted my feet. We'd boxed Louay in by the sales counter, giving him no room to manoeuvre, but considering how slimy he was acting, I half-expected him to transform into a toad and hop away.

"I came here for information, and by your reaction, I assume you have that."

His brown eyes flew wide. "I don't. I don't know anything."

"Running scared is a strange way of securing customers," I said. "I'm guessing you don't get a lot of repeats."

"She said you would come by and hurt me."

Relieved to have clarification on one point at least, I leaned my weight on the counter. "Would *she* be Abigail, by any chance?"

"I don't know her name. She was old. She called me up, put in a request for some herbs and an anti-inflammatory cream, and warned me you would come after me and cause trouble."

I frowned. "Herbs and a cream? What about enchantment stones?"

Now it was his turn to look confused. "What are those?"

I reached into the pocket along my thigh and set one of Abigail's stones on the counter. Louay shot me a look before picking it up, as though he expected me to kill him for touching it. I wouldn't. Not unless he tried to activate it.

His manicured eyebrows climbed towards his hairline. "This is impressive. The magical reading is faint, but you said it was an enchantment stone? So it contains the magic? I've never seen anything like it."

"You don't sell them?"

He shook his head. "I wish I did. I'd make a pretty penny stocking these."

I snatched it out of his hand, but his disappointment quickly faded into resignation. "I wouldn't have the power to create something like that even if I understood how it worked. It must have taken a whole coven to produce it." Uncertainty rippled across his face. "Caroline Taver mentioned she was working on something a few weeks ago. Said it was groundbreaking. She died of a heart attack a few days later."

I marked the stiffening of Emrick's shoulders, the flickering recognition across his features, and made a note to ask him about it later.

The desire was there to lean on Louay harder and drag out any information he might be holding back, but as my magic brushed against his, I realized he was right. Louay made his money selling illegal ingredients—something I would come back to deal with when I had more time—but his power wasn't nearly great enough to create a spell circle in stasis.

A coven, however…

I grabbed my phone to text Poppy.

Your list is a bust. What is your mother involved in these days? Could the Death Raisers have created the stones?

While I waited for her to get back to me, I returned my attention to Louay. "What else can you tell me about this old woman? You say she called you to put in her order. Did she give you an address? Have you delivered it?"

If she had a place nearby, we could stake it out until she returned. Maybe leave her a trap or two as a welcome-home present.

But all hope for that approach was crushed when Louay said, "She asked me to bag the order and leave it outside the store, said she'd be by soon to grab it." He looked at Emrick, then back at me. "I didn't see anyone, but when I checked later, it was gone. I haven't heard from her complaining someone stole it, so I guess she picked it up."

Overall, the morning had been a waste of time. I'd learned that despite Abigail's immortality, she suffered muscle aches. Unless I got close enough to poke her in her arthritic hip, I doubted the information would serve us.

Then again, I supposed it was good to know we were looking at a larger group for the stones. That earned Louay a reprieve.

"Here's some good news," I said. "I'm not going to destroy your back room today. You have one week to clean out all the illegal goods you have back there and close up shop. If you still have anything that would make me want to scrub my eyeballs the next time I swing by, it'll be a different conversation. Abigail may have put the fear of me into you too soon, but she's not wrong that you don't want to get on my bad side. Sound good?"

He nodded but wasn't quick enough to hide the flash of loathing that crept into his face.

I responded with my brightest smile. "If she calls again, will you tell her I stopped by? Tell her I'm getting close, and she won't be able to hide from me forever."

28

Katerina

EMRICK AND I left The Zen Toad, rounded the corner so we were out of sight, then stepped through the afterlife into Poppy's shop, Moon in Venus.

"Did you know that Caroline woman?" I asked.

Emrick peered into a box of crystals. "She told me she'd made some enchantments for a woman in need. It looked like a heart attack, but something about her death… I think Abigail was cleaning up after herself."

"It fits. But if the woman behind the stones is dead, hopefully that means we don't need to worry about them popping up across the province."

Poppy's shop looked almost identical to what it had been before Cindy-Lou Who turned it into a pink, frilly tea boutique, but I noticed a few extra charms and spell books in the display cases and fewer cat skulls on the shelves. I wasn't sure if Murisa or Cuddles was the impetus behind the change in dear Proserpine's decor, but I was glad to see it. With Poppy's family history and her skill in necromancy, she was exactly the sort of person to fall down rabbit holes into darker practices. She'd made the mistake once, and I'd had to drag her out.

Magic for the sake of knowledge was a fine goal, but even with such lofty ambitions, there were points of no return. As long as Muroppy kept each other in check, they would become unstoppable without ever crossing that line.

My phone vibrated against my leg, and I pulled it out to find Poppy's response waiting for me.

Let it go, kitty Kat. The Death Raisers are dead. Hera is more interested in hosting League of Magical Freedom charity balls these days.

Images floated through my mind of Emrick dressed in white and silver leading me across the dance floor at the League's masquerade two months ago. Minutes before I'd gone after Mikhail and nearly watched Barrett suffer third degree burns by potion.

Poppy might have wanted to remove her mother from my suspect list with that comment, but if anything, she'd plunked her right in the middle of it.

**Me: You don't think the League would benefit by taking

me out of the picture?

Three dots danced across the screen, and I waited for her reply.

Poppy: I think having Abigail slaughter a bunch of witches and earn the witch hunters' ire goes against everything they stand for.

"She has a point," Emrick said when I relayed the message.

I huffed. "Fine. I'll put Hera on the back burner for now, but I don't think I'm finished with her yet. Someone's behind all this, and I'm going to figure out who and why. Come on, let's get what we need and head back to Muskoka."

I put my phone away and pressed forward between the bins and shelves. Unlike The Zen Toad's sparsity, Poppy had gone for a homey, cluttered vibe. Being here filled me with a sense of peace I hadn't anticipated. The comforting aroma of sage and sandalwood, the books, the stones, the tarot cards—they had the same effect on me that the smell of fresh bread did when I came home to Maera's baking. It was walking into Adrian's library or bandying insults with Barrett.

Poppy's store had somehow become a safe space, and I was more glad than I could say that the teashop lady had bolted.

I steeled myself against the surge of sentiment. I was here to collect Poppy and Murisa's supplies, and then we'd head back to Adrian's house. Once there, Muroppy could get to work making my family invulnerable to Abigail's attacks, and I could focus on killing an immortal.

It was a solid plan with zero flaws—or so I was determined to believe. I just had to move quickly enough to ensure it stayed that way.

Most of the ingredients Poppy needed would be in her stockroom, the quantity great enough that they wouldn't fit out on the floor. As I made my way towards the back, I paused to check the titles on the bookshelves. "Interesting."

Emrick looked up from his perusal of tiny protection charms nestled in a carved wooden box. "What is?"

"Ms. Lister has shifted focus considerably since the last time I was here. No more dark grimoires. It seems now she prefers educating people on enchanting household objects." I pulled a book free and showed him the cover of *Hearth & Home: Your Guide To Adding Magic to the Everyday*. "I don't know whether to be charmed or sickened by the sweetness. What has Murisa done with the woman who attempted to raise an undead army to protect herself and settled for a zombie cat?"

"To be fair, that woman is still there," Emrick said. "She's just dressing her zombie cat in ribbons."

I laughed at the image his words evoked—Poppy cooing over Cuddles as she groomed his patchy fur, collecting the various bits and bobs that flaked off him even after so many baths and snuggles. It was difficult to put that witch next to the woman who'd once worked with her coven to raise an army of corpses to face off against their rivals.

We reached the storeroom, and I stood in awe of the organization system that awaited me. Poppy had never struck me as the tidiest person, so I didn't know if this was Murisa's influence at work or if Business Poppy was a far cry from Home-Life Poppy. The storeroom was a space of beauty. Metal shelving units lined the walls with bins stacked on bins, everything labelled and colour-coded.

I checked the list, and sure enough, she'd jotted down the corresponding bin colour and number next to each ingredient to make it easier for me to find. Even so, there were at least thirty ingredients on the list. Gathering everything would be no small feat.

"Do you think you can help me track these down or would that be—" I glanced at Emrick, and the question withered on my tongue at the tension in his shoulders. "Right. Never mind. You stay out there and browse. I'll get what we need here."

He gave me a pained look, then walked away, leaving me to power through.

Thankfully, all the herbs Muroppy needed were in bins close to each other, so I gathered those quickly, stuffing the small bins into a large tote bag I found on another shelf. I hoped their stock would be sufficient for what we needed, but by the look of things, they'd already raided most of their stores.

The potions were another story. Based on what I could

interpret from what I was collecting, they would make most of the potions fresh, but there were some bases and standard vials they'd asked for, and it took some rummaging for the footstool to find them on a higher shelf.

Although I did my best to put everything back where I found it, Poppy would probably kill me for the state of her inventory when she returned. Or maybe she wouldn't. Maybe organizing the storeroom was date night for those two. Who was I to judge?

The tote bag was heavy and bulging by the time I had everything. I hauled it over my shoulder and dragged myself from the back room to where Emrick stood at the window, looking out into the mid-morning street. At first, I thought he was taking in the sights, but as I got closer, I noticed his half-raised hand, the balance of his weight on his back foot, the fear in his eyes when he turned towards me.

I opened my mouth to ask what he'd seen when I spotted the tiny ball of blue-white light drifting through the window into the room. The hair on my arms rose as electricity buzzed across my skin.

The faint hiss emanating from the ball tickled the insides of my ears. I hit the floor and threw my arms over my head seconds before the lightning exploded in a burst of arced energy, setting books, display cases, and incense alight.

29

Emrick

I LAUNCHED MYSELF through the flames, grabbed hold of Kat, and rolled us through the afterlife to an alley across from the shop.

By the time we reappeared, the whole building was on fire, with the flames licking upwards towards Poppy's apartment on the second floor.

I helped Kat to her feet, and she clung to my arm as she stared in horror at the blaze that had already consumed most of where we'd stood so recently.

"No," she whispered, then she cast off with being quiet. "*Fuck!* I'm going to kill that bitch, I swear to the gods, Emrick. I've fucking had it."

I put my arm around her shoulder to pull her back, afraid

she would get it into her head to run in and try to save the place. Such a miracle was beyond her.

"Did you see her?" Kat wrenched herself out of my arms to look around the street where passersby had started to amass. "Abigail has to be here. And ball lightning like that?" She caught herself and looked around, dropping her voice for my ears only. "That's the work of a powerful sorceress with a *lot* of control. No spell circles required."

So that answered the question about whether Abigail had been holding back or weakened. How many other secrets was she keeping?

"Do you think she knew we were in there?" I asked, following Kat's lead and scanning the crowd. It was a futile effort. There were dozens of people now, all of them with their phones out instead of retreating to a safe distance. A misjudged decision considering how quickly the fire was spreading.

Sirens rushed towards our location, warning that help was coming. Kat and I had to get out of here. If anyone looked too closely at us, they'd see the shards of glass sparkling in Kat's hair and the singe marks on our clothes.

It had taken me moments to get us out of the store, but our escape had been close. A few more seconds, and we would have been caught in the growing inferno.

"I don't think so," Kat said, replying to my question long after I'd forgotten I'd asked it. "Poppy said she sensed a magical signature outside her store, and the first time Abigail spoke through Rhys, she used Poppy's nickname for me. This attack was a message—like Amelia was—but I doubt she knows the witches aren't here."

I ran my hand down Kat's arm to cup her elbow and turned her towards me. Her blue eyes were wide, shining with fear and grief. I brushed her hair back where it had fallen free of her ponytail, and glass rained onto the ground at our feet. "You outwitted her by sending them to Muskoka. Be proud of yourself for that. She may have stayed ahead of us, but we're catching up."

"For now." Kat rested her palms on my chest. "What if the wind changes again? What if this is the beginning of the end Rhys Saw? He mentioned lightning. He mentioned bodies. What if we've run out of time?"

"The only way we lose is if we give up. We know Abigail is back in Toronto. She's made her move against Poppy—who's next?"

Kat paled. "Adrian and Barrett. We have to get back."

I didn't argue with her. Abigail had made it clear she was aiming for destruction. The only way to fend her off would be for Murisa and Poppy to start their spells, for Barrett to secure the house, and for Kat to stand ready. So far, I hadn't had time to fulfill my promise of training with her, but as soon as we delivered the ingredients to Muroppy—the nickname was rubbing off on me—that would be my first priority.

Kat rested her forehead between her hands, and I circled my arms around her. With my fingertips brushing against the back of her neck to make contact, I stepped us through the afterlife into Adrian's library.

"Katerina?" Adrian was on his feet and striding towards us before the mist had faded. "Are you all right? You reek of smoke."

"Poppy's shop," Kat said, her voice shaking.

"What's wrong with my shop?"

I turned to find Poppy, Murisa, Rhys, and Barrett sitting around the table in the corner. Their presence in this room surprised me—Adrian usually preferred people stay out of his library, keeping the space as his haven against the noise and interruptions of the world. The fact everyone was sitting in here said much about how my friend perceived the seriousness of our situation.

From the way Kat's eyes widened, she also hadn't expected to deliver the bad news so soon. I watched the subtle rise of her chin as she steeled herself. She crossed the room and took Poppy's hand. "It's gone, Pop. I'm so sorry. We were just about to leave, and someone threw a spell into it. The place caught fire, and the flames spread so damned fast. The whole building is gone."

Poppy paled, her skin turning an alarming shade of grey.

Rhys jumped to his feet to help her into her chair.

Murisa poured a glass of water from the pitcher on the table and wrapped her arm around Poppy's shoulders. "Did you get everything we needed?"

Kat pulled the tote bag off her shoulder and set it on the table. "It should all be in here. I emptied a bunch of your bins to get the quantity you asked for."

"That hardly matters now, does it?" Poppy asked, her voice empty, tears spilling down her cheeks. She swiped at them with the back of her hand. "I'm sorry, I'm being stupid."

Kat knelt in front of her and reclaimed her hand. "You're not. That was your home, Poppy. You made that place something special."

"I'd only just moved back in. It's not like I had any sentimental—"

"Stop that," Kat interrupted. "You did. And you should have. You worked hard to build your dream, and this bitchbag stole it from you. We won't let it stand. We're going to find her, and for every hurt she's caused us, we'll make her swallow double. Do you doubt me?"

Poppy blinked, awareness returning to her eyes as they hardened. "No, kitty Kat. I don't doubt you'll rip her a new one for me."

Murisa shifted into her wheelchair, then curled her fingers through Poppy's. "We'll get to work right away with what you brought us. With luck, we'll land on something quickly that will let us inflict maximum damage on Abigail for every strike she makes against us."

"I'll help you get set up," Kat said, then looked down at herself. "After I shower and change."

She glanced at me, and I nodded. Guilt would eat her up until she was sure Poppy didn't blame her for what this woman had done. Rhys followed them out, leaving me, Adrian, and Barrett alone in the room.

"Kat thinks you two will be the next target," I said once the door closed. "Poppy and Murisa avoided getting roasted because they weren't home. It might be something for you to consider."

Adrian sighed and bowed his head. "I'm afraid we're fighting a losing battle."

I crossed my arms. "You don't think Kat can stand against Abigail?"

"I never doubt our dear Katerina, Emrick, you know that," Adrian chided. "I don't mean to say we won't win in the end, but this determination Kat has of protecting us all, of saving everything as we know it—it's doomed to fail."

The conversation he and I had shared the night after Kat took down the blood witch swept over me, and a coil of dread unfurled in my chest. "You've never been the pessimistic sort. You sound like you know this for a certainty."

Adrian replied with a small smile. "Certainty? Of course not. Nothing in this life is ever certain. But I have reason to suspect."

Barrett slammed his hands down on the table, drawing our attention. "Goddammit, Adrian. Will you tell me what the fuck is going on? I've been asking you for days what's bothering you, and you keep dismissing my concerns and telling me nothing is wrong."

"Nothing *is* wrong." Adrian wore his usual barely-there smile but couldn't hide the sadness in his eyes. A lump formed in my throat even as I tried to deny what he was suggesting. "Everything is exactly how it's supposed to be. Just because it hurts, just because it's not how we want things to go, doesn't mean it's not the way it's meant to be."

Barrett strode towards him. "Fuck that. Fuck fate or destiny or whatever the fuck you're talking about. If Kat thinks she has a way to keep this house safe, she'll make sure it happens. And if that fails, my traps will hold this bitch back as well as any magical intervention can. If Abigail is coming for us, we'll fight her off."

"You will," Adrian said without any doubt. "I don't believe this is where your final battle will happen. Only mine."

Barrett clenched his hands at his sides, and his shoulders bunched close to his ears. "What do you mean only yours? What did Rhys tell you?"

His question threw everything into perspective. Rhys must have Seen something weeks ago—the timing lined up with Adrian's cryptic comments that night on his balcony.

Adrian held out his hand to Barrett, but Barrett tightened his fists, doing everything possible to keep his composure.

Adrian dropped his hand. "He Saw enough to make me believe what's coming is inevitable. And it's all right."

To hear him say it aloud—so calmly, so peacefully—shook the world beneath my feet. My immortal friend, a man who'd been around longer than I had, who had seen so much of the world, facing his end with such acceptance. My heart had cracked, was on the verge of shattering, but how could I rail against his calm strength?

"No," Barrett rasped. "It's not all right. How can you say that?"

My old friend's eyes filled with such deep, pained compassion my throat tightened, and my own composure was at risk of slipping. "Ah, James. You knew this wouldn't be forever."

Barrett's jaw hardened. "Because *I* die, not you. I swore to give my life for yours. That's not about to change."

Adrian turned to me. "Emrick, would you give us a moment?"

I didn't want to leave. If my time with this man was coming to an end, I wanted to grab every second of it. Fifteen hundred years hadn't been enough friendship. Another fifteen hundred wouldn't be enough.

But I had to respect his wishes, as he'd always—usually—done for me.

I bowed. "Of course." I wished I could embrace him as the brother he was, but my touch was as fatal to him as it would be to Barrett, and I didn't want to steal any time he had left. Instead, I set my hand over my heart. "Kat's going to fight to get everyone out of this. Don't give up on her."

Adrian mirrored my pose, and for a moment I stood there, staring into his brown-and-crimson eyes, grateful I'd had him in my life for so many years. I hoped he understood how much.

There were no words to express my feelings, so I simply headed towards the door, giving him the time and space to say whatever Barrett needed to hear.

"Oh, and Emrick?"

I stopped and turned, and Adrian's expression was twisted with regret. "Please don't mention anything to Katerina. I don't know how everything is supposed to play out, but I do know if she loses focus, if she tries to protect me at the expense of every-thing else, she will lose *everything*." His brown eyes burned with intensity, driving home the urgency. "After the time comes, when she's angry with you, you can blame me and ask her to have Rhys explain. But until then, promise."

I clenched my teeth, hating the thought of saying nothing. Regardless of what happened, once Kat caught wind that I knew and hadn't told her, she would be furious. Rightfully so. But what else could I do but agree? So far, Rhys's visions had been all too accurate, and as much as Kat would grieve Adrian's loss, it would be nothing to what she'd feel if she sacrificed everything else to save him.

"My lips are sealed."

He nodded his thanks, and I left the room, closing the door tightly behind me with a trembling hand.

Death held this house in its grasp. It was coming for everyone within it, and our only hope was to minimize how many souls it collected.

I couldn't stop it. I couldn't help. All I could do was stand by, watch it happen, and endure Kat's wrath when she found out.

Whoever had survived Palonia, they'd subverted Death with their spell, and unlike what I'd tried to do for Katerina when that spell circle had taken her from me, I wouldn't go to bat for this woman in the afterlife. Abigail deserved whatever Kat threw at her and whatever debt Death demanded for evading its reach as long as she had.

We were going to war, and there would be no mercy.

30

Katerina

SHOWERED AND GLASS-FREE, I paced the length of the dining room where Muroppy had set up shop for their experiments. The extended oak table took up much of the room, and every inch of it was covered in various witchcraft essentials from books to bowls. The curtains across the floor-to-ceiling windows had been pulled open to let in the grey afternoon sunlight, and the glow from the crystal chandelier glittered across the walls.

On the far side of the table sat a plate of sandwiches, and between rounds of pacing, I devoured half of them out of stress. The witches were buried in their notes and tests, murmuring between the two of them, and had completely forgotten Rhys and I were in the room.

That was fine. I didn't need them focused on me—I needed

them concentrating on how to make this house impenetrable. I had no doubt they wouldn't rest until they did. The fire burning in Poppy's eyes swore vengeance, and I was glad it was directed at someone other than me.

At the moment, I would have been tempted to look the other way if she decided to raise all the cemeteries in the Muskoka area to stand against Abigail. My ethics were becoming increasingly skewed the more the woman took from me.

I wondered what Gavin thought about our plans to destroy his grandmother. He hadn't been in the library with everyone when we'd arrived, and I suspected he was in the gym taking out his rage against the world with more solo training.

I glanced at Rhys and found him sitting in the corner of the room staring out over the back garden. His eyes were glazed, his hands slack in his lap. If it weren't for his bright green eyes, I might have thought he'd lapsed into a vision.

I stopped beside him. "How are you holding up?"

He stirred and dragged his gaze to meet mine. "Like I can't form a solid thought. Like every step, every word, is a fight. I can't stand this for much longer, Kat. I'm losing my mind."

"I know." I rested my hand on his shoulder. "I'm doing everything I can to make sure that when the potion wears off, you won't need to take another one."

His brow furrowed as though he were trying to focus on something just out of sight. "My ability isn't totally blocked. I can't See anything, but I feel my Sight trying to reach me. It's coming fast and strong."

"Another vision storm?" I thought of the way his ability had come on him when Mikhail had moved closer to his final plans. Every few minutes, Rhys had lost himself to another vision until we'd been forced to dose him with a sleeping potion to give him a few hours' rest before his brain burned out.

"Not quite that bad," he said, "but not far off. Every few hours, I get this nagging feeling. Like trying to remember something I forgot or see something that only exists in the corner of my eye. Something's coming—something bad—and we don't know what it is because I can't turn around fast enough to make it out."

My heart broke a little more for him. Rhys wanted so badly to be a part of my world and help where he could, and by obscuring his ability, however temporarily, I'd shut him out.

I squeezed his shoulder. "We're at a disadvantage without you. I know that. But you're safe, and that means more to me than anything else. When this is over, we'll continue your training, help you learn how to block unwanted visitors in ways that give you more control. Abigail surprised us by using you, but that was a one—well, a four-shot deal."

Rhys returned his attention out the window, and I turned back to the witches. Poppy had poured a potion into her bowl and was adding a mixture of crushed herbs to it. Murisa's brow furrowed as she pored over the book in front of her, the pages covered in demon sigils.

I was about to ask what in the hells she was researching but was distracted by Emrick stepping into the doorway. He was a vision in his white T-shirt with his white skin and white hair—as though even his clothing had been leached of colour. He nodded his head for me to follow him, and I left Rhys to his staring and the witches to their work.

"Where are we going?" I asked as he led me through the house towards the back doors.

"I told you we'd train."

His face was stoic, a practiced blankness, and I drew to a stop on the edge of the garden. "What's wrong?"

He hesitated before facing me. "We know Abigail will likely strike here next and probably soon. I wish we had more time to make sure you were ready for her, that's all."

I understood his worry. The control she'd had over that ball lightning surpassed anything I was capable of in my current state. I'd worked hard over the past few months to scrape off the rust a century of disuse had formed over my magic, but I was far from what I'd been at my peak.

"Where should we start?"

"Fire," he said. "It's always come easiest for you. Let's focus on your strengths and go from there."

I looked around the garden with concern. "And risk Adrian's

paradise? Is that wise? If we destroy his roses, Abigail might not be our greatest danger."

Emrick flexed his jaw, and his eyes flicked to Adrian's library upstairs. "I don't think he'll mind under the circumstances."

I blinked, having expected some kind of banter in response. Emrick had to be more stressed than I'd realized.

"No, I suppose he wouldn't."

We headed down the path towards the very back of the garden, close to where the beds ended and the dock led down to the boathouse. There were fewer trees here to get caught in any misdirected fireballs, and we were far enough from the house that no one would wander into the fray by accident.

I stood across from Emrick and closed my eyes, sinking into the power that sparked in my blood. I imagined my cells glowing like tiny embers, carrying my magic through my veins to every part of my body. It was the same visual I'd suggested Gavin use during our first sessions together, the same Alodie and Blythe had used when training me.

A shudder ran through me, and the heat evaporated, leaving me freezing despite the sunlight warming my skin.

I was so tired. The chaos of the past few days had taken so much out of me. I'd buried the discomfort under adrenaline and busyness, but now, with the cruel gazes of three traitors glaring at me from the shadows, my strength failed.

I dropped my arms by my sides and stared at Emrick across

the garden. "I don't know if all the training in the world will prepare me to face her."

He stalked towards me and curled his fingers around mine. The contact left me breathless. I looked up to find him staring at our entwined hands. He stroked his thumbs over the backs of my fingers, squeezing tightly, as though to let go would be to lose me.

"Emrick, what's wrong?"

He looked up at me, and I caught the torment raging behind his eyes. "Everything is changing all at once, and there's nothing we can do to slow it down. We have to be ready to change with it. I know you're struggling, but I need you to concentrate, Kat. I need you to be at the top of your game. Because if anything happens to you—"

He cut himself off with a low rumble in his throat and gave himself a shake. "Come on. Throw a fireball at me, all right? You've had enough practice being angry with me that it shouldn't be too difficult."

His smile was forced as he took a few steps backwards, and the continued anguish in his expression pushed me to do as he'd ordered. For his sake, and for everyone else's, I couldn't afford to let my feelings about the past get in the way of my power. The power I'd earned. The power I'd fought so hard to master long after the teachers of Palonia were gone.

This time when my magic rose, I grabbed hold of it and

channelled it into my palms, adding more fuel until the fireball glowed a bright orange against my gloves, casting light into the grey day.

I pulled my hands away from the flames but kept hold of the magic, allowing the fireball to hover over my palms and float out in front of me. It spun in the air, and as I drew my hands farther apart, the fire stretched, becoming more of a long ribbon instead of a ball. Once the ribbon was thin enough, I reached for the end, the flames licking at my runed gloves but never penetrating through the protected leather. With cautious control over the fire, I lashed out with the fiery whip and wrapped it around Emrick's forearm, dragging him off balance before the flames extinguished.

I staggered forward, my heart racing and sweat pooling in the small of my back. I hadn't noticed the drain on my power during the casting, but now fatigue tugged at my limbs.

"Again," he said, backing up to his original spot.

I pushed through the exhaustion and summoned more magic into my hands, once more shaping it into a whip. This one went out before it reached Emrick, and spots danced in my vision at the exertion.

"Dammit, Kat, *again*."

I recognized the desperation behind his tone. It wasn't disappointment or disapproval, but all I could hear was Mae's frustration, Alodie's condescension, Blythe's strained patience.

"I can't, Emrick," I snapped. "I'm tapped out. Abigail's going to show up here and kick my ass, and I won't be able to do a goddamned thing about it because she'll always be stronger than I am."

The despair nearly overwhelmed me. My legs trembled, my hands shook, and I was certain if I tried to draw on more magic, I would vomit all over the grass.

Emrick closed the distance between us. His large hands cupped my face, and before I could take a breath, his mouth claimed mine. His kiss was hungry, heated, filled with every ounce of the terror and anguish that had shown in his eyes and trailed in his words. It cut off all too quickly, leaving my head reeling.

"You can, Katerina. She has no more power than you do—she just believes in herself more. If you can't do that, then believe in me, because *I* know you can make the world burn. Now come on and knock me off my feet."

Fueled purely by stubbornness and Emrick's encouragement, I tapped a deeper well in my magic. We sparred for the rest of the afternoon and well into the night.

Every step of the way, Emrick pushed me harder, doing his best to trip me up. When he noticed I got too comfortable with the flow of our fight, he'd step through the afterlife, forcing me to anticipate his movements. He left me no space for frustration or discouragement. Every time I grew distracted by my failures, he reminded me of all my past wins, from Shogaur a few short weeks ago to the hags in Prague so many centuries ago.

After sunset, Adrian joined us. He kept to the sidelines, and more than once, he and Emrick exchanged meaningful glances that I took to mean I needed to push myself harder. These men knew me—they knew what I was capable of. If I was falling short of their approval, it meant I still had a ways to go to brush the dust off my old skills.

Emrick called it a night shortly after midnight and forced me to go upstairs to shower and sleep, but we were back at it with the sunrise. Today, we changed pace, with less of a focus on my magic and more on my speed and dexterity. Emrick stepped in and out of the afterlife, playing both hunter and hunted as he encouraged me to lean into long-forgotten abilities.

As the hours passed, I was brought back to the old days, when he and Adrian had fought with me. Emrick had done his best to remain hands-off unless the situation became dire or the enemy lacked a soul to interfere with, but Adrian had always been there, fangs extended, claws lengthened, knives in hand when necessary. His movements were like butter, so smooth and quick that few enemies were able to match him. Even at my best, I'd been clunky by comparison.

Sparring with Emrick reminded me of how alive I'd felt back then. How sure of myself. Centuries fell from my shoulders, and I became the Katerina who made magicals tremble. Here with Emrick, nothing else in the world mattered, because who could touch us?

The feeling came to an abrupt stop when a floral scent tickled my nose and a surge of unfamiliar power danced over my skin.

I stumbled in my footing and turned to look over my shoulder.

Emrick was at my side in a heartbeat. The sun had begun to set, a whole day gone, and shadows bled across the garden, obscuring everything from view except for the looming statues Adrian had erected to keep watch over his precious flowers.

"You sensed it, too?" I asked in a low voice.

The ward Muroppy had erected around the property was strong, unwavering, and fresh enough that it would take a significant amount of power for anyone to break through it. But Poppy's shop had been warded, and look what had happened there.

I called to my magic and felt its warmth coil inside my chest, pulsing with every heartbeat until it spilled down my arms and into my hands. My gloves caught it, keeping it close to the surface and ready to be called when I needed it without slipping out of my control in a moment of distraction or surprise.

Emrick stayed close as we stalked through Adrian's garden. Past the dragon, the wolf, and the lovers caught in their eternal dance. Presiding over them all, the demon with the horns and tail, fangs bared, hands widespread.

Adrian. Always with the melodrama.

As we neared the demon, I sensed a change in the air. A vibration that hummed over my skin and raised the tiny hairs on my arms.

A bolt of lightning shot towards me, and only thanks to my recent lessons were my instincts honed enough to dodge it. The bolt struck the demon. Its chest exploded in a hail of stone, and Emrick shoved me away from the flying shards towards the house.

Abigail had arrived.

<h1 style="text-align:center">31</h1>

Katerina

I BURST INTO the house and ran for the dining room, calling for Muroppy. Emrick had stayed outside to pin down where the sorceress was lurking.

Rhys came out of the room first. "She's here, isn't she? There's a pressure in my head like someone's trying to squeeze my brain into pulp."

I believed it. He was squinting at me the way Maera did when a migraine hit.

"Find Barrett and Gavin," I ordered. "Then find your mother and stay at the back of the house. If anything goes wrong, get to the boathouse and use the boat to escape."

Rhys's eyes flew wide. "What? No. Kat, if it's as bad as that—"

I gripped his shoulders. "If it's as bad as that, you have to get to the witch hunters so they can take over."

If I failed, Abigail couldn't be left free to wreak havoc on the world.

A silent battle raged in his mind, each strike coming out in the tic of his cheek and the flex of his jaw until he nodded and hurried off.

I continued to the dining room. "Please tell me you have something. Anything. We've got a sorceress outside the ward, and I'm not in a mood to play nice."

Murisa's thick hair flew around her face where it had fallen from her braid after so many hours of work. She rubbed her fingers in her eyes. "I'm sorry, Kat, but we have nothing. The nullifying potion, the protection spells—everything is *almost there*, but—"

I cursed and spun to face the windows as though that would give me some ideas on what to do. We were empty-handed except for the basics. "So be it. Gather whatever potion vials you have, ready those beetles. We'll make do."

Poppy returned to the table and stuffed a collection of vials into her satchel, taking a quick inventory as she did. "How much time do we—never mind." She squeezed her eyes shut and pressed her palm to her forehead at the same time Murisa groaned and clutched the sides of her head.

"She's attacking the ward," Murisa said. "I'm going to say

we're out of time."

My heart raced. "I'll get Emrick to take me beyond the property line and try to sneak up on her from behind."

Murisa caught my wrist as I strode towards the door. "Be careful, Kat. The force she's using against the ward is intense."

I gritted my teeth. "Be prepared for it to get worse."

Murisa released me, but before I could leave, Barrett came running down the stairs, taser in one hand, his other palm on the hilt of the knife at his hip. Gavin rushed up the hallway from the gym.

"What's the plan?" Barrett asked. His eyes were red and swollen, which shocked me speechless, but we didn't have time for me to ask what had pushed him to show an emotion.

"Poppy and Murisa are getting their potions ready, but they'll need to be close enough to throw them. You and Gavin stay with them, watch their backs. Gavin, get ready to put that training to use."

He scowled but didn't argue with me. I hoped that meant he was ready to bury his grandmother if the opportunity arose.

Emrick appeared behind me. "She's at the front of the house, hidden among the trees. No sign of a demon, but there are at least three ball lightning spells hovering along the ward."

"Fuck me," I breathed. With a bit more pressure, Abigail could push those spells through the ward as easily as she had at Poppy's store. "We need to make her back off until our defences are in place. Take me out there, as close to her as you can, then go to the afterlife."

Emrick's jawline hardened, and his eyes narrowed, but he extended his hand to me. I took it, and in another breath, we stood on the outskirts of Adrian's property. The house was in sight through the trees, the driveway following the treeline.

The sun had dropped below the horizon, deepening the shadows, but I made out the dark figure up ahead. Despite her hunched spine and rolling gait, she moved quickly, and I rushed after her, determined to drag her down before she got closer to the house.

I summoned my magic into my palms and prepared to throw it, but before I could release the fireball, Abigail spun around and hurled another ball of lightning my way. Just like the one in Poppy's shop, it hovered in the air, inching towards me, taunting me with its slowness when I knew just how much destruction it could bring.

Drawing on my own power, I tapped into the stillness in the air and reached for the electricity zipping through the ball. With a cry, I ripped the magic apart, and the lightning dissipated.

Abigail hissed through her teeth and, moving so quickly I could barely keep track, launched a dozen fireballs from her palms.

I reversed the flow of my magic and managed to freeze three

of the flames hurtling towards me. The others kept coming. I threw myself to the ground and covered my head, saving myself by mere inches from getting my hair styled.

Emrick was beside me as soon as I hit the ground, his muscular frame covering me.

"I'm all right," I assured him. "She didn't get me."

He flipped me onto my back and looked me over before hauling me to my feet, his mercurial eyes blazing. "She's almost at the house. The ward is down."

I swore again. Every person who mattered to me was vulnerable. I couldn't be everywhere at once, and Emrick couldn't help.

"You need to leave," I said. "This dance is about to get messy, and I can't have you cutting in."

His jaw flexed, and his grip on my arms tightened. Finally, he kissed me—swift and hard—then vanished into the afterlife.

When I broke through the trees onto the driveway, I found Barrett standing on the front step, gun raised. He aimed his weapon at me, and I lifted my hands as I stumbled to a halt. He cursed and adjusted his aim, never taking his eyes off the treeline.

Gavin stood at the bottom of the steps, fire in his hands, ready to throw. Poppy stood beside him with a vial in each hand, while Murisa sat just outside the front door, tucked behind Barrett, with the remote for her tiny mechanicals on her lap.

Barrett fired a shot, and I turned around in time to see Abigail launch a handful of stones across the gravel driveway before she disappeared again among the trees. The stones blended into the crushed rock almost as soon as they landed, disappearing in the twilight.

My heart thrashed in my chest, and I wiped my sweaty palm on my thigh.

"Everyone get back," I ordered. "She's shrinking the playing field, but we can still dominate it. We need to get on firmer ground."

A voice cried out from the trees, and three stones closest to the house lit up. I barely had time to pull Poppy back before the spell circles unleashed, throwing ribbons of flame into the air that burned hot enough to make my T-shirt cling to my skin. The magical fire caught the eaves of the house, and in seconds, the front pillars of the porch had been consumed.

Gavin rushed down the steps. "Get down!"

I dropped into a crouch, and shots rang out as Barrett fired at the shadow hurrying deeper into the woods. A sharp cry echoed over the flames, and satisfaction roared through me. We'd scored one hit at least. Now it was time to press our advantage.

I looked to Murisa, who nodded and pulled her enchanted beetles out of her bag. As Poppy hurried around Murisa's chair and wheeled her off the porch, Murisa sent the mechanicals over the trees.

Another cry pierced the night, this one farther away, but none of us dropped our guard. Abigail's spell circles had boxed us in, and now she'd tightened the cage with the fire behind us.

Sweat licked the back of my neck as the flames spread. When I checked over my shoulder, Adrian was on the porch, herding Rhys and Maera—who was cradling Cuddles against her chest—in front of him.

The group lined up along the house, away from the fire, away from the trees, but out in the open and asking to be attacked. Gavin, Barrett, Adrian, and Poppy arranged themselves in front of the other three, but I was under no illusions that they would be enough to fend off Abigail if she released another ball of lightning.

A cackle reached us from the woods, and I strode towards it, avoiding the driveway and the remaining stones. Much as it would hurt to destroy these trees, I had to flush her out.

"What's the plan, tesoro?" Adrian asked as he reached my side, keeping pace with me.

"Get everyone to the boathouse," I said without taking my eyes off the woods, wishing I could see more than obscure shapes in the darkness. "We've lost too much ground. The best I can do now is hold her back."

My control over the situation had slipped faster than I'd

imagined. I'd put all our plans in place, but we'd never stood a chance. Abigail had chosen her moment perfectly, and the best we could do was get everyone out alive so we could regroup and come at her again later.

My priority now was giving everyone else time to make it to the boat.

"You should take them and leave her to me," Adrian said. "I can move faster than you can."

I turned on him, breaking my stride. "And do what? You might be the better hunter, but she has fire. And she's immortal."

He bared his fangs. "I'd like to see her breathe without her head attached to her neck. Go, Katerina. If she realizes where we're heading, she'll destroy the entire group with one hit."

He spoke as though he knew for sure that's what she would do, but it made sense. I had no idea where among the trees she was hiding—everyone would be at risk.

A fireball flew over us as Gavin unleashed his magic, and the light from the flames revealed Abigail to my right—where she had a perfect view of the front and back of the house. I summoned ice spikes into my hands and launched them in her direction, summoning more every time the previous ones left my palms.

Adrian flew after her, disappearing into the shadows. Abigail scowled and took off.

"Barrett, lead everyone to the boat!" I commanded, then followed Abigail's path. I started to summon more ice spikes, but let my magic drop before they formed. With Adrian so close, I didn't trust that one of my spikes wouldn't hit the wrong target.

They were heading towards the back of the house. We needed to turn her around and make space for the others to get through. So far, Barrett hadn't been able to move, trapped in the shrinking area of safety between the burning porch and the approaching sorceress.

A bolt of lightning shot out between the trees and struck the ground in front of me. I staggered backwards and realized too late I'd landed in Abigail's minefield. A voice cried out an incantation, another stone lit up, and I threw myself out of the way before the stone opened and lightning arced up and out.

I hit the ground on my shoulder, rolled through the landing, and pushed myself to my feet. Fire swept over my hands, licked up my arms over my gloves, and I held it close, keeping it at the ready.

The lightning had started a second fire that swept over the short grass, blocking the path around the house. Adrian appeared along the edge of the trees, crouched low, his fangs bared. He gave me a subtle shake of his head, and I raised my hands. Somehow Abigail was evading us. As every minute passed, she would heal from whatever injuries she'd sustained—

we had to act fast. If I wanted to give us a clear shot, I had to draw her out.

"How did you escape Palonia?" I called, hoping to trick her into replying so I could land her location. "I watched you die." I stepped between the trees. "It must have come as a shock to learn I didn't."

A twig snapped, and I whipped around, but whoever it was had already run off. "Come on, you have to be as curious as I am. You went through all that trouble to exterminate every last person in Palonia, and I managed to crawl away. Don't you want to know how?"

Movement in my periphery. I drew in my heat and turned my fireballs to ice shards that I threw into the shadows. They struck tree trunks. "I know I have questions. Like how you could have looked us in the eye day after day and pretended you weren't plotting our destruction. How you stomached the fullness of your evil. My son wasn't even twenty months old, you worthless piece of shit."

I sucked in a breath. My anger was distracting me. If she was aiming for some sort of sick revenge, my emotional response would only feed her ego. I had to be cold. Just as the ice had helped me that night in Palonia, a frosty shield would help me here.

More movement. I ran and threw myself at it, not giving Abigail a chance to get away from me again. My fingers closed around a black cotton sleeve. With my fingers twisted in the material, I jerked her closer, and she shrieked and struggled against me. Her magic spread, and fire licked at my fingers. I tried to hold on, but the heat was so great the flames jumped to my clothes. I doused them with frost, which I then spread to hold her. But she released a series of lightning bolts that lit up the sky and sent my system into shock.

A scream of agony lodged in my throat as I collapsed to my knees, my nervous system temporarily paralyzed. Abigail bolted.

Adrian reached my side and helped me up.

"We have to pen her in," I wheezed. "We can't let her escape."

"We'll get her, tesoro. She's bleeding and slowing down. She's not in a place to keep fighting."

I hoped he was right. If she ran, we'd lose our opportunity to stop her, but it would gain us time to prepare. We could gather our resources, form better defences. The next time she came for us, we could destroy her.

Adrian's hand slipped into mine, his cool skin a sweet contrast against my heat. "Come on. She's heading for the road, but maybe we can catch her before she drives off."

We followed her trail, and when Abigail came into view, I pushed myself as hard as I could. Her limp had worsened, and unlike the day at the boardwalk, there was no smugness in the glare she shot at me over her shoulder. We'd doled out some damage, and she was desperate to retreat.

Adrian left my side, moving so quickly I lost sight of him. We were seconds away from stopping her. Victory rushed through me, and my strength returned. I summoned my magic, ready to stop this bitch's heart the way she'd stopped mine.

My friend drew to a sharp stop as he grabbed hold of Abigail's shoulder. I expected her to react with fear, panic, anger… but she smiled—a smile that turned my blood to ice.

In another heartbeat, she hurled a stone towards Barrett where he stood with his gun raised, ready to protect the others. He fired, and Abigail doubled over, but the bitch didn't go down. Adrian's eyes widened as his gaze followed the rock's trajectory. Terror flickered across his face.

He looked at me. "I'm so sorry, Katerina."

And then he released Abigail and vanished, once more moving too quickly for me to track him.

"Adrian!" I shouted, torn between going after him or Abigail.

With her arms clenched around her middle, Abigail stumbled into the shadows. Why had Adrian left her? We had her.

I hesitated only a moment before giving chase, but it was long enough for her to shout the words that activated the spell.

I spun on my heel towards Barrett. The stone was right by his foot, already glowing. There was no way he'd be able to escape it.

The circle lit up, fire spewed from the sigils, and with a cold horror, I watched as Adrian appeared and shoved Barrett out of range.

The spell erupted, and Adrian was trapped in the circle.

Barrett rolled to his feet and screamed so loudly my insides trembled. He sprinted towards Adrian, but Gavin tackled him around the waist and took him to the ground.

The fire raged so hot, so fast, and my screams nearly drowned out the sound of a car engine turning over and tires squealing as Abigail rushed to escape. I dropped to my knees and stared into the flames.

Adrian's beautiful brown eyes, so full of love and life and an infuriating acceptance, met mine, but there was nothing I could do except watch as the fire burned out.

In another moment, my best friend was gone, leaving nothing but ash.

32

Katerina

G RIEF TORE THROUGH me, clawed at my heart, peeled open
old scars.

I launched to my feet and hurled myself towards the charred circle. The temperature dropped, and a pair of arms wrapped around my middle like bands of steel.

"He's gone, Kat," Emrick murmured in my ear.

I knew it, but a large part of me couldn't believe it. It wasn't possible that my forever friend was forever dead. Barely a blink of an eye and his existence erased. Adrian had been a force, his presence enough to fill houses with its greatness. Such greatness couldn't disappear so quickly.

I stopped fighting. Emrick cautiously released me, and on shaking legs, I walked forward. I half-heartedly noted a few unactivated stones nearby, but Abigail had driven away, leaving them as useless as the rest of the gravel.

My feet drew to a stop outside the circle, and I stared down at the emptiness within. There was nothing to save. Nothing to salvage. Adrian was as gone as if he'd never existed.

As Emrick stood behind me with his hand on my shoulder, it registered in the recesses of my mind that I shouldn't have been alone in my shock. The three of us had been partners for over eight hundred years. Why had there been a note of resignation in Emrick's voice? Barely audible beneath his pain, but there.

Embers of anger popped into being beneath the cotton-batting numbness of my horror. I latched on to it, grateful to feel something other than this gnawing agony in my chest.

I slowly turned to face him. His grief-stricken gaze was glued to the blackened scar across the gravel, but no matter how closely I assessed him, there was no surprise at what had happened.

I thought of the glances he and Adrian had exchanged while we'd trained in the garden. I thought of Adrian's cryptic comments, each one sounding more and more like goodbye as I replayed them in my memory.

"He knew. *You* knew something like this was going to happen."

Emrick's face blurred behind my tears, but I caught his

flinch.

I turned towards Barrett, who hadn't moved from where Gavin had helped him to his feet. I thought of his face when he'd come downstairs—all the signs that he'd been crying.

Both of these men had gotten a chance to say a proper goodbye, and neither of them had paid me the same courtesy. The embers of anger flared into an inferno of rage.

"You both knew." I turned back to Emrick and shoved him in the chest. "Why didn't you tell me?"

He didn't try to defend himself. "Adrian made me promise. We all hoped there was a way he'd escape what was coming, but you needed to stay focused on Abigail, not on saving him. You—"

"I could have protected him!" I screamed. "I could have had his back like he's always had mine instead of letting him go after her on his own. I would have—"

The betrayal tore at me, the talons of grief slicing through my innards without any end in sight. Because how could it end? Adrian wouldn't come back to heal this wound. He wouldn't be there to hold my hand and tell me everything would be all right.

I wanted to keep screaming. To blame Emrick for staying silent. To blame Barrett for making himself a target—for putting himself in a position where my oldest friend had sacrificed himself to save his thrall. But I couldn't. If I'd run faster, I could have prevented Abigail from throwing that final stone.

I looked at each of them. Poppy and Murisa held each other as the fire around the house ebbed, the protective spells and sprinkler system doing their job. The fire in the grass had been checked by some lingering snow and caked mud before it had reached the trees.

Gavin had moved between Barrett and me, his hands half-raised. To protect Barrett? Barrett himself stood with his shoulders hunched, his gaze focused on the ground, as though he were ready for me to lash out at him. And why wouldn't he be? He'd been my verbal punching bag for ten years. But I couldn't. Not with Adrian's shadow lingering between us.

Rhys watched me with tears streaming down his cheeks, his arm around Maera's shoulders as she stared at the circle, her expression inscrutable.

Emrick remained behind me, close enough for me to sense him while making no contact. But instead of the comfort his presence usually offered, the absence of our third had torn a chasm through the ground at our feet.

More screams built up inside me, slashing at my heart. If I didn't release them, I was going to implode, and if I stayed where I was, I would take everyone down with me.

Without another word, I bolted. Somewhere beyond the house, Abigail was healing her wounds, glorying in her victory, but I didn't have the energy to go after her. Nine hundred years ago, I'd watched everyone in Palonia collapse, their life force flowing through the air to be absorbed by the traitorous women around their cooking pot.

Today, Adrian had become one more sacrifice. One more loved one these women had stolen from me.

Once I processed what I'd lost—once I unleashed the storm brewing inside me—I would hunt Abigail down, and I wouldn't stop until she'd suffered every agony now shredding me apart. But in this moment, I couldn't think of anything other than my sorrow, the depths of which was greater than I ever thought to experience again.

My magic surged, mixing with the maelstrom of my emotions. There would be no holding it back.

I avoided the house—I couldn't imagine destroying anything else that belonged to Adrian—and redirected myself around the back to the garden. Sparing no glance for the demon statue lying smashed across the path, I headed for the dock and, without stopping, dove into the freezing water.

My muscles tensed at the drop in temperature, but I pushed myself to put distance between me and Adrian's home. I swam deeper, the night sky making it all too easy to lose my sense of direction. For the second time in three days, I gave myself to the current, this time embracing the strain on my lungs and the increasing burn as my body begged for air. The physical pain was a sweet relief compared to the unceasing torment of my heartbreak.

With my body submerged, I reversed the flow of my magic, absorbing all the heat from the water. I drew on more power than I had while training with Emrick. The drain pulled on me, exhausted me, but I didn't let myself stop. My blood warmed to the point of pain as the lake froze, the ice growing thicker and thicker with only an inch of watery space around me, closing in, squeezing me. I couldn't move, there was no air to breathe, but I didn't want to do either. I sat with the pressure, the pain, the loss, and screamed with the full depths of my soul. The sound rippled through the water, sank into the ice, filled the entire lake until I was sure every living creature under the surface screamed with me.

When I'd expelled the last of my air, when my lungs demanded release, I pushed deeper into the pain and pressed my magic outwards, expelling heat instead of absorbing it, pushing my strength against the thick build-up of ice.

My ears popped with the effort. Sweat beaded on my brow, and my heart raced, but I didn't hold back. In every pulse of magic, I added my rage, my sadness, my shame.

Again, I had failed someone I loved.

I had failed *Adrian.*

If I'd tracked down this woman sooner, she never would have had a chance to carry out her threats.

If I'd been faster. If I'd been smarter. If I'd been more

powerful.

But after all these years, I was still the weak little girl who'd let my family down every day in training. I was the pathetic excuse for a Palonian who'd hidden under a layer of ice to stop myself from scratching holes in my skin, preventing the blood from being drawn from my pores as all around me my community fell to a cursed ritual.

Adrian had helped save my life. He'd taught me, supported me, and encouraged me for almost a millennium, and in his final moments, I hadn't been enough to save him.

Another scream built inside me, but I had no air left to give it life. The pressure on my lungs was so great I knew in another few moments I'd lose consciousness. I didn't care. I focused all my attention on my magic until finally the ice melted, heated, *boiled.* Under a burst of power, it exploded outwards, a tidal wave of steaming lake water that struck the dock, the boathouse, the shore, the trees, leaving me crouched and shivering in the epicentre. My clothes had burned away, my hair was singed but already regrowing. I curled my gloved arms around the empty shell of my body, my magical reserves empty.

Mindlessly, thoughtlessly, soullessly, I dragged myself out of the lake, walking the dry path that was already refilling. I felt more ghost than human. Demon, maybe. Certainly not the same person who'd woken up this morning believing I stood a chance of putting Abigail in her place.

I walked through the garden without seeing anything, unable to think about these beautiful beds and how important they'd been to a man who'd never seen them in the daylight, and climbed the back stairs into the house.

The alarms and sprinklers had shut off, but the damage to the foyer was evident from where I stood. The crown moulding was charred and fractured, the hardwood floors black and curling. So much water. The affected sprinklers would have been isolated to the front of the house, but I couldn't bring myself to imagine the damage.

The rest of the house seemed structurally sound, but I wondered if there would be any point in fixing it. Would Barrett choose to stay with Adrian gone?

What would become of the library? The thousands of books accumulated over two thousand years?

I flinched at the thought, rushed to return to my blissful emptiness, and shuffled upstairs to my bedroom.

As I passed Adrian's room, I half-expected him to step out and hail me, to ask me to join him for a drink so we could discuss our next steps.

Who would push me to bare my soul now?

Who would be there to offer me advice based on so many years of wisdom and experience?

A sob caught in my throat, and I cursed my emotions for betraying me. I didn't want to feel this pain. Not again. Not for

Adrian, who was supposed to share eternity with me.

I'd said goodbye to thousands of people in my nine hundred years, but this one hurt as much as those original three hundred.

I bypassed my bed and headed for the corner of my room next to the windows. Goosebumps covered my naked body, but I didn't have the strength to get dressed. I sagged against the wall, dropped to the floor, and bowed my forehead against my knees. As the shivers kicked in, I could do nothing but sit with them, wishing that once they subsided, the foundations of my life would once again be solid but knowing some fractures could never be healed.

33

Emrick

I WANDERED THE afterlife knowing full well Adrian wouldn't be here.

He and I had spent fifteen hundred years discussing our personal philosophies of what happened after Death took someone, and although we differed on many points, we agreed that, as a member of the undead, Adrian's soul had already passed on to wherever it was going to go. The magic that had kept him on this earth for the millennia after his death had simply animated his body.

It had been easy to forget as I'd watched him embrace the simple pleasures and beauties of the mortal world, but no less true.

In the hope that we'd been wrong, I journeyed beyond the

mists, searching the faces of those who had recently died as they waited to pass this in-between plane.

The moment Kat had fled from my presence, Barrett had gone the opposite way, declaring he would take a tour of the perimeter to ensure Abigail had actually left. The man was distraught, barely holding himself together. I suspected one well-intentioned word would push him over the edge. But he stayed focused on the threat as a distraction, and Gavin kept close by his side.

Rhys, Maera, Muroppy, and Cuddles had returned to the house once the fires had abated, all of them claiming they wanted to take in the extent of the damage.

In truth, no one knew what to do. Adrian's final death had shaken us all in different ways, and with Kat gone, they had no one to guide them.

As soon as everyone had left, I'd stepped through the mists. Everything in me longed to go after Kat to make sure she was all right, but the look on her face when she'd realized I'd known what was coming for our friend made me hesitant to seek her out. She was as angry as I'd anticipated. What I hadn't expected was how much I feared losing her because of it.

For centuries, she and Adrian had been my only tethers to my humanity. Without Adrian, Kat was the final string. If she turned away from me…

I shook off the thought, unable to consider the possibility, and turned my attention to my surroundings. The world here was a sharp contrast to the vivid colours and sounds of the mortal world. Here, all was silent, the colours muted into drab greys and murky whites, and although anyone new to the afterlife might see it as the setting of a disturbing dream, there was a comforting beauty in its emptiness. The barren trees, the still water, the fields of dried grass and cracked earth. No wind, no birdsong, no sweet smells of growth or decay that permeated the living world.

I'd come to love this liminal space. Time had no meaning here, allowing me to breathe and reflect. Just like the colours, my grief was also muted, a fraction of the intensity that would hit me when I returned to the place where Adrian and I had spent so many years talking, arguing, *being*.

For now, my sorrow was a hollow ache, the feeling of something sharp having been plunged into my chest and swiftly, mercilessly removed.

Katerina was suffering, and she had no escape beyond the sweet release of sleep—if she allowed herself to take it. Again the urge rose to go to her and offer what comfort I could, but again I hesitated. My explanations for keeping Adrian's secret were ready, my reasoning solid… but I had to prepare for her wrath.

Unable to muster my courage just yet, I walked farther away from the crossroads that would take me back to the mortal world. It had been a long time since I'd come this far, and part of me worried I'd find myself unable to return—especially now, when my fading soul was balanced on such a fragile scale, one that might fall too quickly towards oblivion.

That thought made me stop. As much as I worried about what would happen to me if Kat refused to forgive me and sent me away, I would be leaving her in the same place if I gave myself to this emptiness. I couldn't risk leaving her to grieve alone.

I retraced my steps and wound up on the shores of the river I'd so recently jumped into in a wild attempt to save my sorceress.

The shore was full of souls that I and others in the same servitude had escorted here. Some of them were aware of me, but most stared at or beyond the water, awaiting the ferry that would take them to whatever came next.

This was my realm. It was where my responsibilities began and ended. Increasingly, the tug to remain here felt stronger. As more of me faded, the more the anchor of my soul shifted from the mortal world to this one. When the transition was complete, I wouldn't give a thought to these souls beyond bringing them here and journeying to collect more.

I would no longer feel this grief—but nor would I care about what Kat suffered. Which was why my pain was a gift. It was a reminder that I was still human enough to experience it.

For a long while, I stood and stared at the river. No waves, no ripples, no life within its watery depths. I didn't know how long I stayed, musing on life and love and loss.

You're not dead yet, my friend. With so many years ahead, why do you hesitate to embrace what sparks life in you? Don't hide from passion when passion is what keeps you young. What keeps you free.

Adrian's words drifted over me from centuries past, and I closed my eyes to let his voice rest in my heart, letting it imprint on my soul so I would never forget. Long had he been the voice of wisdom whispering to me in moments of doubt, and I saw no reason for that to change.

"Goodbye, my friend," I said into the ether. "May you finally enjoy the rest you deserve."

34

Katerina

A T SOME POINT, the sun rose. I didn't move from where I sat huddled against the bedroom wall, tracking the shadows as they shifted across the empty garden with every passing hour.

I allowed no thoughts to enter my mind, clinging to the void as though it were the warmest, thickest blanket on the coldest, bitterest night. Every once in a while, an emotion attempted to intrude, but I hid from it until it scurried away.

Soon enough—too soon—I would need to face reality, but every time I inched a toe out of my corner, I was slammed by the reminder of what I faced once I did. The grief left me paralyzed. At least in my numbness, I could breathe, dragging in one breath after another. Aware of my heart beating, of the goosebumps rising and falling on my skin as the clouds played peekaboo with the sun.

Until the sun dipped once more below the horizon, replaced by a beautiful moon that cast its light over the loveliness of Adrian's garden.

A sight he'd never enjoy again.

A whimper escaped me, and I hugged my knees closer to my chest, shrinking smaller, wishing that the smaller I became, the smaller my grief might become.

Someone knocked on the door. It was the first time anyone had tried to seek me out all day, and I wished they'd given it a few more hours. Days. Weeks. However long it took me to process the vastness of the change that had shaken my life.

Light spilled across the room from the hallway as the door opened. I didn't bother to look away from the window to find out who it was. Unless it was Adrian, magically revived, I didn't care.

Soft steps padded across the carpet, and a figure stopped a few feet in front of me. In my peripheral vision, I took in grey socks and a pair of men's jeans. Blue, so not Barrett. That was as far as my processing brain would go.

"Get up," Gavin said.

His voice wasn't harsh, nor was it sympathetic. Either might have provoked a dangerous reaction. Instead, he spoke with a matter-of-factness that glided across my tumultuous emotions, leaving them unstirred. His levelheadedness stood against the tempest raging within me, and it was strangely soothing.

I didn't answer him. My dry tongue had glued itself to the roof of my mouth, but even if it hadn't, there were only so many ways I could politely tell him to fuck off.

"I know you're hurting right now," he said in that same level tone, "but you're not the only one in this house suffering. You have to get up, get showered, and get moving."

I clenched my teeth, and the muscles in my jaw spasmed after so many hours of stillness.

"I know what you're going through, Kat. Believe me, you don't get to be a nurse for eight years and not see every kind of loss and pain and grief. You've had the heart punched out of your body, and that fucking sucks, but unfortunately, you're not in a position where you can let it break you."

My silence persisted, though I was beginning to vibrate with the effort of hanging on to my blissful emptiness.

He approached and sat on the side of my bed.

"I'm serious, Kat." His voice was softer now if no less steady. "The people in this house are lost without you. The revelation that magic exists has ruined my life on so many fucking levels I don't know how to get past it, and the fact that this woman is a blood relation? That fucks me up most of all. But she's out there somewhere, still a threat, and no one knows how to move against her. Everyone is hiding in busy work, but there's only so long that'll play before Abigail recovers and attacks again. If you don't get up to lead us, we won't be prepared, and you'll lose more than just Adrian."

My shoulders cracked as I raised my arms to clutch the sides of my head. I didn't want to hear this. How could I lead anyone else when I couldn't see beyond this dark corner of my room?

And to walk out of here, to be confronted with reminders of Adrian at every step, knowing his association with them had been cut off?

"This house will always be empty without him," Gavin said. "There's no length of time you can sit in the dark and expect the pain of that emptiness not to hit hard."

If I didn't know better, I'd think he could read my mind. It was why experience sometimes came off as magic. My situation wasn't unique. I wasn't the first person to be trapped in a house of memories, not wanting to move lest the illusion of normality go up in a puff of smoke.

But knowing it and accepting it were two separate things. I longed to remain in my cocoon of stasis for a while longer, but word by word, the sorcerer was pulling me out.

The first tears spilled down my cheeks. All day, I hadn't let myself cry, knowing once I started, it would be impossible for me to stop. But Gavin's presence, his calm, rational, professional approach, had broken through the walls I'd built to keep the world at bay.

"Rallying your people and going after this woman will do more for your grief than getting stuck here. I didn't know Adrian long, but I think it's what he would have preferred." He hesitated, and at first I thought he was giving me a chance to catch my breath after that blow to the solar plexus, but then he added, "I also think Barrett needs to see you. I think he needs to know you don't blame him."

I didn't know if I was in a place to alleviate Barrett's guilt. Not when a small, irrational part of me *did* blame him. Not nearly as much as I blamed myself, but my shame was desperate to lay the fault somewhere.

Abigail was the most obvious target, but she wasn't here. And until I looked her in the eye, she was too enormous—too ethereal—to make out clearly.

Yet if I was in pain, I could only imagine what Barrett was suffering. And like me, he wouldn't let anyone hold his hand. After all this time, I had to accept we had something in common.

"Maera made cookies."

It was Gavin's last-ditch effort. He'd been patient with every new argument while I'd given him nothing, and bribery with baked goods was all he had left. If I stayed silent, if I refused to move, he would have no choice but to leave, and I could stay in my corner to watch the sun and shadows play hide and seek in

Adrian's garden for another day.

My treasonous stomach gurgled, giving away my awakening appetite, and with the reminder that I was not, in fact, one of the stone statues that guarded the garden paths, I sucked in a breath and raised my head. Gavin watched me, unfazed by my nudity, his expression neutral, waiting to see what I'd do. Would I show up for my team or keep my head in the sand?

The truth bombs he'd dropped had destroyed my numbness, and to keep hiding would be an act of cowardice I would never forgive myself for.

I'd failed Adrian, but I wouldn't lose anyone else to Abigail's games.

"Let the others know I'll be down in ten minutes," I said, my voice rough. "We need to have a meeting. With cookies."

Barrett wasn't in the dining room when I came downstairs—showered and dressed—but his was the only absence. Rhys, Maera, Poppy, Murisa, and Gavin sat around the large table, while Emrick lurked against the far wall with his hands behind his back.

He met my gaze as I came in, but I looked away, not yet ready to see my grief reflected in his eyes.

Rhys rose from his chair when he saw me, and Maera put

an extra cookie on my plate before she set the tray in the middle of the table for people to grab more as they wanted. I intended to stake my claim on at least half of them.

Poppy stood and threw her arms around me, and Murisa reached out to take my hand. Not wanting to miss out on the action, Cuddles pounced from under the table and sank his teeth into my ankle. It might have hurt, but one of his teeth snagged in my sock and fell out.

"How are you doing?" Murisa asked as she pried Cuddles from around my foot and plonked him in her lap. Her tone was closer to curiosity than pity, which I appreciated.

"I'll be better when this woman is in the ground. By the sound of those screams, we managed to hurt her—hopefully enough that she'll need time to recover—but where do we stand on making sure she doesn't get back up?"

Poppy turned her head to wipe her eyes with her crimson-painted nails—in honour of Adrian, I was sure—and returned to her seat next to Murisa.

Murisa gestured to the spell paraphernalia spread across the table around the cookies. "We've set everything up for another go at the tracking spell on the off chance we can get to her first next time. Using what we have left of Gavin's blood, we'll be able to get around the blocks she's placed on herself."

I liked this idea. So far she'd kept us on the back foot, but I was ready to upset the balance. "Not that I doubt you, but we can't afford to leave gaps. Where do our defences stand?"

Poppy glowered at the table. "The bitch broke through our ward too easily. We've recast it, and she'll find a nasty surprise if she tries to strip it down."

"That's a good start. What about the demon? It didn't make an appearance last night, but we have to be prepared for it." I didn't look forward to facing both Abigail and her demon, but if we wanted to take her down, we needed it there.

"Work in progress, I'm afraid. We need his name before we can plan for him, and we're still searching."

"What about the enchanted stones?"

Murisa frowned. "Like I said earlier, we're close to being able to nullify—"

I raised my gaze to hers. "I'm not talking about nullifying them. I'm talking about replicating them."

Silence fell on the room, the tension palpable.

Poppy cleared her throat. "That would be getting into some pretty violent magic. The past three years, you've threatened to kill me for going anywhere near that kind of stuff."

"I know. I'm a raging hypocrite." I wasn't about to apologize or feel ashamed for stretching my morals. Not when Adrian's ashes lined the driveway. "Can you do it?"

Poppy looked uncertain, but Murisa offered an embarrassed grin. "When I was figuring out how to shut them down, I *may* have poked around into how they were made. I should be able to reverse engineer them."

Poppy brushed her fingers over Murisa's cheek and leaned in to kiss her. When she pulled away, her eyes glowed with pride. "You are an absolute madwoman."

Murisa laughed and pushed her away. Then she caught my eye, and when her smile faded into sadness, my heart clenched. Adrian wouldn't want anyone hiding their moments of joy because of his final death.

Life is for living, mia Katerina.

I sucked in a breath as his words came to me, so clearly it was like he sat beside me, and closed my eyes against the shot of pain.

When I opened them again, all eyes were on me, and I did my best to tuck my broken pieces together. "You two work on that and let me know when you have something workable. Gavin, your presence in that fight helped us. You managed to hold her off. Whether she was expecting you or not, she wasn't prepared for both of us. I want you and Barrett to keep training. You won't be able to match her, but you don't have to. All you need to do is help me split her attention until we deal with her demon and spot an opening to take her down."

He kept his expression carefully blank, his displeasure at my announcement loud enough without him uttering a syllable. But he didn't argue or refuse. I didn't know if that meant he was making progress on his road to acceptance or if he knew better than to oppose me on this.

"Rhys, how's your head?" I asked, turning to him next.

He winced and gave a slow shrug. "Clearing, I think. The squeeze isn't so bad now."

"Good. We won't be topping up the potion." Maera sucked in a breath, but I shook my head. "We need to know what Abigail's next move is. If Rhys can get us a few hints, we have no choice but to take the risk. You stay close to him. Raise the flag if the bitch tries to use him again."

She paled, but Rhys nodded. "I'll do what I can."

I turned in my chair to face Emrick. His gaze was soft on me, open, braced for me to lash out. But I didn't have space in my heart to be angry with him right now. Later, we'd talk. For now, I needed him. "You stay with me. Depending on the results of the tracking spell, we might need to travel quickly."

He dropped his chin in a nod, and I turned back to the table. "We need to be ready for her to direct the next move. No slacking off, no dropping our guard. Every second she gives us is an extra second for us to work towards stopping her. Let's make the most of it."

35

Katerina

WITH OUR PLANS made and everyone focused on their assigned tasks, I followed Maera to the kitchen. The cookies had torn the bandage off my hunger, and what I needed now was something more substantial. I couldn't be weak the next time we faced Abigail.

As I pawed through the fridge to find something that grabbed my interest, Maera sank into a chair at the kitchen table. Vaguely I was aware of the way she picked at her nails and at a stain on the placemat. I discovered some leftover Thai curry, neatly labelled and dated, and popped it in the microwave. The moment the microwave pinged, I tucked into the food as though I'd never enjoyed a meal before. The spices danced across my palate, and my stomach hugged me from within.

The flavours paled and the sauce turned to ash on my tongue when I looked up to find Maera staring at me with so much guilt I was amazed she could sit upright.

"What is it?" I asked.

"He begged me not to tell you, Kat, but I can't keep it a secret anymore."

My bowl nearly slipped from my fingers. I set the half-eaten curry on the counter and crossed my arms where I stood. "What secret?"

"Adrian knew."

The lump in my throat that had so recently shrunk swelled again, coated in spices that made my eyes sting. "I know. He warned Emrick and Barrett." As my housekeeper dropped her gaze, her meaning sank in. "How long?"

Maera wiped the tears from her cheeks. "A few months."

The food revolted in my stomach, and I drew in a deep breath to keep it down. Months. Months and he'd said nothing. "How?"

"Rhys."

Every word out of her mouth was another punch to my stomach. Barrett had been right that they were avoiding him. Rhys's second sight had shown Adrian dying, and *no one had told me?*

"When?" It didn't matter, but I needed to know how long my friends had lied to me.

"During that vision storm. He was Seeing so much so quickly. Most of the visions were about Mikhail, but some went further into the future. Sometimes he saw Adrian in the fire. Sometimes he saw you shielding Adrian while the rest of us burned. There was never a third option."

My legs went numb, and I leaned my weight on the counter. Adrian or everyone else. That was why he'd made Emrick promise to say nothing. He'd sacrificed himself to save the rest of the family.

There was something else, something more she wasn't saying, but I wasn't sure I wanted to hear it.

Two months. He had known for two months that his end was coming, and instead of worrying me, he'd offered his advice, his comfort, and his constant love and support as though everything was normal.

I wanted to be angry with him. I wanted to be *furious* that he'd kept this from me and left me to be blindsided. But the man had known me too well. Despite the odds, I would have tried to save him, and he'd known exactly how well I'd have handled the alternative.

My heart squeezed, and my breath came in shallow wheezes. I was going to be sick. I was going to pass out.

Maera was on her feet, reaching for me, and I stepped away from her. Maybe I could come to understand Adrian's reasons in time, but the betrayal was too fresh. She and Rhys had lied to me. The two people I relied on to keep me honest, keep me human, had held back information they knew would devastate me.

I couldn't look at her. Wasn't sure if I'd ever be able to look at her. My already fractured world had developed another crack. Any more of them, and I was liable to fall into the deepest, darkest void that would be impossible to escape.

I started towards the door, needing to get away, but Maera called after me. "He was tired, Kat."

I froze on the threshold but didn't turn around.

"That's what he said when Rhys told him. We tried to convince him to tell you while we had enough time to find a solution to save everyone, and he told us that after being around for so long, he was exhausted. He'd become everything he'd always feared he'd be, wasting time trying to find excuses to keep living. He didn't want to leave you—or James, or Emrick—but he said if this was his final opportunity to do something useful with this life, then there would be no better way for him to go."

I closed my eyes and tried to breathe through the ache.

"He didn't want me to tell you for all those reasons. He knew your love for him would cause you to overlook the only important fact—that this is what he wanted."

I didn't want to listen to anything else. Didn't want to believe it. Didn't want to consider that my old friend had grown tired of spending his life alongside mine.

Without responding, without turning around or acknowledging her explanation, I continued on my way, fighting the desire to return to my room and pull the covers over my head.

On my way upstairs, Emrick stepped into the stairwell behind me. He said nothing as he followed me down the hallway, and I sensed his hesitation before he crossed the threshold into the darkness of my bedroom.

He caught my eye, and in the silver depths, I found his permission to vent my rage. He believed he deserved it and wanted me to let loose.

My thoughts were primed to fight. The words were on my tongue to scream and attack him until the rage settled. But even as I formed my accusations, they stuck in my throat. Adrian had given Emrick his last request, and Emrick had respected it. I was angry, but not with him. Not with any of them anymore.

My emotions roiled, running out of control, so I shut them down—everything except the fire in my blood that refused to go out. But there were other ways to vent that flicker of turmoil.

I didn't bother turning on the lights. The curtains were open, and the moonlight shone through. That was enough brightness for me.

Without words, I grabbed Emrick's hand and pulled him inside, pushing the door closed behind him. He remained stiff under my touch, more than once pulling back, and I knew what he was doing. He wanted to talk. He wanted to pull me out of my silence to get the explosion over with, but I had no interest in doing that.

Instead, I pulled my sweater over my head and tossed it onto the floor. In quick succession, I added my shirt, leggings, and underwear to the pile.

"Kat." Emrick's voice was soft as my lips brushed against his neck. I nipped at the hollow of his throat, and he groaned. "Are you sure—"

"Shut up and kiss me."

I didn't need to ask him twice. He wrapped one arm around my waist and coiled the fingers of his other hand in my hair as he bent his head to claim my mouth. I twined my arms around his neck, and a moment later, my legs circled his waist. His hard length pressed through his pants against my core, and I rolled my hips against him, needing him closer, needing the mindlessness of that fire more than I needed air.

I'd tried sitting in a dark corner, and that hadn't helped. I'd tried focusing on what lay ahead and spending time with my unexpected family, and that had made things so much worse.

I craved oblivion, if only temporarily.

Emrick carried me to the bed and gently laid me down,

stretching out on top of me. His kisses grew tender, his touch a sweet caress as the hand that had been rough in my hair skated down the side of my face, over my neck, and skirted my breast to clasp my waist.

I arched my hips and deepened our kiss, not wanting tender. Not wanting soft or romantic.

But every time I tried to speed things up, Emrick pulled back, until finally I shoved him away in frustration. Or I tried to. The stubborn man would not be shoved.

"I know what you're doing," he murmured against my neck. His lips were so close to my ear his deep voice sent vibrations running along my nerves, through my chest, and into my lower belly. "I won't let you."

I huffed. "Won't let me what? Find some satisfaction in the middle of so much misery and chaos?"

He angled his head to look up at me with his gleaming silver eyes. "I won't let you use me to hide from whatever you're feeling."

His words wrapped around my heart and squeezed, and I sucked in a sharp breath. Cold set in, and against my chattering teeth, I sat up and dragged my knees to my chest. Emrick turned onto his side, head propped on his hand. His other hand trailed up my shin, and he pressed a kiss against my calf. My skin steamed under his touch, the shocks of electricity popping and surging, offering light in the darkness, but I couldn't bring myself to enjoy it.

"I don't care if you use me as a distraction." He trailed more kisses up my leg, which awoke a stirring of deeper desire, something that burned lower and hotter than my desperation of a few minutes ago. "I don't care if you use me for pleasure or to satisfy yourself. But I won't let you hide. I don't want you numb and distant." His lips continued up my thigh and across my hip as his hand brushed over my skin in ways that gave me goosebumps. "Be here with me, Kat."

His mouth closed on my nipple, and I gasped as I arched into him, the last of my emptiness fading under his touch.

This time when his mouth met mine, I responded body and soul. I slid my fingers under the bottom of his shirt and pulled it over his head, revealing the dips and valleys of his muscular chest, his flat stomach, the defined vee that disappeared under his jeans. I clawed at his back, drawing him closer to me, and his fingers curled into the thick of my hips as he angled himself between my legs. His kisses grew more heated, his hands urgent in their explorations that left me squirming beneath him.

As always, he knew exactly what I needed—better than I did myself. By the time I got his pants off and he slid inside me, I was ready to fall apart at the seams.

Again he slowed, rocking his hips in a deeper, undulating roll, and with each wave, I crested closer to my climax, hanging on to him, certain that if I let him go, I'd explode into a million pieces.

His breath grew ragged, and he increased his tempo. I met each thrust, driving myself closer to the edge of the cliff, ready to throw myself into oblivion for a few sweet seconds.

But not alone.

Not this time.

Emrick's lips brushed against mine as he braced himself on his arms and stared into my eyes. Together we reached our peak, losing ourselves in each other—not numb but full of life. As I cupped Emrick's face and pulled him down to taste him again, I appreciated how lucky I was to have experienced the love of this man who refused to leave me behind.

Mae, Alodie, and Blythe may have been happy at the thought of binding themselves to a demon for the sake of claiming forever. But as I curled myself in Emrick's arms, his chest pressed against my back, his embrace so tight around me I felt all my broken pieces fuse back together, I realized just how lost I would be without him.

And how much I pitied the woman who wanted me dead.

Grandmother's gnarled fingers twisted through my thick black hair, weaving the tresses into small braids that would hide among the rest of the loose locks.

"You've always had such beautiful hair. Like mine when I was younger."

"I'm surprised you remember it," I teased.

Gran tugged on the braid. "Don't be cheeky. Remember that I can make you look a fright if you're not kind to your poor, decrepit grandmother."

I laughed and patted her wrinkled hand. For all her years, Gran was in good shape. The magic ran strong and true in her veins, and I was certain she would still be around when Rowan was old enough to remember her.

"You wouldn't do that to me," I said. "The people in this village already want to toss me out. Making me look like a lake monster would spur them on."

She sighed. "Ah, nephene, *you put such pressure on yourself. No one in Palonia wants to cast you out. Your teachers only want to help you, and the others… well, they're simply too busy to know what to do with you.*"

None of which made me feel better.

Gran squeezed my shoulder. "Your future may be too murky for me to See clearly, but from what I've managed to glean from my visions, you have greatness before you. More than you'll know what to do with."

I snorted my opinion of her visions. She was a skilled Seer, but her second sight was known to lead her astray.

Her hands went slack on my shoulders, and I turned around to *find her blue eyes had gone white as a vision came upon her.*

"Blood in the moon. Blood in the grass. Dead grass. Betrayal."
She sucked in a breath as her eyes widened, and she grabbed my
hands. "Trouble is coming to this family, nephene. You alone will
stand against it. I See it."

"When, Gran?" Fear speared my heart. How was I supposed
to stop it when I couldn't even summon a fireball into my hands?
"What am I supposed to do?"

She closed her eyes, searching for more answers, then shook her
head. "It's not clear. But you have to be strong, my dearest girl. For
all of us, you have to be strong."

I jerked awake with my face soaked in tears, my naked body
trembling, and a scream on my lips. Emrick's arms were already
around me, the smell of him soothing me with its closeness and
familiarity.

My chest felt hollow, my ribs cracking with the suction as
they tried to close in on the gaping hole where my heart should
have been. I curled in on myself, leaning into Emrick as he
held me tighter. The warmth of his bare chest soaked into me,
chasing away the chill. I wrapped my hands around his forearm
where it locked around my middle and held tight.

He nuzzled the nape of my neck. "Where did you go?"

"Palonia," I whispered. "Always Palonia. I'd forgotten that conversation with my grandmother. She had a vision about the festival night a few months before it happened. She told me I would be the only person to stand against the traitors. I thought she meant I'd face them when it happened—but she was Seeing so many years into the future. I swore they were dead. To discover at least one of them is alive—that she's suddenly *here*… How is it possible?"

"Muroppy will figure out who summoned them," he said against my hair.

"Do you think it's another coincidence? Some witch dabbling in dark magic who happened to summon the demon bound to an immortal sorceress who's set so many horrible events in motion?"

Saying it aloud, I appreciated the unlikelihood.

"But if everything was planned…"

More questions I didn't have the energy to ask right now.

Until we learned something new, there was nothing we could do but wait until we had—or made—an opportunity to face Abigail again.

The clock on the wall ticked with the passing minutes where we said nothing, both of us lying in the blissful silence of the here and now where nothing was trying to kill us.

"I can't let her win again," I said, the sound coming out choked. "I won't let her take everything from me."

"She won't, Kat." His reply was low and assured. "No matter what, she won't steal anything else from us."

Us.

Such a small word that made such a difference as the emptiness inside me lessened.

It was true. Unlike what had happened in Palonia, I wasn't the only survivor. Everyone in this house had reason to hate the woman who'd assaulted the bedrock of our lives and livelihoods, and we were all of us strong in our own rights. I might be the only person with the power to stand against her directly, but together we were a force.

We would be ready to fight.

36

Katerina

STILL FEELING LOST, chased by my past and afraid of my future, I left my room a few hours later and padded down the hallway. Emrick had disappeared to escort another soul in need, and without him beside me, my bedroom felt too cold and quiet.

With no clear destination in mind, I found myself wandering towards the library.

The door was open, and I wondered if someone else had already gone in. I slowed my approach to brace myself for the wave of pain about to hit.

I imagined the empty armchairs by the window, the dark hearth, the lines of books, hoping to dilute the blow when I saw them in reality. I anticipated the coldness, the stillness in a room I'd always known to be full of warmth and life.

All the anticipating in the world couldn't save me from the way the air was sucked out of my body when I stepped inside.

The room was empty, and it was like the energy had been vacuumed out of the space without Adrian here to fuel it. No one had opened the curtains at sunset, leaving everything draped in darkness. Stifled.

I wrenched the curtains open and cranked the window, letting in the soft April breeze that carried scents of lake water and new growth. The moonlight tempered the emptiness, and I rested my hand on the back of Adrian's armchair, half-expecting to feel his hand settle on top of mine.

Unable to deal with the memories looming in the shadows, I turned on the table lamp between the chairs. A book sat next to the lamp. The same copy of Swift's *Gulliver's Travels* that had been there two months ago. The day Adrian had shoved Barrett into my life and given me the push to come out of hibernation.

At the time, I'd wondered if he and Barrett were reading it together. By the placement of the bookmark, they'd made some progress through it but hadn't finished. All those days Barrett had joined me on the hunt had been days I'd stolen him away from Adrian, and a fresh wave of guilt washed over me.

I dropped into Adrian's chair, breathed in the scent of his cologne, and tried to imagine what he would say if he were here.

But I couldn't find his voice. I'd fought so hard to keep thoughts of him out for the past day that now I feared I'd pushed his memory too far.

A moment of panic hit me as it sank in that I would never spend my evenings with him again, and I squeezed my eyes shut to sit with that spear in my heart.

The soft hiss of a door sliding open cut through the silence. My ears twitched at the brush of footsteps crossing the room and the creak of leather as someone settled in the other armchair.

Once I caught my breath and got my tears under control, I looked up, expecting to find Emrick sitting there. But it wasn't his familiar, comforting paleness that had taken the seat. Instead, it was a black-clad, black-mooded Barrett who was attempting to bore deep holes in the woven rug with his black stare.

For a while, we sat in silence. I hadn't realized how much having Barrett close by would be a balm on my tormented soul. Adrian had loved this man enough to sacrifice himself for him. Our issues aside, he had stood by my friend for a decade despite his loathing of the world Adrian was a part of.

My throat ached, my heart bled, but I managed to rise above my sorrow enough to say, "I'm sorry for your loss."

Although Barrett's dark eyes glistened, his tears didn't fall. His jaw flexed as he clenched his teeth.

I returned my gaze to the floor, certain he wouldn't reply

but not in a rush for him to leave. A few minutes later, he surprised me.

"He shouldn't have done it." His voice was gruff, a low rumble I strained to decipher. "Knocked me out of the way, I mean."

His shoulders were tense, and he leaned faintly away from me, as though expecting me to agree with him and readying himself for the hit. The foolish man. Regardless of what tensions existed between us, I would never sully my friend's feelings like that.

"I understand why he did. He cared about you. Loved you. The moment Abigail threw that stone, no one could have stopped him."

He stiffened, a single tear sliding onto his cheek as his eyes widened. He needed more, but I couldn't offer anything else yet. The words I wanted to say were blocked by my feelings around them—my anger that such a sacrifice had been necessary, my guilt that anyone else had been involved—and I fought a battle of wills to find my tongue.

"Adrian was his own man. Stubborn, passionate, brave. He put the people he loved ahead of himself. Always. The moment you were in danger, there was no pause for consideration. His only thought was ensuring your safety." A sob escaped me, and I bowed my head. "I'm so sorry it came to this. I'm so sorry I didn't stop her long before now."

My apology came out as a whisper, and I clutched my hand to my chest, squeezing it into a fist and pressing it against my sternum to keep my bleeding heart from spilling between my ribs.

"We're going to kill that bitch," Barrett growled.

I sucked in a breath and forced myself to sit up. Tears wet my cheeks, but I looked him in the eye. "We are."

He stared at me, and after a moment, he nodded and stretched out his legs. Without another word, he picked up *Gulliver's Travels* and opened it to the bookmarked page.

All of a sudden, I was no longer sitting in this room but being walked through a dance in Adrian's Florentine estate over eight hundred years ago. The pressure of Adrian's hand against mine was so solid, I could almost believe it was real, and my vision blurred as he spun me in a wide circle.

He and Emrick talked while we danced. We'd just taken down a giant, and Adrian was lamenting that the hunt had begun to lose its thrill.

"I'm not sure what I'll do when the day comes that I stop enjoying it."

"Lock yourself in your library listening to the latest songs and drinking vintage blood, I'm sure," Emrick said.

Adrian groaned. "If that day comes, kill me yourself, old friend. Don't let me languish in this world with no better way to spend my time than by spending time."

All these years, I'd thought he was happy. To a point, I believed he had been—with Barrett, surrounded by the people he loved. But he also believed he'd served his purpose and that his role on this earth was finished.

I thought of what Maera had said about how Adrian hadn't worked to prevent Rhys's vision because he'd been ready to go. I thought of the acceptance in his eyes the moment before the flames consumed him. He'd made his choice.

It broke me that I hadn't seen his wishes for myself. That I'd been so caught up in needing him that I hadn't considered what *he* needed.

In this, I'd failed him as well. For the sake of his memory, his love for me, his years of always being there, I had to be the strong one now and accept his decision.

My heart fractured once again as his loss hit me, but with the pain came a mild, barely-there solace. For now, that would have to be enough.

"Read to me?" I asked.

Barrett stilled, then relaxed and picked up where he and my friend had left off. Hearing the words roll off his tongue, I could imagine the two of them sitting here on a night much like this one. The thought made me feel strangely comforted—the idea that part of the man I'd known for a thousand years remained beside me in this staunch, brooding soldier who could barely tolerate me at the best of times.

I didn't know what the future held for my relationship with Barrett, but right now, until Abigail was nothing more than a bloodstain on the ground, we were allies.

For you, my friend.

We owed Adrian that much.

37

Emrick

I RETURNED FROM another tour of the afterlife an hour later, just in time to enter the dining room behind Katerina and Barrett.

"I'll grab Gavin for a bout of training," he said, and Kat nodded as he strode away.

It was clear at a glance that the atmosphere between them had changed. Although they stood in close enough proximity that sparks of tension should have been flying, all I sensed was peace. Whether it was the effect of a temporary truce or a permanent foundational shift, only time would tell. For today, I appreciated how necessary it was that they were on the same page. Abigail had struck a brutal blow—one that could have sundered the strong ties this family had formed and made it impossible for them to rally against her. Instead, it had brought them closer.

Or so I hoped.

It was hard to miss how Kat struggled to look Maera in the eye, or how the smile she gave Rhys was brittle when he asked how she was doing.

I had my own feelings about Rhys's and Maera's silence—feelings that bounced between anger on Kat's behalf and understanding—but my opinions didn't matter. Adrian had tasked them with the same silence he'd sworn me to, and they'd trusted his logic in this as they had in all things. But now my friend was dead, and his logic would no longer play a role in our lives.

My breath caught in my throat as a wave of grief crashed over me, and I held it until the spasm in my chest eased.

"Okay," Kat said as she reached the head of the table. "Update me."

Muroppy sat to her left, while Maera and Rhys sat across from them.

I circled the room and leaned against the wall behind Kat. I had nothing to offer at this meeting, no way to help beyond the odd question, but that didn't mean I wouldn't support her however I could every step of the way.

"We've figured out how the stones work," Murisa said, her eyes shining.

My interest peaked. Was there nothing these witches

couldn't do?

She reached into a pouch and sent a black stone skittering across the table. Kat picked it up and spun it through her fingers. I tensed, my memories of those stones too fresh and too painful to see them with neutrality.

Kat's brow furrowed, and her throat bobbed. She cleared it without any demonstrative reaction and tossed it back. "How?"

"Easy." Poppy slid it towards herself and threw it into the air to catch it. "The spell is in complete stasis until activated. You could hurl these into a fire, and nothing would happen to them. Say the right words, and *boom*." She spread her palms wide to mimic the resulting explosion. "My suggestion is we shove one of these up Abigail's—"

"Poppy," Murisa warned.

Poppy crossed her arms. "What? You think anyone here would stop me?"

She looked to Kat, who shrugged. "I wouldn't get in your way."

"Maera might have a few things to say about it," Murisa pointed out.

"Would you?" Poppy asked, turning to her.

Maera's expression darkened. "I'd help pin her down."

Cuddles bared his teeth and let out a low hiss, making his own opinion known.

A chill settled over the room—so cold it made me shiver.

The anger spilling through every one of these people was palpable. Most of us had lost a man who'd been a guiding force for the better part of our lives, Murisa and Poppy had nearly succumbed to Abigail's magic, and Gavin was related to the woman.

Abigail's greatest mistake was pissing off the wrong group—the sort who wouldn't cower under her assault but would devote everything they had to retaliation. The only question now was if their plan would be enough to stop a woman who had likely spent centuries in hell.

Again, my uselessness tugged at me, made me want to flee to the afterlife so I wouldn't have to face it, but I stayed where I was. If any opportunity came up for me to play a part, I wouldn't run from it.

"If we're preparing for the endgame, we need to focus on Abigail's demon," Kat said, drawing the conversation back to her mental checklist. "Where are we with that?"

Murisa flipped her thumb over her notebook. "We need another hour or two. We've pared down the list to a few options for Abigail's bond. Demons she and the other two might have considered safe bets for the binding."

Maera frowned. "There are lists?"

Poppy nodded. "Dark web shit. All summoners add to it every time they attempt a summons, whether it fails or not. They leave tips on what demons to avoid, which to use, the best lures, the best forms of control. Most of the names listed are low-level demons that stick around for a day or a week to help with a particular problem. Summoner makes a pact, gets what they want, deals with the consequences."

"It's not a comprehensive list," Murisa admitted, "but with what I've learned, I've cross-referenced some of my tomes to rule out other options. It was slow-going, but now that I've limited it to a handful of names, we can cast tracking spells to latch on to the demon's energy and find out who and where it is. Unless we get lucky, and Abigail lets the name slip."

Kat and Adrian had done their fair share of demon hunting over the years but never with the advantage of the internet. She had to be grateful someone else was willing to take on the research. Especially a tech witch like Murisa, who, I had no doubt, had found a way to automate the most tedious aspects of the process.

"I helped as much as I could." Rhys sat hunched in his chair as though he didn't have the strength to sit up, but the circles under his eyes had faded, and some brightness had returned to his meadow-greens. He must have gotten some sleep while Kat and I were upstairs because he looked more alive than he had for the past couple of days. I hoped that meant the potion had cleared his system. Kat's reasons for blocking his second sight had been sound, but I felt better knowing we might receive early notice if Abigail returned.

"Any visions yet?" Kat asked gently.

"No, but not for lack of ability, I don't think. I sense… something, but I haven't wanted to chase it in case it's Abigail trying to lure me in. I've been getting—I want to call it hot-cold vibes while Murisa and Poppy go through the list."

Murisa smiled. "It's been helpful in eliminating our options."

"What about the possibility that Abigail spent time in the infernal realms?" I asked, bracing myself for the sensation of some new part of me fading away. A small breath escaped me when nothing happened.

Murisa offered an apologetic shrug. "There's some evidence to suggest more than one summoner has gone that route. Every such case reads like a deal gone bad. An overlooked or poorly worded term of the agreement. Nothing about any of them being summoned back, though."

Kat rubbed her brow. "I don't see Mae, Blythe, or Alodie making that kind of mistake. They would have gone through every word of the ritual before agreeing to anything. But there was a lot going on. Maybe they missed something."

Poppy shuddered. "There are lots of mentions of summoners who managed to open a window to the infernal realms. Enough to let them peer inside. None of them walked away lucid."

A moment's silence fell over the table as everyone considered what it would mean if Abigail had spent centuries there. It explained her unpredictability and her cruelty. Getting ahead of her would be no small feat.

Cuddles hopped onto Poppy's lap, and she stroked her fingers through his long tufts of fur like some fiendish villain in a spy movie. "What we do know is that it has to be a solidly mid-level demon. Not nearly as difficult to destroy as Shogaur or as challenging to keep out of anyone's head, which is good news. That point brings us to…" She reached into Murisa's satchel and drew out a handful of thin silver chains. Each chain had a wire cage attached to it with a black stone inside. I tagged the stone as either obsidian or black tourmaline. "You thought obsidian was useful? How about hyped-up *uber* obsidian?"

Kat picked up one of the amulets and twisted the wire through her fingers. "You managed to make something to protect us from Abigail?"

"You bet your perky ass we did. The energy field on these babies will disperse any magic that comes within range, spreading it out enough to remove the damage."

I blinked in awe at the tiny stone fragments. Seriously, were these witches human?

"I didn't think you'd find a way to make it happen," Kat admitted.

Poppy snorted. "Learn to give us some credit, kitty Kat. Between the two of us, there's nothing we can't do."

I believed it.

She looped her fingers through Murisa's, and the other witch beamed at her.

"What's their limit?" Kat asked, and Poppy's smile fell.

"Unfortunately, only one or two good hits."

Kat pressed her lips together and nodded. "We'll need to position ourselves well."

I clenched my fists behind me, practically hearing the thoughts whirring through her head. She was trying to figure out who she could leave behind without risking her win. She didn't want to put anyone in danger, even if it meant leaving herself vulnerable.

I saw it, and I would be ready to step in if she made that call. Last resort only, but I would not let Abigail finish what she'd started in Palonia.

Kat massaged her temples. "All right, so we have the best possible defence and offence to stand against this woman. Now we have to find her."

"We'll set up what we need for the tracking spells," Poppy said. "We were about to do it when you called the meeting, so your timing is perfect."

As she stood up and started gathering her ingredients, a faint stirring in the air made me stiffen. My attention jumped to Rhys. Gone were the green eyes and slouched posture of a moment ago. Now he sat straight and stiff as a board, and his eyes were muted under a film of white.

"Hills and water and empty stretches of pain and blood."

Kat rose from her seat so quickly the chair toppled, and she backed up until she bumped into my chest. I slid my fingers through hers.

"What did you say?" she whispered.

"You in an open field surrounded by hills. Campers come here often, tamping down the grass, putting their boats on the water, but now it's silent. Empty. Filled with ghosts." He sagged forward on the table, and Maera rushed to throw her arm around him before he could fall to the floor.

My heart hammered against my ribs as I processed Rhys's premonition, the meaning as clear to me as it obviously was to Kat. We both knew the place he described—the hills in the Lake District. I forced myself to swallow, to work some moisture back into my lips.

Barrett stepped into the dining room with Gavin close behind him. Their expressions were grim, and Barrett held a wrapped package in his hands. "We went out to check the traps. This was sitting by your car."

He set the package on the table. The brown paper was the same kind Abigail had used to wrap the stone so many days ago, but the box was much larger in size, maybe five inches by seven. Even so, no one was about to take chances. Murisa and Poppy murmured a few words under their breath while Murisa cut her thumb and smeared the blood across the paper. A faint shimmer surrounded the package, then disappeared.

"Whatever's inside, it's contained by a ward now." Poppy gently picked it up and handed it to Kat, who accepted it with shaking hands.

A light floral scent wafted off the paper as Kat tore it open to reveal a box, this one plain cardboard.

Sucking in deep breaths, she set it on the table and pulled open the lid.

Inside was a cup made of thick, dark stone.

She wavered on her feet, and I caught her elbow to steady her.

Tears spilled down her cheeks as she pulled out the cup and set it on the table beside the box.

A plain, drab, empty cup. Nothing special about it.

Yet even so, the reek of its previous contents hit me as though it were full—the stink of rot buried beneath spices, strong enough that everyone who took a sip curled their lip and tried to spit it out.

I'd seen this cup—and smelled those contents—only once before, and so far, Death had left the memory intact. I pictured hundreds of sorcerers laughing and enjoying their revelry around the scattered bonfires while three women made their way through the crowd encouraging people to drink. Everyone had gotten a taste, from the oldest man to the youngest babe. Part of the harvest rites, they'd said. A single drop on the tongue was all it took.

I'd been the only one to abstain—the only one they'd allowed to abstain.

"What is this?" Poppy asked, leaning closer to get a better look but wise enough not to touch it. "Some Holy Grail shit or something?"

"No," Kat said. "No one would make it their life's mission to track this down. Not unless they wanted to find themselves bound to a demon and living forever."

Poppy frowned and looked from the cup to Kat to me. But it wasn't my place to explain.

Murisa picked up the box and peered inside. "There's something else in here."

She reached in and pulled out a folded slip of paper, which she offered first to Kat, then, when she didn't take it, to me.

Kat wobbled again and squeezed her eyes shut as I read out the single sentence written in spidery handwriting.

I'm waiting for you.

Kat let out a slow, measured breath. "I should have known she'd force me to go back."

Maera blinked as she stroked her fingers through Rhys's hair. "Back where?"

"Palonia," Kat said, her voice as empty as Rhys's had been. "She's leading me home."

38

Katerina

Palonia - September 1147

As the sun set, the festival rites began in earnest. Gran tucked her hand under my arm and gave it a squeeze, and Kyla bounced our little brother on her knee. Tegan, six years old, was watching the festivities with the wide eyes of a novice. This wasn't his first big festival, but it was the first time he was old enough to appreciate the revelries. Our other two brothers were off somewhere causing chaos, no doubt.

"It's time!" Alodie shouted as she joined our small party. She thrust a flask in my face. "Drink up."

She sounded more than a little tipsy as she wobbled on her feet.

I took the cup, and the sharp, sour smell of the wine made me wrinkle my nose. "Gods, Alodie, what is this?"

"The ritual wine! I made it myself." She nudged my arm. "Go on. You don't want to anger the gods. Everyone gets a sip."

I cleared my throat to get rid of the sickly smell of spirits on her breath. They mixed unpleasantly with the hint of lavender water she must have bathed in this morning. She made no move to back off, and if she stayed close any longer, I worried I might gag.

To get her away from me, I took a sip, then spat on the ground, gasping for air. The lingering flavour was salty and foul, and I spat again as I handed the cup back to her. "Sweet mother, Alodie, what did you put in here? Feces?"

Her face fell. "Why does everyone keep saying that? Too many spices? I thought I did such a good job this year." Her grin returned, and she winked. "Ah well, wine is wine, am I right? The effects are the same. Come on, everyone. One sip to honour the gods!"

She passed the cup around to my family. Kyla retched into the grass, and even Gran wrinkled her nose in distaste. When Shep dipped his coated finger into Rowan's mouth, my baby boy's face squished with disgust. He writhed to get out of my grip and escape the taste. I didn't blame him.

As soon as Alodie finished torturing my family, she spun away and danced towards another group.

"Tonight, after she passes out, we'll set fire to anything that's left," Shep said. "No one should have to suffer that evil again. She makes people miserable enough without the wine."

We shared a laugh at Alodie's expense and turned our attention to a group of dancers who had created balls of fire in their hands, tossing them back and forth within a circle made of whip-like flames from another group.

"I wish I could do that," I sighed.

Shep kissed my hair. "One day, love."

My mouth felt dry and more than a little dirty from Alodie's brew. "Does anyone have anything good to drink?"

"Not here, but I know Callum's hoarding a barrel for cooking," Kyla said. "Why don't you go charm him into sneaking you a skin? He's always had a soft spot for you."

Shep winked at me. "You have my blessing if it means rinsing this taste out of my mouth."

I handed Rowan to him and headed across the field towards one of the larger cooking pots. A dozen people stood around it waiting for their bowls to be filled, and Callum shot me a look over his fuzzy eyebrows as he ladled out the stew.

"Back for more food?" he asked.

"Something to drink. We need to wash out Alodie's blend."

Laughter ran through the line as everyone grimaced and spat, agreeing with my assessment.

Callum grunted and snuck me the small leather skin off his

belt. "Here, but don't spread around I gave it to you, or I'll have the whole village badgering me."

I grinned at him and took a swig of the red. "Much better."

He swatted his arm and gave it a scratch. "Damn bugs. You'd think all the fire smoke would keep them away, but the last few minutes they haven't left me alone."

"You taste too sweet." I kissed his cheek before heading back to my family. Mother and Father had joined the others, and Kyla watched me eagerly as I approached.

"Anything?" she asked.

"Just this." I tossed her the flask. "Don't be greedy."

Kyla sipped the wine as she scratched her belly.

Rowan squirmed in Shep's arms, his face red. Small noises of discomfort gurgled in his throat.

"Want your momma?" Shep asked.

I took my baby and held him to my breast, but his little hands pushed me away, and the gurgles turned to whimpers.

"What's wrong, little one?" I bounced him gently in my arms.

It didn't help. He reached up and scratched at his neck, squalling now.

I looked to Shep. "Has he been like this long?"

He shook his head, forehead drawn in concern. "No, he was fine. I saw him scratching a little, but he laughed like it tickled."

Rowan was twisting so strongly I didn't trust myself to stand and hold him.

"Let his grandmother try," Mother said.

She took him and balanced him on her knee. His bawling started Tegan going, and Kyla held our brother close to calm him.

"Did he roll in something?" I asked. "Rashweed, maybe?"

I knelt and searched my son's delicate skin for any sign of nettle stings, but it was difficult to make anything out between the fading light and flickering bonfires.

Mother couldn't restrain Rowan anymore either. His neck bled, and he had started scratching his arm.

Worry fluttered in my chest. "I don't like this. I'm going to find Mae and have her take a look at him."

"It's probably bug bites," Father assured me with a hand on my shoulder. "I've started itching, too. It's the time of year for biting flies."

"Owie!" Tegan yelled, scratching his chest.

I didn't know if his symptoms were real or if he was mirroring Rowan, but I didn't want to wait until they'd both scratched themselves bloody.

"I'd rather be sure," I said, and no one else stepped in to stop me. "I'll be back in a minute."

But Mae proved harder to find than I'd hoped. Having seen her with Alodie and Blythe not long ago, I hurried first to the younger woman's home only to find it empty.

I headed back into the crowds, determined to track her down. It seemed most of the children were suffering the same sudden skin irritation. Like Rowan, they squirmed as their parents tried to figure out what was wrong, but the longer I watched, the more I realized the problem wasn't limited to the children. Everyone had started scratching—some absently, some with a fury.

There were a few who found humour in the discomfort of others, who laughed at their plight. The laughter soon faded and confusion took its place as they fell prey to the same mysterious condition.

The sound of nails on skin buzzed in my head, and I lifted my hands to cover my ears. With my arms half-raised, I froze. My wrist was red.

Had I been scratching?

I must have been, but I didn't remember being itchy. Now that I was thinking about it, my skin caught fire. I tried not to scratch, used the heel of my palm to rub instead, but it didn't help. Soon there was blood under my nails, and a spot on my leg grew uncomfortable.

Around me, people were contorting to reach the itchiest places, expressions of confusion morphing into grimaces of pain. Some people removed items of clothing to get directly at the source. Breast, stomach, back, behind the knee, the sting struck anywhere.

I needed to get back to my family. I wanted my mother and to make sure Rowan was okay. But the more I moved, the worse the itch became until my whole body burned.

I fell to my knees. The cold earth soothed, but the prickle of dead grass tortured me. I couldn't scratch hard enough to make it stop.

What was happening?

My heart pounded with fear, and tears welled in my eyes.

Voices filled my head. A repetitive chant, soft as a whisper. I closed my eyes to listen and got caught in the monotony as it became a balm on the pain.

Then the pain returned, worse than before. I begged the voices to stop, but the pins-and-needles sensation spread to cover my entire body. I sank forward onto my hands and buried my fingers in the earth. I had to stop scratching.

With a scream, I opened my eyes. If I found the source of the chant, if I could see them, if they could see they weren't helping, they would stop. They had to stop.

It took a while—the voices seemed to echo from all directions—but eventually I spotted three women standing on a fell-top by a large pot. They stood apart from each other with their eyes closed, their voices flowing in unison.

I thought I was trapped in some illusion, that the itching, the burning pain had warped my senses. But now I recognized the voices in my head.

Blythe, Alodie, and Mae were unaffected by the mania. They were calm and itch-free, lost in the chant.

My heart flooded with relief. Mae was all right, and she was already acting. We needed to give her time to work her spell.

The burn intensified, and the chanting in my head grew louder. I couldn't hold back my screams. My blood was boiling. I needed to cool down.

In my distress, I tried to find something to focus on and seized on the chant. I couldn't make out what they were saying, but the words didn't matter. The rhythm was all I needed. I forced my breathing to match the flow of their speech and managed to step outside my body, away from the pain.

My temperature dropped, and with the rush of cold came a sweet cessation of agony. Numbness took over as frost covered my hands and the ground around me, then crept up my arms and legs like crystalline vines.

A shiver ran through me, and I gloried in it. After so many years of feeling like a failure, my unique and utterly useless skill of channelling my magic inwards instead of projecting it outwards finally had purpose.

As I got colder, my faculties returned, letting me make out what was happening.

I didn't know why, or how, but the three women were not trying to help. They were the cause. Somehow their chant had worked its way into our veins.

The rancid taste in my mouth grew stronger as bile churned in my stomach, and horror struck me again. Alodie's vile drink. It had been for a ritual but not one that had anything to do with the harvest or the gods.

They were harvesting *us*.

The screams of my kin grew louder, becoming wails of torment and terror, and I knew I had to stop the spell. But what could I do, frozen to the ground as I was, with magic weaker than my six-year-old brother's?

Blood trickled from where I'd scratched through the skin on my forearm, and I watched in fascination as it separated into small beads. On my frosted hand, it turned to ice, but from everyone else, their spilled blood gathered in puffs of red cloud. In swirls and drifts, it moved towards the sorceresses. So much of the blood mist clung to me as it passed, soft as a fine rain, until my pale skin, my clothing, the hair on my arms were coated in a shimmering red, stinking of metal and death.

The chant came to a crescendo, and at the climax, the three women sliced into their own arms and held out their hands to accept the sacrifice. The blood in the air soared towards them, encircling them, entering them.

In my mind, the voices went quiet, the power of the rhythm gone, and although I still had the impulse to scratch, still ached and screamed, it was nothing compared to what the rest of my people suffered.

I had never felt so helpless.

I couldn't see my family from where I knelt, but it broke my heart to watch the others. It hurt more than the burn of my skin. Their blood left them—I felt the pull in my own body and couldn't imagine the torture they felt—and in their state, there was nothing they could do but scratch and spill more. My sanity cracked at the thought that Rowan might be suffering along with them, the torment of that image a thousand times worse than the physical agony I endured.

Screams filled my ears. My people fell. I heaved the contents of my full stomach onto the frost-covered ground, the magic having spread from my hands to form a wide circle around me.

Little by little, the cries fell silent, and with every voice lost, my chest broke open a little more. My heart shattered, the pieces cutting my insides like dagger-sharp shards, slicing me open from within until I forgot how to breathe.

The people nearest me collapsed, and eventually my view to the dales beyond them cleared to reveal a sea of bodies. Some writhed in pain, their fingernails tearing holes in their flesh, while others already lay still.

I watched my grandmother crumple to the ground, and a wail tore out of me as I caught sight of familiar clothes on familiar bodies at her feet. Everyone gone—my baby boy, my little brother.

More shrieks clogged my lungs, too many to expel.

Drawn by movement to my left, my gaze shifted of its own volition to watch Mae, Alodie, and Blythe throw their hands up in victory. The light of the bonfires danced over them, transforming their shadows into great, shuddering monsters. Their cheers echoed the screams of terror of the people they'd sacrificed.

Yet as I watched, their faces changed, becoming lined with the same horror that had been written on the faces of their victims. Mae fell first. Blythe's eyes widened, and she flailed out her arms to grab at nothing before she collapsed. Alodie stood the longest and seemed to be pulling herself away from some unseen force, then she too dropped.

I closed my eyes and forced myself to look away, not wanting to feel grief at their deaths. They deserved whatever came for them.

Somehow, I remained. Alive. Alone.

39

Katerina

THE MEMORY OF that last night in Palonia chased me for the next twelve hours.

I buried the images in the task of arranging flights and packing whatever potions and weapons we might need, but I couldn't escape the pull into the past.

And now I stood in silence, so close to where my worst nightmare had taken place. The empty hills stretched out in front of me, the green grass blowing in the soft wind, the crystalline lake rippling across the surface.

For now, I was alone. Murisa and Poppy would remain at the B&B as they took on Abigail's demon from afar, while Rhys, Gavin, and Barrett were on my trail, keeping their distance, allowing me to scout ahead.

So much had changed in these hills. There were houses where there had been rock and footpaths where there had been grass.

Even the water had changed—the banks having eroded. The perfect mirror reflection of its surface had lost some of its purity, stained with pollution.

I wondered at my surprise to find things so different, as if I'd expected everything to stay the same.

Then I heard bleating and laughed through the tears that had unknowingly gathered behind my eyelids. The Herdwick sheep were still here, anyway.

My laughter and the familiarity of the woollen bundles, some of them overly shaggy and ranging from dark brown to light grey, cut through my tension, and I carried on, positive now that I knew the way. These were my hills—my fells—and although I'd only spent twenty-four years here, it was the only place my heart of hearts considered home.

The sun grew hotter as the hours went on, but I picked my way slowly, ready for traps, for enchanted stones, for magic to come flying at me. By the time I reached the crest above what had been Palonia, sweat dripped down my face and tickled the backs of my knees. The only thing out of the ordinary was the lack of people. At this time of day and this time of year, these fells should have been dotted with tourists, hikers, or people looking to soak in the beauty of the area. But there was no one.

As though everyone sensed the presence of evil and thought it wisest to stay away.

I didn't doubt Abigail was here somewhere, watching me alongside her demon. Our plan—as all my plans seemed to be—was hastily thrown together and depended on many elements outside our power, and I prayed I was able to keep everything on track. I had to keep Abigail's attention on me to give the others time to get into position. Protected by their amulets, the guys would scatter our fresh batch of enchanted stones around the fells, keeping a call open with Muroppy in case I was lucky enough to wheedle the demon's name from Abigail's shrivelled mouth. Once we dealt with her demon, we could finally deal with her.

The fact that Barrett had agreed to carry the stones was evidence of his determination to tear this woman to shreds. I worried how Gavin would handle facing family, but he assured me Abigail could throw the word *grandmother* around as much as she chose. Since she'd never been in his life, she meant nothing to him.

Rhys had cautiously attempted to trigger another vision, but nothing had come. Only a sense that we were walking into something big.

I knew it. Emotionally. Magically. Psychologically. The fight I faced would hit me on every level. But I finally had a chance to avenge my family and fulfill the promise I'd made to my grandmother to keep everyone safe. Back then, she'd rested her hand on my arm and told me that was beyond anyone's power. She'd been right, of course. Then.

Not today.

I squeezed my hands at my sides and summoned my magic, resisting the tug of the past trying to drag me back through the years.

Time ticked by, and I remained in my place, looking down on the bare fields and finding no trace of anything ever having been here. I didn't know if it would have been easier to see a hint of my childhood or the nothingness in front of me that meant only my memories existed.

No magic lingered in the air or in the soil. Nature had done her job in wiping it out. In the emptiness, I might have found it impossible to believe I hadn't dreamed those long-lost years.

The wind blew, and for an instant, I caught a familiar smell—a hint of lavender the women used to steep in their washing water. I closed my eyes, and, like an illusion, they were there. Below me were the rows of thatched houses, the whinny of horses in the stables, children laughing.

A breeze brushed my cheek, and it was Kyla running past me, laughing as she stripped the shirt over her fourteen-year-old head. "Come on, Kate, I'll race you to the water!"

The scent of gasoline from some unseen caravan became the smell of cooking fires, and the call of swans became the clanging gong announcing the supper hour.

The wind in my hair was my mother running her fingers through its lengths, lamenting its tangles and knots. "You really should take better care of this mess, Katerina. You'll catch a bird if you're not careful."

Grandmother standing beside us, chiding Momma for being overbearing.

The tears drying on my cheeks were Shep's kisses the day I told him I carried his child.

All this I remembered, imagined, just by standing on a patch of earth that had once been filled with life. It was reassuring to know they were still here. That their magic and memories had joined with the essence of the earth and would never truly be gone.

In their own way, they stood with me to face what was to come.

Embracing a wave of courage, I descended the fell and strode to the middle of the empty field, my feet following old lanes out of habit.

I walked past the dining hall and the council hall that had never been finished, past my house where I had lived so comfortably in a single room with nine other people. Visions of my clan followed me, coming and going as the memories of each place flowed.

It was when I reached the dale where my world had fallen

apart that my knees trembled again, the images that had hung around me for the past day nearly overpowering me. I wanted to leave, but there was nowhere to go. This was where I had to be.

Bile rose in my throat, and my skin started to itch, as though the effects of the centuries-old ritual lingered.

Here, only one memory remained for me, each frame of the scene seared into my mind like the dragon tattooed on my thigh. I saw where each body lay. I saw my arms drenched in my people's blood as the mist rose around me.

I saw Emrick crouched over the last remaining corpse as he turned it to dirt.

Today, he was waiting at the B&B with Muroppy. As much as I'd wanted him with me to lend me courage, I'd stayed strong. Before leaving, I'd curled my fingers into the front of his shirt and clung to him, wishing I could keep him close. But if he was here when Abigail arrived, he would feel the need to help me, promise be damned. The only safe place for him was far away from me.

"I love you, *mîn hiertan*," he'd whispered against my hair. "Please be safe."

His voice, filled with love and fear, drifted around me and settled in my centre, bolstering me.

I wasn't about to collapse. I wasn't about to run screaming.

I'd worried I might when I'd arrived in Ambleside and made the journey towards my past, but now that I was here, I felt nothing but rage. Rage against the woman who'd caused me such pain and who, eight hundred and fifty years later, continued to torment me. The woman who apparently hated me so much she'd chosen to waste her immortality stripping away everything I loved.

What a sad, miserable life she led.

Had led. Past tense. Because after today, she wouldn't be breathing.

The smell reached me before anything else, the scent of lavender growing stronger. Almost sickening. It was the same scent that had taunted me outside the burning occult shop, in the hotel in Toronto, in the warehouse outside Oakville.

Abigail was here.

The traitor who'd murdered my family.

The woman who should have been dead.

"Well, well, Kate," a frail voice said. "I wondered if you'd show."

I forced myself to turn around and face her. In the light of the fading afternoon, she wasn't hidden in shadows. There were no trees, no crowds, nothing for her to duck behind. Except for a face I didn't recognize.

Her grey hair was pulled into a thick braid that fell over her shoulder, and lipstick—a shade of pink that did nothing for her complexion—stained her wrinkled lips. She grinned, revealing crooked yellow teeth.

I blinked at her, searching for the woman I knew beneath all those wrinkles, but the only similarity was the cruel glint in her eyes. The one I remembered all too well as threatening a bad time ahead.

The teacher who'd made me believe I would always be a failure.

Alodie.

Her eyes brightened as she watched my recognition dawn.

"Do you know how many times I've walked past you, and you had no idea? Do you know how *long* I've waited for this moment? Decades, Katerina."

My thoughts were too frazzled to form words, too many questions tumbling over each other. The first one to spill out was, "Why?"

Why are you still alive?

Why are you old?

Why are you trying to kill me?

Why now?

It didn't matter which one she answered as long as she tore down the veil of my ignorance.

Her grin widened, and the air crackled with electricity as she summoned lightning into her palms. She had no gloves to help channel her power, and the sparks crept up her arms until the sleeves of her pale blue cardigan smoked.

"I can't believe you're still wearing those gloves," she hissed, as though she'd read my mind. "How ironic that of everything you took with you, it should be those."

She threw out a lightning bolt, and I lurched out of the way, rolling across the grass and jumping back to my feet in a crouch, ready to leap again. She was coming in strong, but that could only help us. If she was focused on hurting me, I hoped she wouldn't notice the others approaching.

"You should have stayed in the infernal realms," I said, stating it as fact to test Emrick's theory.

She barked out a cry of frustration and let loose another bolt, but I was already moving, drawing fire into my hands. Emrick and I had spent more time training before our flight to England. My body was loose, my magic primed, but it wouldn't benefit me for Abigail—*Alodie*—to know that yet.

"You summoned Shogaur." I ran a circle around her to keep her off balance. She tottered on her bad left leg but didn't fall. "How did you know about him?"

"Gossip spreads quickly in hell," she spat. More lightning, this time immediately ahead of me. I veered to the side and teetered on the edge of the fell. The earth was scorched black where I'd almost stood.

"What about the ritual?" I pushed. "You gave it to Mikhail. Did you want company for the rest of your long, lonely life?"

I reversed the flow of my magic and set my hand on the ground. Frost zipped across the grass and covered Alodie's orthopedic running shoes in a lacy pattern. She scowled at me and danced away from it. I had to remember she was more spry than she appeared. She'd darted through the trees around Adrian's house like a woman in her prime.

"He wouldn't have lived long. He would have been bound to the same demon we were, and the moment he reached the pinnacle of the ritual, I would have killed him and taken the power for myself. Turned back time and been what you are."

"Why?" I asked. "Why are you old? You look three times your age."

Alodie's expression contorted with more unrestrained fury. "That spell was supposed to bind us to eternal life—eternal *youth*. We were supposed to summon the demon to this plane, link our souls to it, and keep it chained. As long as that demon survived, we would channel its power, its stasis, its immortality. Instead, this bastard dragged us to hell, and it's all your fault!"

Confusion hit me with more punch than her lightning bolt. She blamed *me* for their failure?

A flash of light made me turn my head to take in the hulking creature that stood behind me. It wasn't nearly as tall as Shogaur, its skin grey and peeling. The reek of sulphur blocked out the sweeter aromas of the felltop air, and I worked hard not to gag.

"Mae and Blythe chose to fall rather than be dragged into that reeking pit, but I"—she jabbed her finger into her chest—"I accepted the sacrifice. I knew what I would gain." She pulled her teeth back in a snarl. "But what did I get? Centuries in a sulphuric prison. I was bound, yes, but imprisoned. For eight hundred4 years, Katerina. Immortal. Beautiful. *Waiting*."

As far as I was concerned, she'd earned every year of torment.

"Until finally—finally—Fegor was summoned, and I was free."

There it was. We had the name. I prayed that my team was close enough to have heard it and that Muroppy knew what to do with it. All I could do now was keep going, keep Alodie's eyes on me—make myself the target so the others could set their trap.

I sent my thoughts to Emrick, hoping with everything I was that I would see him again.

"You can imagine my horror when, as the years passed, I began to age," Alodie continued, squeezing her hand into a fist. "At first, I thought it was the shift to this polluted air that turned my red hair grey and added wrinkles to my flawless skin. I thought it was the exposure to these electronic devices that have become more pervasive than all the magic in Palonia."

Her lip curled. "And then to find out within a year of my freedom that *you* had survived. That *you* had maintained your youth and your power, bonded to some *spirit*. Useless, magic-less, spineless *you*. Whatever you did to get in our way, you'll make up for it now."

She followed her spew of hatred with a lightning blast that shot in all directions, leaving me nowhere to run. I turned at the last moment and was struck in the arm instead of the chest.

The pain of electricity dancing along my nerves was unbearable, and I didn't bother trying to hold back my screams as I fought against the full burst of its charge.

Alodie cackled, but she hadn't anticipated the fact that I'd learned more than a few tricks since our old training days. Her spell circles had caught me off guard, but I'd expected this attack. Clenching my teeth against the agony, I grabbed hold of my magic and used it to turn hers against her, redirecting the electrical charge.

She shrieked and flew backwards into the grass, her frail form slumping into the dirt. She spat out blood as she rolled from her back onto her stomach and attempted to push herself up. A wheezing noise reached me from where she wobbled to her feet, and it took a while for me to realize she was laughing.

Strong arms wrapped around my middle, trapping my hands. Alodie's accusations had left me too stunned to notice her demon's approach, and I cursed my lack of awareness. The reek of sulphur wafted up my nose, tickling my gag reflex. I struggled against the demon, but its iron grip was too tight. Channelling magic through my arms, I pumped fire along the surface of my skin. Fegor's arms heated, turned molten red, but it didn't react. The bastard was impervious, and I was wasting energy.

Alodie rose to her feet, limped towards me, and wrapped her hands around my throat.

"For years, I tried to kill you, until I realized you had to be the reason everything went wrong. I want my youth back. I want my *life* back. It's time to return what you stole."

A deep dread awoke in my gut as I guessed what was coming. Sure enough, she pulled out a vial filled with a familiar red liquid. The hand around my throat grew hot, hotter, and when I opened my mouth to scream, she used her other thumb to pop the cork on the vial and poured the foul drink into my mouth. I choked on the disgusting potion and spat it into her face, but just like with Mikhail, I knew it was too late. Enough had made it into my system that I was vulnerable to her ritual.

"You think you have enough time to cast it?" I wheezed.

Her sneer widened, and her lips moved in a soundless incantation. All around us, pillars of fire shot into the sky as she set off the enchanted stones she must have planted ahead of time. "I have all the time I need. No one's getting through to you. Goodbye, Kate."

40

Katerina

THE HEAT FROM the circle of fire caused sweat to bead on my brow and Alodie's makeup to drip down her face. Unfortunately, her discomfort didn't prevent her from chanting the familiar words under her breath.

Unlike Mikhail, she didn't turn the ritual into a big production. She wasn't performing, she was carrying out a task, each word quick and steady.

I swung my legs back, landing solid kicks near the demon's knees, but its hold didn't loosen. I tried more fire with the same results. I reversed my heat to summon ice into my hands, but the space between me and the demon's chest was too tight to wield the ice shards I'd formed, and the demon showed no more response to being frozen than it had to being burned. I was stuck, and as Alodie chanted, a burning itch swept over my skin.

My heart raced. My stomach churned. The heat from the fires did nothing to help my rising anxiety. The activated spell circles would keep Barrett and the others from reaching the valley, and the timer was running down for me. With the speed of Alodie's chanting, I gave myself three minutes, if I was lucky, before she reached the pinnacle of the ritual. And this time, it didn't matter if I covered my whole body in frost. She didn't need me to scratch myself raw. All she had to do was slice my throat with the knife peeking out from under her cardigan and she'd get what she wanted.

A scream escaped me as the itch, the desire—the *need*—to tear my fingers into my flesh to relieve the agony grew worse. I squirmed in Fegor's grasp, gagged at the stink of sulphur creeping up my nose, and tried to block out Alodie's voice grating against my ears.

Over her left shoulder, a tall, slender figure with a mop of red hair prowled along the edge of the fire. My reinforcements were here. Relief, fear, and exhilaration poured through me, but I forced myself to keep squirming, raising my screams to block out any sounds that might alert Alodie to the fact that we weren't alone on the felltop.

Had they heard Fegor's name? Were Muroppy performing miracles back at the B&B? With no way to ask, I could only continue playing my part and cross my fingers my rash plan worked.

Alodie's chant grew louder, faster, and my vision wavered. Black crept along the edges, making it harder to focus on Rhys as he ran in a crouch along the outside of the fiery circle. There was still no sign of Barrett or Gavin, and I hoped they knew how tight our time was.

A sudden hiss cut through Alodie's rapid chant—not from her but from behind me. Fegor's grip tightened so much I lost the ability to breathe, and its grey, clammy skin grew warm, hot, scalding. I screamed again, this time not having to force its pitch as my shirt smoked and my skin steamed.

A bright white light flashed, and I squeezed my eyes shut, leaving me unprepared to hit the ground before I slammed against it.

Alodie cursed, breaking the ritual, and I rolled onto my back to find Fegor trapped in a stasis circle, the glowing cage of magic having bound it to the spot. Muroppy had come through. Now we had to kill it.

Enjoying the reprieve from the maddening itch, I summoned my ice, ready to drive a shard into its throat and tear off its head. The zing of electricity drew my attention back to Alodie just in time to avoid a lightning bolt before it hit me in the back. I dropped to the ground and rolled away from the strike before returning her attack with one of my own. She dodged it, but missed my follow-up. Fire spread across her cardigan, and she stripped it off before the flames spread.

"Why now?" I asked, needing to hold her attention.

She looked down her nose at me, an expression I remembered too well. "I'm in constant pain, Kate. My hip is going out on me, my knee is shot, my eyesight is failing. I'm aging, and I'll keep aging. I will never die. Do you know what a nightmare that is? I was given this chance with you, and I don't intend to squander it."

All around us, the pillars of fire began to peter out, as though someone had flicked a switch on her enchanted stones. My eye fell on Barrett. He'd dressed in drab colours to blend in with the scenery and was running from stone to stone, spraying each one with some kind of pink liquid in a spray bottle. A nullifying potion.

Before Alodie could pin Barrett down, another voice called out from our right. "Hey, Grandma! Long time no see."

Gavin stepped into view. He was dressed in black, his expression twisted in disdain. I wanted to use his distraction to attack the demon, but Alodie was in my way.

Her eye twitched. "You. Apparently this is my day to face all my past mistakes."

Fury flashed through me along with the desire to throw her words back at her, but this exchange had nothing to do with me.

"Your mother was supposed to be my solution, and wasn't, and *you* should have been Shogaur's tool," Alodie spat. "It's all you were ever good for."

If her cutting words hit home, Gavin didn't show it. He pulled his lips back in a sneer. "Too bad for you, I've never been one to play by someone else's rules. I'll tell Mom not to expect you at the next family reunion."

He launched a giant fireball at Alodie, and it struck her full on. She stumbled backwards and hit the ground, and I charged towards Fegor.

But Alodie hadn't let up her practice during her time away. She summoned her own fire to consume her grandson's, and in less time than it took for me to draw magic into my palms, she was on her feet, hurling two fireballs at me and Gavin.

Gavin ducked and rolled, but she threw a lightning bolt after her fire, and I only had time to shout before the lightning struck him in the chest. He flew beyond the fell and out of sight. I ran to where he'd stood and stared at his body lying still at the bottom of the incline.

Why wasn't he moving? Had the amulet failed?

Red smeared my vision, and I turned back to Alodie. She didn't look smug over her win—she looked pissed.

"It ends here, Kate," she rasped. "After I destroy you, I'm taking the rest of your friends down as well, just to spite your memory. I hope you rest in eternal torment knowing how badly you failed."

More lightning sparked between her palms, and I responded

by summoning my fire whip. She raised her hands to unleash her spell, and I lashed out, wrapping the whip around her arm and redirecting the bolt towards her demon. She cried out in pain as the demon slumped to the ground, the stink of char joining that of sulphur.

But both were back on their feet too quickly, and the demon was making progress pressing its way through the stasis circle. Already an arm was out, its talons raking the air towards me.

I had to put that demon down.

I braced for Alodie to aim her next assault at me, but she feinted and launched her lightning to the right. Rhys cried out as sparks rippled over his body, and he tumbled out of sight behind the rise with—in my opinion—exaggerated jerkiness. I cried out and ran towards him, but when I looked over the side, he was nowhere to be seen. I hoped that meant he'd been able to dart away and not that he'd rolled too far for me to find him.

On shaking legs, my heart thrashing against my ribs, I turned back to Alodie and summoned lightning of my own. The bolts arced across the fell, but Alodie caught one and absorbed it before it struck her. The sparks flickered over her hands before they disappeared, and without stopping to catch her breath, she raised her hand and muttered a word in Fegor's direction.

The stasis circle faded, leaving it free to lurch towards me. It made to grab me, but I shifted the source of my magic, tapping into the moisture that danced in the air. I summoned ice crystals into my hands and launched them at the demon's eyes. They latched to its skull, and frost spread over its head and down its arms. With the demon at a disadvantage, I prepared to throw my shards, but another bolt of lightning hit me in the side and sent me airborne.

The air whooshed out of me as I hit the ground, and my thoughts scattered, rushing to piece themselves together. When I sat up, Abigail stood between me and Fegor. She was so damn strong. For all my training, all my growth, I was no match for her.

My muscles ached. I stretched out my arms and back, popping the joints to relieve the tension, giving my flesh and bone time to heal. My magic might not compare with hers, but I was still here, still fighting. As long as I could direct this battle, we stood a chance. My team was out there dropping stones of our own. One good fiery spell circle would be enough to take her down once her demon was dead—I just had to keep the pressure on.

She threw a burst of lightning at me, and I rolled out of the way and onto my feet. I lobbed a fireball in her direction. She switched from lightning to fire, grabbed my spell and whirled it back at me. I dodged to the side, and the fire sailed over the fell to hit the mere below. It landed with a sizzle, steam wafting up into the beautiful afternoon sunlight.

Barrett appeared over the western rise. He dropped his chin

in a nod and vanished again. Our stones were in place—now to get Alodie into our trap. Once the demon was removed from the equation, it would be her turn.

I shot a few tiny fireballs at Alodie's feet, pushing her backwards, farther away from Barrett. She smirked at my show of weakening power, but I ignored her amusement and continued my barrage. It was barely enough to warm her toes, but it was all I needed.

"Surrender, Alodie. I can do you the favour of making your end painless."

She barked a laugh. "Kill me? No, no, Kate. Not after all this time. I didn't make deals with a bunch of pitiful mundanes only to hand myself over to you willingly."

I balked. Mundanes?

She scowled, but her frown slid into a sly smile when she noticed Barrett creeping across the fell.

"Watch out!" I shouted, but not quickly enough as a lightning bolt flew out and struck him in the chest. I screamed as he collapsed to the ground, his hands clasped to his middle, his face contorted in pain.

"You may have gained some power, but you're still weak, aren't you, Kate?" Alodie hobbled in Barrett's direction, favouring her left hip. "Weak enough that you turn to your pets to help you. Never willing to fight your own battles."

Rhys appeared over the next rise, and confusion filled

Alodie's expression. She fired a lightning bolt his way, but he was paying attention and rolled down to avoid the hit. Unfortunately, he rolled towards us instead of away, putting him directly in Alodie's line of fire.

My pulse raced as I threw another fireball to draw her attention back to me. Barrett shook himself off and rose to his feet, and this time uncertainty flickered across Alodie's eyes as she backed away from him.

She couldn't know that my team had lost their protection against her. I had to keep her focused on me to give them time to escape.

"They're not useless." I stepped towards her. "You may think you know me, but I've come a long way since the poor, sad, failed student in Palonia." Another step closer. "Tell me who summoned Fegor."

Again I phrased it as a statement. I couldn't believe someone had summoned her demon by chance. Not after everything that had followed.

Her uncertainty fled as she laughed. The air between us shimmered seconds before an intense blast of energy burst from her hands and shoved me backwards—right next to the glimmer of an enchanted stone she'd yet to activate.

She'd managed to get me into her minefield, and if I didn't want to go the way of Adrian with one misstep, I had to get her into ours.

"You're going to kill me, anyway," I said. "What does it matter if you tell me? Don't you want me to know who betrayed me? Again?"

Alodie laughed but shook her head as she pumped more magic into her hands and pressed in on me. I checked over my shoulder and cursed. There were at least three glittering stones for me to navigate around or risk getting fried if Alodie set them off.

"Oh, Katerina. Always feeling sorry for yourself. Does it matter who sent me? So many people want you dead. I'm just the lucky one who gets to deliver the final blow."

She raised her hands, and I raised mine, aware that I'd have to expend most of my remaining power to fend off the coming onslaught. Before she grabbed hold of her lightning bolts, her scream of rage rent the air, and a flash of white light even brighter than before wiped out my vision.

When it cleared, the demon was on its knees, trapped in another stasis circle—but this time, the light didn't stay white. It darkened to a deep, blood red, and Fegor threw itself at the sides of the cage, desperate to get out.

"No!" Alodie shouted. She raised her hand to counter the magic, and I gathered my power to flick a tiny fireball at her hair.

She shrieked and slapped at her head, and her opportunity to save the demon binding her to this earth passed without action. The light brightened, and the cage closed in, the lines of the circle slicing through its body like so many knives. The demon roared with such intense fury my bones trembled.

In another breath, the demon's severed remains littered the grass. The light faded, the circle disappeared... and Alodie was mortal.

She clutched her burned head and backed away from me, directly into our scattering of stones.

Behind me, Barrett, Rhys, and Gavin came up over the rise. They kept their distance, knowing the broken sorceress in front of us was far from helpless, but I appreciated their support.

On exhausted legs, I walked towards her. "Who sent you after me, Alodie? You have nothing to lose by telling me. It's too late for that."

She looked down at the ground, alarm written in her eyes as she took in the dark rocks near her feet, their magic primed and waiting. Disbelief, uncertainty. I read the questions spinning through her head. Had I gotten my hands on the same arsenal she'd used against us? Would I have the courage to activate them?

My smile spread, and I hoped it hid the tremble in my hands. My heart ached. I was facing the woman who had killed my family, who had killed Adrian, and I felt none of the satisfaction I'd imagined I would.

I'd hoped for closure, but as I stared into clear brown eyes filled with concern for herself and hatred of me, I accepted I wouldn't get it from her.

The pain in my heart hardened, swept away beneath a current of rage, and I crossed the last few feet between us until I stood less than an inch away. "Who. Sent. You? Who else wants me dead?"

The corner of her lip curled. "Seems to me that's a waste of a question, Katerina. I wonder if you'll ask the right one in time. Think of me when they come for you—it won't be long now."

She winked at me, and dread filled my stomach as she dropped a rock at her feet. One of hers that she'd held back. She spoke the incantation, and the stone lit up.

"No!" I reached out to grab her, desperate not to let her steal my vengeance. But I was already too late.

It took seconds.

Seconds for Barrett to grab me around the middle and jerk me backwards.

Seconds for Gavin to roll Rhys through the grass and down the fell away from the blossoming spell circles.

Seconds for the flames to erupt and capture Alodie the same way they had Adrian.

Her screams filled the silent pockets of the area as the fire engulfed her. The stench of burning flesh seeped into my nose and poured down the back of my throat, leaving me gasping for breath so I didn't vomit.

But as soon as those seconds had passed, there was no trace of the woman who had haunted me for centuries. Of the sorceress who had stolen my family from me.

With the death of her screams came the final death of my past.

41

Emrick

I PACED THE length of the living room of the Sleeping Maiden, the bed-and-breakfast Kat had rented out for the weekend.

Murisa was asleep on the couch with her head on Poppy's lap, and Poppy watched me with narrowed eyes. "You're making me dizzy. Kat's got this. You know she does."

I wanted to believe her. Everything in me refused to conceive of any other possibility. But why hadn't she contacted us yet?

We'd heard everything that had happened on those hills—right until the end. Barrett had kept his phone on, slinking close enough to listen but staying far enough away to relay what he learned without being noticed. He'd passed along the demon's name and Abigail's threats. The close call with that fucking ritual. He'd warned Muroppy when the demon escaped the stasis circle. Without him, the witches wouldn't have known to recast it and follow it up with a more offensive attack.

Then the call had cut out, and we'd heard nothing since.

It had been half an hour since Murisa had cast the spell to kill the demon. It had taken everything out of her to do it from such a distance, but Poppy had lent her strength, and they'd succeeded.

So why hadn't we heard from the others? They were supposed to have called as soon as the fight was over. I sensed the pull of Abigail's soul on the edge of the afterlife, so I knew she was dead—the bitch could wait—and the tether in my chest remained strong… so where was Kat?

Thoughts of Death stealing her away from me again ripped their claws through my composure. I paced another round, tearing at my hair, checking the clock over the mantel, peering out the window for any sign of Kat's rental car driving up the road.

The floor creaked above us as the landlady went about her business. We'd asked her for privacy, and she'd wisely complied. I wasn't sure the woman could have handled the candle smoke and smells that had come from the witches' various attempts to bind the demon.

What if Abigail had bested them? Yes, she was dead, but that didn't mean she hadn't stolen my life in the process. Kat had gone in prepared for anything, but I knew she'd also been prepared to fail.

I raised my hand to summon the mist. "I'm going to take a look."

"No, you're not," Poppy said, as if she could stop me. "You promised kitty Kat you'd stay here. What if you see something you don't like? You step in and lose your soul. Then Kat will be all mopey and pathetic, and we won't be able to do anything with her."

"And if something's happened to her?" I shot back.

She shrugged. "You'll disappear into the afterlife and do your moping somewhere else."

Her words were casual, but her fingers were stiff as they stroked through Murisa's hair. She was no more relaxed about the delay than I was.

All the more reason to take a quick look. Hands off, I promised myself.

I raised my hand again just as the front door opened and Barrett strode in carrying Kat in his arms. She was awake, if barely, and in rough shape. Her clothes were burned, and large red welts marred her neck. Anger prickled under my skin along with the wish that I could do more to Abigail's soul than escort her into the afterlife.

Death must have known it or had staked its claim. My awareness of the sorceress's soul vanished in a blink—no longer my problem. Maybe for the best, but a growl of unsatisfied rage rumbled through me.

"What the hell, guys?" Poppy said. "I count four of you, and you all have hands. Where was our fucking phone call?"

"Phones got fried," Barrett said.

Rhys and Gavin shuffled in behind them, neither looking any worse for wear beyond exhaustion and shock. Rhys pulled out his phone—what was left of it—and tossed it on the coffee table. "We all got a dose of Alodie's lightning. The amulets kept us alive—the tech wasn't so lucky."

Kat tapped Barrett's shoulder, and he set her down. She reached for me, and I caught her as her legs gave out from under her.

"I'm all right," she said. "Tired, but fine. The rest of me will heal."

"Who was it?" Not that it mattered, but I thought it important that she say the name.

"Alodie. Direct attacks to the last. Mae and Blythe never made it to the infernal realms."

I covered her face in gentle kisses before reaching her lips and pulling her tight against me. Our kiss deepened, growing more urgent, until Poppy cleared her throat.

Kat looked towards them with a feeble smile. "Your timing was perfect, Muroppy."

Poppy grinned. "Glad to hear it, kitty Kat." Then she snorted. "Muroppy."

"There's no better team," Murisa said around a yawn as she sat up and stretched her arms over her head.

Kat looked around at all of them. "I'm glad that team is mine."

I bundled her against me and dropped into the nearest chair. She rested her head against my shoulder, her forehead tucked into the crook of my neck. "It's over. She's gone for good." She rolled her head towards Gavin as he came around to settle on the couch. "I'm sorry your grandmother tried to kill you. And called you good for nothing. She's wrong, you know. You were pretty heroic today."

I looked him over, spotted the burn marks on his shirt. Muroppy's amulet had done its job, but it had been close. I tightened my arms around Kat. If Gavin had taken such a hit, Kat must have taken a hundred times worse.

"I'm glad to have the mystery of her cleared up," he said. "There were always questions. Never a family occasion where she wasn't mentioned. Now I'll know, even if no one else does. There's some closure to that."

"I'm glad." Kat smiled, but I heard the underlying note in her voice. Sorrow. Jealousy?

I pressed another kiss into her hair.

"I should call Mum." Rhys's voice was gravelly with fatigue as he shuffled out of the room.

Barrett clenched his jaw, and my thoughts travelled the

same direction his must have gone. He didn't have anyone to check in with. His family was here—with us—whether he liked it or not.

"You guys did really good," Kat said to him. "I worried for a minute you'd thought better of helping me."

Barrett crossed his arms, his expression blank. "I got what I wanted out of it. The bitch suffered."

"Not as much as she should have," Gavin said. "She chose her own end, and that pisses me off."

No one argued with him.

"What now?" Murisa looked around the room as though braced for some new threat to barge through the door.

"Now we take a breath," Kat said. "Then we go home and finish cleaning up Alodie's mess. Poppy needs to set up a new shop, Adrian—Adrian's house needs to be renovated and his library salvaged."

Barrett nodded. "I've got appointments booked already. Shouldn't take more than a few weeks to get it all back to the way it was."

"You're going to stay?" I asked, surprised. I would have thought he'd leave the magical world behind now that his tie to it had been severed.

He nodded and shoved his hands in his pockets as he turned to look out the window. "It's my home."

We ignored the huskiness of his emotion, giving him a

moment, and silence descended on the room.

Unlike the last time, when we'd sat around the dining table in Adrian's half-burned house, this silence was calm. The threat was gone, our friend had been avenged. It was the best outcome.

Yet Kat never relaxed in my arms, and by the way she chewed on the side of her thumb, her thoughts were anywhere but in the room. For the time being, I let it slide, but I had a feeling our problems were far from over.

42

Katerina

THE NEXT MORNING, those not able to travel by the Emrick Express headed to the airport to fly home. I'd said goodbye at the door of the B&B, then asked Emrick to take me into the fells.

He didn't say anything, but understanding flowed off him as though he were sending it through our tether. Along with no small amount of concern for me and my mental state.

Which was probably fair. Right now, my mental state was as much a question mark to myself as it was to him.

In all the years I'd run through what I would say to the women who'd stolen my son from me, it had never played out the way it had yesterday. I'd ranted and raved at them. Tore at their eyes with my fingernails to vent the centuries of fury and grief that had chased me across the world.

Then I'd killed them. Over and over again. In so many ways, I'd lost track. My favourite had been letting my fire slowly creep over their limbs, consuming them the way Shogaur's Crusaders had nearly defeated me.

I'd imagined feeling victorious. Satisfied. Relieved.

Instead, I felt empty.

And, in ways I couldn't begin to comprehend, sad.

For a moment, I cleared my thoughts, closed my eyes, and breathed in the familiar air of a place that, I realized now, was no longer my home.

Palonia had been a part of my life for barely a fraction of a second compared to how much I'd seen and experienced since then. Something that, despite all the passing years, hadn't sunk in until today.

To my fractured heart, it had only been weeks ago that I'd danced on these fields with Kyla. That Shep had put his arms around me. That I'd held Rowan to my breast and made him giggle with kisses.

Weeks since my sister had dared me to challenge the cockatrice homing in on our territory and we'd nearly burned down the village.

My brothers' laughter, my parents' lectures, my grandmother's gentle words of wisdom.

Their voices echoed in the rustle of the wind in the grass

and the bleating of the sheep as the creatures returned to their grazing, the danger over.

Tears rolled down my cheeks, hot and heavy but silent. And as each one fell, I said my goodbyes to those I'd lost. Not tucking them back in their precious boxes to deal with later, but an actual, proper goodbye for the first time in eight hundred and fifty years. It was something I'd never had the courage to do, too afraid that once I put them behind me, I would be left with nothing.

But that was no longer true. I had as much now as I'd had then, and although I'd lost Adrian, one of my two anchors in this world, I knew his voice—like Gran's, like Mother's and Rowan's, even like Alodie's—would linger a long while, never truly disappearing so long as I remembered him.

Emrick stood silently at my side. His strength and closeness bolstered me. He said nothing and made no contact, allowing me whatever space I needed, but the fact that he was here for this made it possible for me to open my eyes and appreciate the detachment I'd finally gained from this place.

Already, with the demon gone and Alodie nothing more than ash in the grass, the sense of stasis had vanished. Boats were out on the water, hikers wandered the banks, and all was as it should be.

Without the sorcerers of Palonia marring its new purpose. Our day was over. Had been for a long time.

Perhaps it was time to consider what came next.

But that would be a conversation for later because Alodie had left me with one more riddle that needed to be solved: who had summoned Fegor and pushed Alodie in my direction? What other threat was out there putting my family in danger?

I wouldn't find the answers here.

When I stretched out my hand, Emrick's fingers curled around mine. I looked down at our palms pressed together and compared the paleness of my skin to the whiteness of his. At least it hadn't gotten worse. He'd kept his promise and stayed away. Even when Alodie had nearly stripped my life from me with that ritual, he'd kept his distance. This time.

We had to find a solution to that problem as well. We couldn't spend eternity walking on eggshells, never sure what the last straw would be. Maybe Murisa and Poppy would have a few ideas. Or maybe there was something in Adrian's library we'd missed. With whatever time we had before the next storm raged, I would use it wisely.

And I would start by celebrating our survival.

"Take me home?" I asked.

Emrick drew me closer, wrapped his arms around my waist so his chest was flush against my back, and laid a kiss in the crook of my neck. The contact buzzed along my skin, burrowed into my veins, flowed through my blood, and the world faded as Emrick took me away from my past, where I hoped it would rest for good.

Thank You for Reading

Thank you so much for taking a chance on an independent author. We're living in a wonderful age where it's easy to upload a book to the internet, but that doesn't reflect the blood, sweat, and tears that go into making a book the best version it can be. It takes time, patience, perseverance, and to have the final result end up in a new reader's hands is the best reward. You are the reason we keep writing, so thank you.

If you enjoyed the read, please help support the author by leaving a review at the retailer where you purchased the book. Reviews make a world of difference for an author, helping us reach new audiences and bringing more people into the worlds you've spent time in.

For exclusive character content, announcements, promotions, and special offers, sign up for Krista's mailing list at https://www.kristawalshauthor.com/pages/about-the-author

Acknowledgements

This book was a doozy. Every series has a trouble child, and for so many reasons, this one was it for the Immortal Sorceress. Why? Well, I blame Adrian.

In spite of it all, we finally reached the finish line, and I have a few people to thank for making it happen.

Kate Sparkes for holding my hand through every editing pass, even as I cried and screamed and threw empty tissue boxes at the wall.

The FAKAs and the Blood & Pulp gang for the support, encouragement, brainstorming, feedback, and push to accept the final draft as final.

My editor, Christopher Barnes, for helping me wrangle the pacing of those first few chapters.

My ARC team, my street team, and my beta readers. You are the best cheerleading squad I could wish to have. With you behind me, even the troublingest of trouble childs don't seem as daunting.

My Patrons, whose feedback on my weekly teasers made me believe I was on the right track with this book.

Chris Reddie, my wonderful husband and partner in all things. You propped me up on my worst days and helped me limp along to the end. And my beautiful, wonderful daughter, who makes me laugh through the worst frustrations.

Finally, my readers. Thank you so much for coming back. Hold on to your seats. The final two books are about to get wild.

About the Author

Known for witty, vivid characters, Krista Walsh never has more fun than getting them into trouble and taking her time getting them out.

When not writing, she can be found reading, gaming, or watching a film – anything to get lost in a good story.

She currently lives in Ottawa, Ontario with her husband, toddler, and epileptic blue heeler.

You can find her at www.kristawalshauthor.com or at the local Second Cup coffee shop... but only if you come bearing a Vanilla Bean Latte, half-sweet.

Other Works by Krista Walsh

Epic Fantasy
The Meratis Trilogy
The Cadis Trilogy
The Nayis Trilogy

Urban Fantasy
The Dark Descendants
The Ghostmaker Trilogy
The Immortal Sorceress Series